AN ALASKAN
WEDDING

Visit us at www.boldstrokesbooks.com

By the Author

Cowgirl

An Alaskan Wedding

AN ALASKAN WEDDING

by

Nance Sparks

2021

AN ALASKAN WEDDING

ISBN 13: 978-1-63679-053-4

This Trade Paperback Original Is Published By
Bold Strokes Books, Inc.
P.O. Box 249
Valley Falls, NY 12185

First Edition: November 2021

CREDITS
EDITORS: Victoria Villaseñor and Cindy Cresap
PRODUCTION DESIGN: Susan Ramundo
COVER DESIGN BY Tammy Seidick

Acknowledgments

I'd like to acknowledge all of the hardworking people at Bold Strokes Books who have helped me make my dream a reality. Thank you for taking a chance on me.

CHAPTER ONE

A ndrea stared at herself in the full-length mirror. She turned to the left and then to the right debating whether to wear her hair up or down for the wedding. She liked the way the burgundy dress offset her strawberry blond hair. If she left her hair down, it was just long enough to cover her shoulders but wasn't so long to hide the pretty deep vee detail of the back. She spun around in front of the mirror once more, admiring the way the dress flowed with each movement. She was thrilled with how it fit her figure, as if tailor-made for her body. Her breasts looked full and perky, showing off just enough cleavage, and she loved how it hugged her ass just right. The shoulder straps were thin, and when she held her hair up, she felt like her neck and shoulders looked sleek and elegant. She twirled around in an effort to catch glimpses of herself in the mirror and decided that her hair should definitely be up to make the most of the skin on show. She spun once more and thought to add a pair of dangling earrings and maybe some sort of choker necklace. Yes, that was the look she was going for. She needed an evening of feeling sleek and elegant.

"Whoa Mom, you look hot!"

Andrea spun around to see her older daughter standing in the doorway. It didn't seem possible that she was already fourteen, and if she closed her eyes, she could still see the newborn infant cradled in her arms. Now, Sydney was taller than she was. Her short brown hair was neat and trim except for the long, shaggy bangs that hid half of her face and most of her striking green eyes. It was a style that Sydney loved, and it suited her relaxed personality. The same relaxed personality that had her dressed in a football jersey, faded jeans, and multicolored Chuck Taylor shoes. Sydney walked into the bedroom and flopped down onto the bed.

"Thanks, Syd. Okay, opinion time, hair up or down?" Andrea turned toward her and posed.

"That's some dress. Aunt Sara has great taste. Up, yeah, definitely up. It screams hot mom. Who knows, you might even get lucky." Sydney wiggled her eyebrows and smiled.

"Sydney Anne Daniels, what am I going to do with you?" Andrea shook her head. If only she could be so lucky as to get lucky. It had been so long since she'd been the focus of anyone's attention. She'd all but forgotten what it felt like. She stepped out of the dress and returned it to the hanger.

"Um, Mom, please tell me you're not wearing granny panties under that dress. You'll never get lucky if that's what the dude sees. He'll have flashbacks of his mom, or worse, his grandma and run off screaming!" Sydney quickly leaned back to avoid Andrea's playful backhand swat.

"I have nicer things already packed, thank you very much, and getting lucky isn't my goal, Syd, it's a vacation." Andrea pulled the loose-fitting T-shirt over her head and then wiggled back into her yoga pants.

"A child-free vacation. I'd be your wingman if you'd take me with you instead of dumping me off with Dad and Cathy. Geez, Mom, definitely don't take that outfit. It throws the 'hot mom' right out the window!"

Andrea looked at herself in the mirror. Sydney was right, definitely not a hot mom outfit. More like a frumpy working mom with two teenage kids where everything was more of a priority than her appearance. She decided to reevaluate what was packed in the three suitcases. Maybe she could go for a bit more of the hot mom look while on vacation.

"Do you really feel like I'm dumping you with Dad?" Andrea flopped on the bed next to Sydney and brushed her hair out of her eyes.

"I don't know, maybe a little. An entire week over there is going to feel like forever, and he's not as much fun on the weekdays as he is as weekend dad. He just yells for us to do our homework so he can watch his shows in peace. Besides, I won't have my own room or my stuff and he's always too tired after work to take us anywhere so we can hang out with our friends. Why can't we come with you?"

"Well, for starters, school just began, and four school days is too much time to miss this early in the year. Besides, I'll be busy helping Sara with stuff and the wedding is only for adults. Occasionally, moms need a little break, some adult only time."

"Hold up, you need a break from your own children? And here I thought we brought nothing but joy to your life!"

Andrea ruffled her hair. She sighed and looked at the ceiling. She did love being a mom and she loved her career as a registered nurse, but those two things shouldn't be all that defined who she was. She craved some time on her own to remember what it felt like to be Andrea again and not simply Mom or nurse.

"Mom, do you regret having us? Do you wish you'd never had kids?" Sydney pulled her from her thoughts.

"What? No, no regrets, never regrets. You and Olivia are my treasures, not regrets."

"Treasures that you want to dump at Dad's for an adults-only party in Alaska!"

"A vacation doesn't mean that there's regret. Why do you ask that?" Andrea twisted on her side to see Sydney's eyes.

"Well, sometimes you look sad, and I heard you on the phone with Sara saying that this wasn't how you expected your life to turn out."

"Oh, sweet baby girl, that had nothing to do with you and Olivia. I love you both with all my heart. Just because I need a break doesn't mean I regret having you and your sister. You were both fantastic surprises, not regrets."

"Fantastic surprises you need a break from," Sydney said with a half grin.

"You're relentless!" Andrea thought for a moment. "Ya know how sometimes, when you have a big report due at school and you've worked super hard on it, and while it's not quite finished, you ask if you can go hang out with Amelia or someone? You need a little time away from it, so you can come back with a fresh perspective and knock it out of the park? It's like that. I just need a little break so I can come back with a fresh perspective."

"Your life is like always having to work on a big report? Well, that's gotta suck!"

"Syd, my life is nonstop laundry and short-order cook and taxi service and work, which includes lots of long shifts, and I wouldn't trade any of it for the world, but sometimes parents just need a little fun with other adults who need to get away from laundry and cooking and work—"

"Okay, okay, I get it. I'll go finish packing. I guess I can handle a week with Dad and Cathy." Sydney rolled over on the bed and into Andrea's open arms. She snuggled into Andrea's shoulder. "I hope you have lots of fun, Mom. I love you."

"Thanks, Syd. I love you, too, with all my heart."

"Oh, is it snuggle time?" Olivia asked from the hallway. She ran and launched herself onto the bed.

"You're the reason Mom needs a vacation." Sydney pushed Olivia off to the side.

"I am not. You're the reason and stop pushing me. Mom, Sydney won't let me in the snuggle pile."

Andrea rolled over the top of Sydney, enjoying how she giggled while being squished into the mattress and then dropped between the girls and wrapped her arm around each of them. The doorbell chimed from the hallway.

"I love you two goofballs! That's probably your father. Come on. Let's get going."

Within an hour, the girls were off with Scott, and Andrea had the house all to herself. She poured a little whiskey on the rocks and made her way back to her bedroom. She needed to finish packing.

She had an early flight, and at this time tomorrow night she'd be lounging in a resort in Alaska resting up for her best friend's wedding. She was excited to stand at Sara's side and watch her get married, perhaps even a tad envious. She'd always dreamt of a big wedding with the flowy white dress, but instead she'd had a courthouse wedding while trying to hide a baby bump. It was true, her life hadn't turned out as she'd expected, and certainly not what she expected at Sydney's age, but she loved her daughters and wouldn't change that for anything in the world.

CHAPTER TWO

Good afternoon, passengers. This is your captain speaking. I'd like to welcome you to Fairbanks, Alaska, where it's sunny and sixty-three degrees. Skies should be clear for the next week or so which is perfect for those of you here to sneak a peek of the northern lights. We ask that you remain seated until the plane comes to a complete stop at the gate. Please take care when opening the overhead bins as luggage may have shifted during the flight. We would like to wish you a great stay here in Alaska."

Riley ran through her mental checklist while waiting to exit the plane. She always arrived a day early to get settled at the hotel, check out the venues, and prep her gear. She was especially excited about this trip. Shooting in Alaska was a bucket list trip. The scenery, the wildlife, and then the northern lights. She'd always dreamt of shooting the floating curtain of almost mythical color that shifted through the sky. Mid-September was the perfect time to capture everything she wanted to see, especially if the weather held true. A couple of days on the job and then she'd have an entire week to explore the landscape.

She checked into the Moose Lodge Resort, dropped her suitcases in her room, and then hopped back into the rental car to meet the couple at the reception hall just north of town. The navigation system alerted her of a right turn ahead, but Riley's attention was captured by a large moose eating lilies in a pond off to the left. She pressed gently on the brakes, hoping to stop the car without scaring off the moose. Successful, she climbed over the seat, opened the camera case, and attached a large zoom lens to her camera. Her heart hammered in her chest with the excitement of seeing such a magnificent creature right in front of her. She climbed back over the seat and lowered the driver's window. With one quick adjustment of the camera settings, she focused and engaged the shutter. A glance at the display screen made her smile. What a great shot of the moose with greenery draping from either side of its mouth. She raised the camera again, zoomed in and took a few more shots. The late afternoon sun was perfect, illuminating the muscular features of the animal and glistening its reflection in the still water. She glanced at the clock and realized she'd be late if she didn't get to the venue soon. Riley capped the lens and put the car into drive.

She pulled into the parking lot and instantly understood why the brides had picked this hall for the reception. It was every bit the trademark Alaskan experience. The building was crafted with large diameter logs and tall, steeply pitched roof lines. A large wooden deck appeared to wrap around the building, offering incredible views of a lake and the dense woods beyond. Native rock chimneys at either end of the building completed the picturesque setting. Riley swapped the telephoto lens for a portrait lens and made her way inside.

She stepped through the entryway into a rustic wonderland. The inside of the roof was open and exposed. Tall logs supported the timber trusses in the vast open space. Large river rock from the chimney continued down into the hall expanding into massive fireplaces on two of the outer walls. Another wall was lined with floor to ceiling windows offering a romantic view of the lake. This was going to be a fun location to shoot.

"Excuse me, are you the photographer?"

Riley spun around. A tall, slender woman with short, slicked back platinum blond hair approached from the same entryway she'd just walked through a few minutes earlier.

"Yes, that's right. I'm Riley." She held her hand out in greeting.

"Hi, Riley, I'm Kay Martin, one of the brides. Sara is back at the hotel keeping family entertained. I appreciate you taking the time to meet me out here today. Your work is impressive, and you can't imagine my excitement to hear you were available to capture everything about our special day. Sometimes it all lines up perfectly, doesn't it? However, there's been a bit of a change in venue for the ceremony. What is it they say, happy wife, happy life? Anyway, we saw this building in person yesterday and decided to move the ceremony here instead of the small church in town. Luckily, the other side of the building was still available to rent. Other than that, the itinerary I sent you holds true. So, everything will move from the hotel to this location tomorrow starting at about one o'clock in the afternoon. There are dressing rooms at the far end where we'll do the hair and makeup shoots. The divider will be up for the ceremony, and this side of the hall will be set up to host the reception with the bar over here and the dance stage right in the center. After the ceremony, they'll convert that space from row seating to large round tables for dining and a place to visit away from the loud music." Kay walked around the room indicating the arrangements.

Riley was impressed at the organization and detail, as well as by how calm Kay seemed. "It all sounds magical. The ceremony is at five in the afternoon, correct? Perhaps we could take some time before or afterward for a small shoot down by the lake? The lighting would be picture-perfect that time of day."

"I'll pass the idea by Sara, but it sounds wonderful to me. Let's plan on it. Do you have any other questions?"

"No, I believe I'm all set. We'll do some posed shots during the welcome party and prior to the ceremony. Otherwise, I'll pop in and out of the other activities listed on the itinerary. I tend to stay in the shadows and only use flash when absolutely necessary. Whatever you're doing over the next couple of days, try your best to be natural and ignore my presence. Hopefully, my style won't impede on your activities too much."

"Your style is why we hired you. I'm super excited to see what you capture." Kay smiled.

"I hope you'll be pleased. Do you mind if I stick around for a bit?" Riley asked. "I'd like to see where the sun will set for tomorrow and what the hall will look like when it's lit for the event after dark."

"I don't think that will be a problem. The owners are decorating and setting up the seating for the wedding. I'll let them know you're sticking around and to check with you before locking up. I'm sure they can set up the lighting so you can see what you'll be working with."

"Perfect. Thank you. I'll see you tomorrow at seven for the welcome party. Have a great night."

"You, too. Thanks again for traveling all this way." Kay stepped forward and shook Riley's hand.

"It's my pleasure." Riley smiled and watched Kay head to the far side of the hall. She moved gracefully, and her lines would work well in the photos.

She strolled out onto the large deck overlooking the lake. The sun was dropping low in the sky, quickly stealing the golden glow from the landscape. The lake was a perfect mirror, offering a reflection of the tree line and the landscape beyond. She pulled her camera off her shoulder, setting up a shot of the sky and the lake. She checked the display screen. The reflection of the trees and the sky in the water was everything she'd hoped for. She stood out there watching the changing light. When she'd first started in this profession, she'd taken a ton of pictures of the same scene as the light changed, trying to capture just the right moment. But over time, she learned what light worked and what light didn't, and simply enjoyed the moments in between.

As darkness crept in, she saw an opportunity for another shot of the lake. In lieu of a tripod, she used the deck railing and a shutter timer to steady her shot given the low light. She loved the thin ribbon of gold sandwiched between the dark night sky and deep blue of the water. Before long, the sun dropped completely below the horizon. Riley stood on the deck a moment longer hoping for a glimpse of the northern lights. Instead, the stars emerged in the cloudless sky, and while it wasn't the northern lights, it was an impressive sight to witness with so little light pollution. She could have hung out there all night watching the landscape take on different lighting but decided to finish her work inside so the owner wouldn't have to wait on her.

Riley explored the lodge from different angles capturing test shots along the way. She picked out locations for her portable flash stands to offer good lighting of the two brides and guests without destroying the romantic lighting of the event. Within an hour, she'd completed her task. She thanked the owner for her time before heading out to the parking lot.

The sparkling night sky once again captured her attention. Thousands of twinkling stars looked as if they could be plucked from above if she merely stood on her tiptoes. She reached up in a feigned attempt to wrap her fingers around one and then lowered her hand. What would she wish for? Was there anything about her life she'd like to change? Nothing specific came to mind. She had an amazing career that took her all over the country. Sure, there were times when she wished for someone to share it with, but it wasn't difficult to find a short-term solution to that issue either. Not that her hotel room guests had an interest in photography or exploring the countryside with her, but the bed was warm for the evening and she enjoyed that too.

CHAPTER THREE

Andrea stepped out of the cab and took in the massive log buildings that made up the Moose Lodge Resort. It was a huge facility located just outside of Fairbanks. If it looked half this good inside, she'd consider canceling the scenic tour package and spend the entire week here lounging in the heated indoor pool and Jacuzzi. She could learn how to use her new camera another time. She turned back toward the entrance just as a hotel worker appeared through the glass doors with a rolling cart. He helped her load the three suitcases and two carry-on bags. She looked at the luggage and wondered if she had packed enough for her short week. If not, they must have stores somewhere in Alaska.

"Squee! You made it!"

Sara ran across the lobby and almost fell into Andrea's arms. She wasn't used to seeing Sara's dark brown hair free from the tight braid she wore at work. Her hair had gotten long, and the natural soft wave gave it a healthy bounce with each step. Her dark brown eyes were sparkling too. If happiness could be a look, this would be it.

"Are you ever a sight for sore eyes. Oh my God, my family is already making me nuts! Is it time for cocktails?"

"After a nine-hour flight that included a layover with a barking lap poodle and a screaming infant, it's definitely time for a cocktail. Where's Kay? She's usually your family buffer," Andrea asked, walking arm in arm with Sara up to the check in counter.

"She's meeting with the caterer. She's determined to make sure everything is perfect for tomorrow. We flipped venues for the wedding at the last second. Oh my God, we drove over and saw the reception hall and instantly knew the ceremony had to be there instead of at the tiny church in town, so the wedding and reception will be in the same huge building tomorrow. Just wait until you see this place! It's even more amazing than this lodge, and that's saying something."

"Welcome to Moose Lodge Resort. Do you have a reservation?"

"Thank you, yes, the reservation is under Andrea Daniels." Andrea handed the clerk her driver's license.

"Ah, here you are. We have you in room three fifteen and it looks like we already have your credit card on file. Shall I have your bags sent up to your room?"

"Please, that would be fantastic." Andrea accepted her driver's license back and the key card for her room. She reached into her purse and handed the gentleman with the luggage cart a twenty. "Thank you very much."

He smiled and nodded before making his way to the elevator with her luggage.

"I have time for a drink, and then I have to run. Come on, the bar is this way." Sara grabbed hold of Andrea's hand and led her down the hall. "The welcome party is in that big room over there at seven tonight. There will be lots of food and booze so don't eat too much between now and then."

"Do you need help setting anything up for tonight?" Andrea asked.

"Nope, you just have to show up and have fun. The hotel events people are doing the setup and break down. God, I am so happy you're here!"

"Me too. I can't tell you the last time I traveled anywhere, let alone anywhere by myself."

"Thank you for agreeing to be my maid of honor. I can't think of anyone else I'd rather have at my side when I say I do," Sara said.

"I think your sisters would like you to say otherwise, but I'm honored you asked me, and my dress is *perfect*! Sydney called me a hot mom."

"Sweetie, you are a hot mom."

"That's kind of you to say. I'm so thankful that they finally found traveling nurses to cover both of us. I was starting to get a little nervous that I wouldn't be able to leave. I do wonder how our floor at the hospital is faring without the two of us. You know the med carts will be completely rearranged when we get back."

"Who gives a shit. We are on *vacation*! We'll fix the med carts when we get back. Come on, just think about it, no kids, no ex-husband, and no work. Just several heavenly days of pure Andrea time! So, what do you have planned for the few days after the wedding?" Sara slid into the far side of a small booth for two.

Andrea slid into the seat across from her. "I have to remember what I *like* to do first! It's been a long time since I've had any time to myself. I do have a scenic tour scheduled and I brought some books to read."

"Oh, that's a good start. Hot romances?" Sara wiggled her eyebrows up and down.

Andrea flinched. "Um, not exactly. The updated drug interaction guide and another one about migrating into leadership r—"

"*Do not* spend your vacation reading that crap. You don't have to be the responsible one all the time. How about you let your hair down and have some fun? Maybe read fifty shades of something steamy." Sara's eyes seemed to glisten. "Look at me, I'm getting married and then enjoying two weeks of sex and cocktails and more sex, and we even brought an assortment of toys! Oh hey, maybe that's what you need. Ya know, go on a little pony ride, maybe a little whiskey, something to get those hips a rockin'."

"I'm open to anything." Andrea laughed. "I have plenty of time after the wedding to do whatever I want to." She always enjoyed Sara's way of unedited conversation.

"Hi, I'm Cat, I'll be your server this afternoon. What'll you have?"

Andrea looked up into bright blue smiling eyes. Cat looked very young, almost too young to tend bar. She also looked much too young to have so many tattoos, but there they were, intricate designs that sprawled across her chest and up the sides of her neck. Her black tank top showed off the colorful artwork and complemented her jet-black hair. She looked a little rough-and-tumble in the skintight black jeans, but with an air of confidence that Andrea instantly admired.

Andrea smiled back. "Hi, Cat, I'll have a Southern Comfort old-fashioned, sweet please."

"Nice choice and will it be the usual for the not so blushing bride?" She looked over to Sara.

"Hey, sexy. No, not the usual this time. I think I'll have what she's having. That sounds good. Thanks."

"Comin' right up, an extra cherry or two for you." Cat turned and made her way behind the bar.

"A regular here already I see. When did you get into town?" Andrea asked.

"The day before yesterday, and yes, I may have snuck down here a few times already."

Andrea raised her eyebrows and tilted her head.

"Okay, fine, I'm running a tab. Cat has a strong pour, especially if you tip well, and I tip very well. Trust me, you'll like the drink." Sara laughed.

"Then, I shall tip well too." Andrea smiled.

"Oh, maybe that's what you need!" Sara looked from Cat back to Andrea.

"Excuse me?" Andrea tilted her head, confused.

"You don't need to ride a pony; you need to play with a cat!"

"Hey now, I decide who gets to play with the Cat." Cat smiled mischievously as she placed the two drinks on the table.

"You'll have to excuse my friend here. She's on a mission to give me the perfect vacation." Andrea shook her head, knowing full well she was probably fifty shades of red.

"Oh, I could definitely make your vacation purrfect, darlin', but the bride here might get jealous. Maybe we should include her, too? Just think of it, a bunch of arms and legs all tangled up together." Cat reached over and ran her finger down Andrea's forearm. Then, she leaned down and tenderly kissed Sara's cheek. "Too bad you're getting married, sweets, 'cause I'd jump the fence to play with you.

I bet you'd make this Cat purr up a storm." Cat ran a finger along Sara's jawline and then tapped her chin with the tip of her finger before spinning and walking back behind the bar.

"Okay, a strong pour and fucking hot!" Sara whispered across the table.

"Yeah, no wonder you're tipping so good," Andrea said and then drained half of her drink. Hot was an understatement. Andrea felt flush from the top of her head all the way down to her toes. The thought of finding someone to play with on vacation suddenly sounded like a fun idea. No strings, no attachment. Just a reminder that she was a woman who might be interesting for a night or two.

CHAPTER FOUR

The venue for the welcome party was well thought out. Games of large block Jenga, Connect Four, and indoor cornhole were set up around the room as social ice breakers. Servers wandered around the room offering a variety of appetizers in addition to a full buffet table and an open bar. It seemed the brides had thought of everything to welcome their friends and relatives who had traveled so far for their special day.

Riley had a couple of flash stands set up in strategic locations and photographed people as they arrived. She also made her way around the room catching candid shots of those playing games or guests simply sitting at tables lost in deep discussion. It was relaxed and fun, and she loved doing what she did.

And then she picked up on a voice, a laugh, that she recognized from a lifetime ago.

Wide-eyed, she found herself completely frozen in her tracks. Goose bumps erupted on her arms and the hair prickled up on the back of her neck. She knew that voice, without a doubt she knew that voice. The sound of that laugh used to melt her heart. It had been so long since she'd seen her. Riley lowered the camera, turned, and searched the crowd for the source as she looked from person to person. She heard it again but was pulled away by the arrival of the brides to the welcome party. Her heart was thumping with the possibility. Nevertheless, she forced herself to focus on the job. Once the brides had made their entrance into the event space and posed for a few shots, Riley faded back into the crowd determined to find the one person who had broken her heart.

Her camera allowed her to approach every small group that came along. Each person was eager to halt any conversation, raise a glass, and pose for a picture. She'd covered most of the room when she finally spotted her.

Riley could hardly believe her eyes. It was her. It was really her. Somehow, she was here in Alaska and standing less than twenty feet away. Riley stood there staring, unable to move. Andrea turned away from the bar, slowly lowering a rocks glass from her lips. She was wearing a sexy black cocktail dress that hugged her curvy figure perfectly. Elegant, sensual, graceful, beautiful, Riley couldn't pick a word because Andrea was all of them and so much more. She raised her camera and captured a shot of her raw beauty. Andrea gradually scanned the crowd. Riley kept shooting. As Andrea's gaze approached, Riley lowered the camera, glanced at the display screen, and then continued to shoot.

Their eyes met briefly, and Riley held the shutter button and continued to shoot. She offered Andrea her trademark half smile and a slight nod before Andrea scanned beyond her. Just as quickly, her focus snapped right back, as though suddenly understanding who she'd just seen. Andrea cocked her head slightly to the side, her expression one of shock and bewilderment. Her free hand covered her mouth, and her eyes grew wide.

Riley quickly raised the camera and captured that moment of recognition. The way her eyes lit up with surprise and then the true treat of seeing those deep dimples appear with that broad smile made Riley's heart race. It was a smile that could capture anyone's attention and one she'd seen in her dreams over the years. She felt everything, every emotion that Andrea was expressing and more. She took three more shots of absolute beauty. These wouldn't be shared with her clients. They'd be for her alone. When she lowered the camera, Andrea was closing the distance between them. Her astonishment was almost completely concealed by that same flirtatious smirk from years gone by.

"Riley Canon? Oh, please tell me it's you. Is it really you?" Andrea asked.

Riley smiled and nodded. It was all the encouragement that Andrea needed to brush Riley's cheek with her fingertips. The tender touch sent an electrical current to every cell in her body. She drew in a sharp breath to steady her heart rate.

"Andrea Haney, my sweet Andi, it's so good to see you." Riley shifted the camera so it hung behind her. She stepped forward, and before she could fully extend her arms, Andrea stepped into her embrace. It felt incredible to hold her again. Riley inhaled deeply, taking in the scent of Andrea's perfume. It was a new scent, different than what she wore years ago, still it was lovely, completely intoxicating yet not overpowering. It suited her perfectly. Riley inhaled again, hoping to remember every detail of this moment. She savored how amazing it felt to hold her again after all these years. It was pure electricity. Andrea must have felt it too since she shivered in the embrace. Eventually and way too soon, Andrea stepped back but left her free hand resting on Riley's shoulder. The touch continued the powerful connection, even through her jacket.

"Andi, you're still absolutely beautiful. How have you been? How do you know the brides?"

"How I've missed you calling me Andi. No one else calls me that. Though, it hasn't been Haney for a long time. It's Daniels." Andrea smiled. "I'm friends with Sara. I'm her maid of honor. Kay, the other bride, grew up here in Fairbanks, and her family begged them to get married out here. I'd ask you the same question, but that camera gives away your secret." She paused and looked Riley up and down. "I can't believe you're standing here in front of me. What a small world! You're rocking that suit."

"Thank you." Riley felt the color rushing to her cheeks. "I try to blend in."

"Well, I'm sorry to break it to you, sweetheart, but you're not blending. You totally caught my eye. Damn, you look good. Are you a world-famous photographer now?" Andrea asked.

"I don't know about the famous part, but I still love it and it earns me a good living. Speaking of which, I should get back to it.

I'm done around nine tonight. Could I come find you? Maybe we could grab a drink and catch up?"

"I'd like that," Andrea said, her eyes warm and tender.

"Wonderful! I'll find you when I'm finished." Riley instinctively went to step forward for a kiss and caught herself. She cupped Andrea's cheek in her hand, caressing her skin with her thumb. "I know I should go, but I really don't want to walk away."

"I don't want you to walk away either," Andrea said.

Riley smiled and forced herself to turn away. She worked her way around the room trying desperately to calm her racing heart and focus on the job at hand, but knowing Andi was in the room made it extremely difficult. It had been so long, and life had moved on, but seeing her again brought everything flooding back.

Chapter Five

Andrea's hands were shaking, and her heart was pounding wildly in her chest. She drained the whiskey from her glass and went back to the bar and ordered a double on the rocks. She picked up the glass and made her way over to a quiet table off to the side. She took a seat and tapped the rim of her glass wondering if Riley had ever forgiven her. Completely lost in thought, she gasped and jumped in her seat when Sara bent down and draped her arm around her shoulders.

"I saw you with the photographer, and that hug, whoa, totally smokin' hot! Talk about a full body embrace. I was seriously fanning myself. So, are you finally thinking about jumping the fence, or just the photographer? She's a hot, hot, hotty."

"Sara, it's *her*. Holy shit, after all this time, it's her. She's here. You hired Riley, *my* Riley. Did you set all of this up?" Andrea's voice was shaky.

"Set what up? I don't understand. Riley Canon is the most sought-after photographer for lesbian weddings. She gets these candid shots that no one ever expects. Her work is brilliant. She flies all over the country. We were ecstatic that she was even available. Hey, what's going on? What am I missing?" Sara sat in the open seat next to Andrea. She reached over and took Andrea's shaking hand.

"Sara, *that's her*," Andrea said, the reality of it all finally sinking in.

"Honey, I've been drinking all day long. You've gotta give me more."

"You know how you keep teasing me about jumping the fence and I always respond that I walk on the top rail so I can enjoy both sides?"

"But you don't walk on the top rail, sweetie. You and Scott got divorced and you went out to pasture, like an old gray mare."

"You know, sometimes you can be a real dick."

"I know, but my honesty is what you love most about me. So, how does the photographer fit in, exactly?"

"Where do I start? We met on the first day of kindergarten. She was this super shy kid who wouldn't let go of her mom's leg. I took her hand and told her my name and she told me hers. We sat together at the same table, and we were inseparable from that point on. We did everything with each other, always staying at one house or the other. Each year, I'd go on camping trips with her family for Memorial Day and Labor Day and then we'd enjoy sunbathing on the dock at the lake house up north for my family's vacation in the summers. As we grew older, deeper feelings developed between us. We'd hold hands under the blanket while watching movies and would curl up in each other's arms at night on sleepovers. God, we'd talk for hours, all the time, about anything and everything. There was this apple tree in the woods behind the elementary school, we called it our spot. It's where we shared our first kiss. A quick little peck at first, ya know, to see what it felt like and then a longer kiss and I swear it was like the Fourth of July erupted inside my body. Shivers and fireworks everywhere. She was all of my firsts, my first love, my first experience, my first everything." Andrea picked up her whiskey and tipped the glass back. "You and Kay hired *my* Riley to shoot your wedding."

"Holy fuck." Sara picked up Andrea's glass and held it up to the bartender and then held up two fingers. He nodded and quickly showed up with the two rocks glasses of whiskey. "Kay is definitely getting lucky tonight. She was in charge of the photographer, and this earns her a triple gold star. Shit, Andrea, I had no idea. Why haven't you ever shared this with me?"

"It never came up. My life went down a different path." Andrea looked up, hoping that explanation would suffice.

"I call bullshit. We've been besties for far too long and this is definitely something you share with your *lesbian* best friend."

"You've never told me about your first or anyone prior to Kay."

"I was drunk off my ass and barely remember my first. Yes, I was that teenager. So, what happened? Why on earth would you let something like that go? I need so many more details!"

"Oh, details? You want more details? Okay, my parents went out one night and were supposed to be out late. We finally had the entire house to ourselves and could share a real experience instead of just touching under the covers, inside our pajamas. Safe to say we were seriously enjoying ourselves. Until my parents came home early. Apparently, when I'm on the edge, I can be extremely vocal. They kicked in my bedroom door and pulled Riley's face out from between my legs. It was the most amazing orgasm that I never got to have. Everything ended at that moment: the sleepovers, the vacations, everything. My parents wouldn't talk with me about it. Riley was banned from my life. I was grounded for months, forbidden from seeing her and couldn't go anywhere that she might be. I lost my best friend, my first love, my everything, all in a split second. It was devastating. I can't remember a time in my life when I felt more lost or alone." She stopped to take a sip of her drink as the memories hit hard. "Then there's Scott. He kept asking me out and asking me out until finally at the end of my senior year I said yes and went to a party with him. I was so lonely. It felt good to be desired, to be the focus of someone's attention again. One alcohol-filled evening led to the back seat of his dad's car. The condom broke and poof, everything changed. How's that for details?"

"Double. Holy. Fuck. How could I not know this about you after all these years? Who are you?" Sara blinked a few times and then tipped back the contents of her rocks glass. "Whoa, that burns. How can you drink that shit straight?" She tapped her palm against her chest and coughed again. "Okay, so you're an adult now. Why keep up the facade?"

"No facade, I honestly felt like I was doing the right thing, the responsible thing. I married Scott a few months before Syd was born, and then we had Olivia a couple of years later. I worked really hard to keep my family together, tried to make it work. When it didn't, well, by then, I had school and two kids and then a full-time job. Besides, I haven't met another human being who rocked my world like she did. I'm sorry I never told you about her. It was just part of me that got buried trying to figure out my life after I ended up pregnant. It hurt so much back then and I had no one but myself to blame."

"Well, maybe it's time to unbury it. Maybe it's time to stop blaming yourself for one small moment in time." Sara reached across the table and took hold of Andrea's hand. "You have your entire vacation to figure it out. Maybe this is your second chance. Time for some soul searching. Figure out what it is that you need. What it is that you want."

"I've already hurt her so deeply. I have no right to even ask her for the time of day, let alone consider anything more. Besides, no way she's single. She's too incredible." Andrea buried her face in her hands.

"You won't find any of that out sitting over here shooting doubles of whiskey. Go talk to her." Sara reached across the table and pulled Andrea's hands away from her face. "Are you listening to me?"

"I will. She's going to find me when she's done working. We'll catch up then." Andrea smiled.

"One more thing, and I'm only saying this because you're my very best friend in the entire universe. Don't you dare do anything to fuck up my wedding pictures!" Sara squeezed her hand.

"Has anyone told you that you can really ruin a heartfelt moment?" Andrea shook her head.

"Only everyone who knows me!" Sara squeezed her cheeks.

"There you are!" Kay walked up to the table. "We've been challenged in a Jenga game. You in?"

"Go. Kick some Jenga ass. We'll catch up later." Andrea smiled.

"Honey, I have so many more questions and I need so many more details!" Sara leaned forward and kissed Andrea's cheek. "Come on over and join in on the fun when you're ready. Love you, sweets."

"I will. I love you too." Andrea shook her head and watched Sara make her way across the room. She looked past Sara and caught sight of Riley staring at her before disappearing behind the camera and moving around the room again.

Andrea took a sip of whiskey and thought back to the last time that she'd been the focus of that lens. The noise in the room seemed to fade away, and suddenly she was sitting beneath the apple tree in their favorite spot deep in the woods behind the elementary school. She remembered how much it hurt to see the tears well up in Riley's eyes. She hadn't thought about that evening in years, yet every single detail came flooding back. The pain in Riley's eyes, the tears sliding down her cheeks. She still felt so much guilt for causing all of it. She tipped back the last of her whiskey. That evening by the apple tree had been the last time she'd seen Riley, and it was surprising how Riley still had that same incredible effect on her. Her body remembered. The moment she saw Riley, her body thrummed with desire for her touch, her caress. Riley had known, even as a teenager, how to take her to places that no other had ever been able to do. What it would be like to experience that with Riley now? Could it be as powerful as it had felt back then?

CHAPTER SIX

Shortly after nine, Riley was able to make her way into the back room where her equipment tote was stored. She sat in the seat next to her gear and rubbed her face with her hands. Her heart was still thumping wildly in her chest. Every time she'd looked up, she was aware of the hazel eyes watching her every move. It had made it so hard to focus on the job. She had to get it together, since tomorrow would be a fourteen-hour day of the same thing. Once upon a time, they had been completely in love. Granted, it had been the love of a teenager; wild, consuming, and dramatically perfect. As an adult she understood that, but God, it was so good to see her again after all these years. Riley took a deep breath and focused on putting her gear away properly. She'd worry about the job tomorrow. Tonight, she needed to finish up so she could spend some time with a certain stunning woman in a sexy black dress.

She spotted her right away, chatting with the two brides and a few family members around a larger table. The room was emptying out and the servers were cleaning up the last few items on the buffet table. Riley's stomach grumbled reminding her that she hadn't stopped tonight to eat. Well, too late now. She walked over to the bar and ordered Jack on the rocks. She sipped the whiskey and watched Andrea interact with her friends. She could hear her laughing at something that had been said. It was so good to hear that laugh again. She looked around the room once again for Scott. She hadn't seen him all night, but it was Andrea Daniels now. He must be around here somewhere. She wasn't sure she could deal with seeing them together as a couple. Despite the years, the hurt was still very real. Riley took a deep breath and then another swig of Jack. She'd deal with it when he came around.

Andrea twisted in her chair, their eyes met, and a huge smile spread across her face. She leaned into Sara and said something and then stood and made her way toward the bar. She still had that same sexy swagger that had her ass swinging fluidly from side to side.

"How long have you been standing there?" Andrea asked.

"Just a minute or two."

"Why didn't you come over? I've been waiting for you."

"I didn't want to interrupt. I'm the photographer, not a guest." Riley felt Andrea's fingers curl around her own. Her heart rate shot up.

"Well, you're off duty now aren't you? Consider yourself my plus-one. Let's grab a drink and find a table."

Riley picked up her refilled glass and rested her free hand on Andrea's lower back. She felt Andrea shiver and take in a sharp breath of air. Riley squeezed her eyes shut. *It's Daniels, remember?* She pulled her hand away and focused on making her way to a table in the corner.

"You didn't have to move your hand. It felt nice to have it rest there again."

"It's not my place. So, where's Scott? I haven't seen him this evening?" Riley tried to keep her tone neutral. After all these years, he was still one of her least favorite people on the planet.

"He's probably at home with his wife." Andrea looked over and smiled. "We're divorced."

Riley stopped and looked into Andrea's eyes. She didn't try to hide her smile. Electricity popped and arched between them. The look in Andrea's eyes told her that she felt it too. She pulled a chair out for Andrea and then took the seat next to her.

"It's so great to see you." Andrea's smile turned shy and she played with her glass.

"How have you been?" Riley asked.

"I've been good. You?"

"Can't complain. It's hard to believe it's been fifteen years since I last saw you. It was the evening before I left for college, also the day you told me you were pregnant. I never found out if you had a boy or a girl?"

"A girl. Actually, I have two daughters. Sydney, the older, is fourteen, and Olivia just turned twelve. Syd's all tomboy. She plays volleyball in the fall, swims in the winter, and then it's softball in the spring. I laugh sometimes because she loves the same sports that you did in high school. I'd swear you were her mom if that was at all possible. She reminds me so much of you. Same dark brown hair, same piercing green eyes. I can't look at her and not see you, though she was blessed with my dimples when she smiles." Andrea smiled and the dimples appeared. "Liv is more like me. She's more of a girly girl. Strawberry blond and hazel eyes to boot. She wants to be on the cheer squad and takes two different dance classes."

"How long were you and Scott married?" Even if they were divorced, his name left a bitter taste in her mouth. She tried to wash it down with a sip of whiskey.

Andrea grew quiet for a moment. She looked down into her glass and swirled the ice around in circles. "He should have gone off to school before Sydney was born, but the parental collective urged him to stay and attend community college. A year later, he quit college and we moved to Wisconsin when he was promoted at work. We were so young and full of resentment toward each other for the predicament we found ourselves in. It was a loveless marriage. I guess you can't force feelings. We'd nitpick and argue and then we kinda stopped talking altogether. It was like we coexisted, just going through the motions out of obligation. After a while, I don't even think we were even friends anymore. I tried, we both tried, but after a couple of years we finally admitted that it wasn't going to work." Andrea scratched her chin and inhaled deeply.

Riley could see the emotion on her face. She'd always been an open book. Her eyes gave away her secrets. It seemed there was more she needed to say, so Riley remained quiet and waited.

"Syd was almost two when we called it quits. I'd even put a deposit down on an apartment. I hadn't been feeling well, and I thought it was just the stress of it all, but it kept getting worse, not better. I went to the doctors and low and behold, I was pregnant with Olivia. We tried once more, to keep the family together, but it didn't take long to realize that we were doing more harm than good. It wasn't healthy for either of us to live like that. All said and done, it was a little over four years. I kept the name for the kids. He's a good dad and we got along much better once we were apart. His wife, Cathy, is a good person and she treats the kids well. They live close by and we share custody." Andrea smiled. "I didn't mean to dump all of that on you. It was certainly a long answer to a simple question. I guess I wanted you to know it wasn't—Shit, I'm sorry I said so much. I'm rambling. I'm nervous. I don't know why I'm nervous, but I am. It's so good to see you."

"It's good to see you too. Don't be nervous, I'm still just me. And you? Did you remarry after the divorce?" Riley asked. It wasn't subtle, but she didn't care. She needed to know.

"No, not remarried and not seeing anyone right now. Really, nothing serious since the divorce. The girls are both busy with sports and after-school things. My job keeps me busy too. I finally went to college. I took night classes for years and years. That's how I met Sara. We were in the same program and now we work together. I'm a registered nurse." Andrea lifted her glass to her lips.

"I bet you make a great nurse." Riley smiled, trying not to stare at Andrea's lips on the glass. "Do you enjoy it?"

"I do. It's a demanding job and also quite rewarding. I'm up for the shift supervisor position."

"They'd be lucky to have you. You'll have to let me know when you find out." It was presumptuous, perhaps, to assume they'd stay in contact after this, but why not?

"What about you? Where are you living these days?" Andrea reached across the table and touched the back of Riley's hand.

"My furniture lives in Illinois, just west of Chicago. I bought an old warehouse and converted it. The photography studio is downstairs, and I live in the loft above. It works for the time being. I travel quite a bit doing custom shoots. Luckily, I have Jodie. I honestly don't know what I'd do without her. She travels too, so I can have a break now and then. She also runs the studio when I'm out of town."

Andrea pulled her hand back. "I kind of figured you'd have someone to share your life with. She's a lucky lady. How long have you two been together?" She continued to play with her glass.

"Wait. What? Jodie? No, we're not a couple. We're amazing friends and we work great together but nothing more than that. I met her on campus in Missouri. We were both in the photography program at school and shared a dorm room that first year. She's got a great eye for the shot. When my studio took off and the work became more than I could handle, she agreed to help me out on a few jobs. It worked out so well that she ended up moving to Illinois. She was supposed to work this wedding with me, but another wedding had been postponed a week so we ended up double booked. She's in New Mexico."

"If not Jodie, then—"

Riley smiled. "It's kind of like you said, nothing serious at the moment."

"Really? How is that even possible?"

"Well, I travel a lot. Only being around for a few days a month doesn't make me the best relationship material."

"Don't you get lonely?"

Riley looked down at her drink. Sure, there were times when she was lonely, even when there was a warm body next to her. She usually tried to stay busy enough that she could ignore the loneliness and the emptiness. But admitting that opened up an area for conversation she didn't want to get into.

"Unless you're not alone in all of those hotel beds." Andrea's eyebrow quirked when Riley didn't answer. "Look at you. I bet you have to beat the women off with a stick."

"I wouldn't exactly say that. My job is to disappear into the background. I do my best work when people don't notice I'm around. Those are the shots my clients pay for."

"I'm glad you lowered the camera and let me see that it was you. I still can't believe you're here." Andrea yawned into the back of her hand. "Excuse me. I think the day is catching up with me. I just flew in this afternoon."

"It's a hell of a flight over isn't it?" Riley smiled.

The table buzzed twice and then a ringer sounded.

"Oh, crap, I think that's me." Andrea opened her handbag and pulled out her phone. "It's one of my daughters, would you excuse me?" Andrea tucked her handbag under her arm after accepting the call. "Hello."

She stepped away from the table. Riley picked up her drink and leaned back in her chair watching Andrea's expression. There seemed to be great concern with what was being said on the other end of the call. She didn't mean to eavesdrop, but she couldn't help it, since Andrea hadn't gone far from the table.

"Liv, honey, calm down. Sweetie, no, I cannot just come and get you. I'm three thousand miles away. Isn't it after midnight there? What are you doing up? What? Can you get your dad? Olivia, put your father on the phone so I can figure out what's going on." Andrea pinched the bridge of her nose. "Sweetie, you have to calm down so you can tell me what happened."

She kept talking but her words trailed off as she walked across the room and out the double doors. Riley sat there for some time sipping on her drink. The servers finished clearing the tables and started breaking down the room. When Andrea still hadn't returned, Riley went into the back room and collected her rolling equipment tote and camera bag. She walked back across the vast space as slowly as possible hoping Andrea would show back up. She made it all the way to the elevators without an Andrea sighting. Sighing, she pressed the button for the fourth floor. *What the hell was that about?* Part of her wanted to wait longer, but the thought of Andrea not showing up at all was a disappointment that she wasn't ready to face. Kids complicated everything. Andrea was no more available than she'd been fifteen years ago.

CHAPTER SEVEN

"Welcome to the spa. Are you part of the wedding party?" A tall, slender young man asked from behind the counter.

"Hello, yes I'm part of the Sara Hernandez and Kay Martin wedding party. My name is Andrea Daniels."

"Right this way, Ms. Daniels. The brides are already here."

He led her through frosted glass doors. "That first door on the left is the changing room. There are lockers available for your belongings. You can undress to your desired level of comfort. Robes and slippers in the cloth tote are yours to keep, a gift from the brides. Once you change, you'll proceed out the door on the far side of the room labeled Spa and that's where you'll find the brides."

"Thank you. You've been very helpful."

Andrea stepped into the changing room. It was a dimly lit aromatherapy haven of lavender and mint. She sat down and took a moment to breathe. Lavender was supposed to be calming, but it wasn't working. She was a jumble of thoughts and emotions. She stripped down completely and hung her clothes up in the locker before donning her new robe and slippers. She wasn't sure what all was on the agenda, but Sara had let it slip that a full massage was part of the morning and she could definitely use a massage. Maybe that would help.

"You're here!" Sara and Kay were already in the Jacuzzi holding flutes of champagne.

"Of course, I'm here. Where else would I be?" Andrea sat in a chair near the Jacuzzi tub.

"Oh, I don't know, maybe spending some time with a certain photographer. Where did you two disappear to last night? I forgot my purse behind the bar, and when I came down to get it the room was dark and empty." Sara asked, a glint in her eye. "Did you get naked and have some fun?"

"Not so much." Andrea sat farther back in the chair and crossed her legs. "It's like the universe cannot cut me a break when it comes to Riley. We no sooner sat down and started talking, next thing you know, Olivia's on the phone in full-blown meltdown mode. It took forever to get her to calm down. When I finally got back to the table, Riley was gone. I can't imagine what she must be thinking right now."

"Oh, shit. What happened with my little Livy?" Sara asked.

"Your little Livy had a seriously traumatizing day yesterday. Definitely rates in the scarred for life category."

"Seriously? Shit, is she okay?" Sara sat up in the bubbles with a concerned look on her face.

"Olivia started her period after lunch at school, first one ever, and I guess it was a bit of a mess."

"Oh, no!" Kay smiled sympathetically.

"Oh, yeah, I'm totally in the doghouse for not being there. Cathy was with Syd at the first away volleyball game, which was over an hour north and she didn't answer her phone, so Liv asked Scott to take her to the store. He wanted to know why. She refused to tell him. Well, you know Scott, he wasn't going to take her anywhere if she wasn't willing to tell him exactly why she needed to go. There was a whole lot of screaming and tears and Scott's yelling in the background for her to get off the phone and go to bed. Then, Liv asks me to tell her dad why she needs to go to the store because it's too embarrassing. Once I finally got him on the phone, I started giggling while trying to explain her predicament and then Scott starts laughing and then I'm laughing, like snort laughing."

She nodded when Kay shook her head. "Right? Olivia lost her shit all over again. Let me just say, I will not be winning any mother of the year awards, I can tell you that much. Finally, Scott says to go enjoy my vacation, that Cathy has stuff in the bathroom, and he'd take care of it. I was like *score,* maybe Riley hasn't completely given up on me. So, I'm just outside of the double doors and I get another frantic call, more crying, more screaming because apparently all Cathy has in the cupboard are the super plus tampons *without the fucking applicator.* Like that's going to work for a twelve-year-old! Olivia is done asking Scott for anything and insists I explain *over the phone* how tampons work. I mean come on, really, I'd had way too much whiskey for that conversation. Instead, I tell her the wad of toilet paper trick and she hung up on me." She sighed and closed her eyes. "At this point Riley is nowhere to be found and I get a third call. Thank God Cathy finally showed up and had pads on a different shelf." She finally took a breath. "Fuck my life, parenting is hard."

"And that is why we are not having children," Kay said to Sara before bursting out into laughter. "Come on in and join us. Chilled champagne and hot jetted water are a match made in heaven. It will cure what ails you." Kay held up a full flute of champagne.

"Shit, Andrea, that sucks!" Sara said between giggles.

"I thought we were getting massages, so I'm afraid I'm extremely underdressed for the Jacuzzi."

"Massages are next, but we've reserved the entire spa. No strangers. We're naked too. It's a huge Jacuzzi." Kay smiled and stood up. "See? Naked. Come on in. It will make you feel better."

Andrea lifted her robe as she stepped into the Jacuzzi and then turned away from Sara and Kay before removing it completely. She lowered herself the rest of the way into the steaming hot water. It did feel incredible. Kay handed her a flute of champagne. A few more of these and Andrea wouldn't care who saw her naked. The conversation was light and fun. Everything needed for a relaxing wedding day, until a flash went off and then another. Andrea looked down to be sure her boobs weren't floating on top of the bubbles. There were not enough bubbles to hide everything she wished to stay hidden. She spun around trying to find the source of the flash. She knew it had to be Riley, but she wasn't prepared to be photographed while lounging in the Jacuzzi, naked.

"Are you serious?" Andrea whisper-shouted across the tub and then kicked Sara beneath the bubbles. Kay grunted, but it didn't really matter who she kicked.

"We never know when or where she's going to show up. It was all part of the contract. It's called 'Candid Photography' for a reason. It's why she's the best," Kay said. "And kick Sara next time."

"Shit, I'm sorry about that, Kay. Sara, I owe you one, or perhaps two given the smirk on your face." Andrea wanted to drop completely below the bubbles. This would all be over today, but how on earth was she going to get out of the hot tub now? "Will she be photographing the massages, too?"

"Who knows? She has free rein on all activities until ten o'clock tonight. She gets an itinerary and we get the best wedding shots ever." Sara smiled. "Though, I think we should get a discount because ninety percent of the shots are going to be of you. I wonder if she snagged a couple of shots when you dropped that robe. It was hot. Kind of mysterious and seductive."

"You really can be such a dick sometimes!" Andrea shook her head.

"It's what you love most about me." Sara blew some bubbles at Andrea's face.

"Either one of you could have mentioned this yesterday when we talked at the welcome party."

"We agreed not to tell anyone. It's *candid photography* not posed for photography! Just relax and enjoy your day. No nudies, that we can promise." Kay started to giggle again.

"Well, at least none that we'll get to see." Sara winked.

"I don't think either one of you would care if she saw you nude." Andrea glared at Sara. "I, on the other hand, am at least twenty pounds heavier than the last time she saw me naked. Shit, probably more like thirty."

"It's easier if you don't think about it. Just be natural. It really will make for the best photographs," Kay said. "You should see the stunning shots on her site."

"Oh, yeah, just be natural, easy for you to say. You're getting married in a few hours." Andrea finished her glass of champagne. "Refill, please." She pushed the glass into Sara's hand.

"Did you try to find her after the Olivia meltdown last night?" Kay asked.

"Yes, but the front desk wouldn't give me her room number. I looked everywhere this morning too, but no luck. I did write her a note and begged the front desk to be sure she got it. Hopefully, we can talk tonight."

"Riley? If you're still hiding in here somewhere, Andrea would like to talk to you. She's sorry she was called away last night. Flash once if you heard me." Sara spoke loudly to the room so that it echoed, then winked and wiggled her eyebrows.

They waited in silence for a moment before Andrea splashed Sara. "And you continue to be a dick!"

"Yeah, and it continues to be what you love most about me. Salute." Sara lifted her glass in the air before taking a sip.

Andrea shook her head. Sara was so bold and outspoken, something she wasn't. Still, she was disappointed that Riley hadn't appeared from the shadows.

"Sara tells me she was your first love?" Kay asked. "I always thought you were straight. If I'd known you swung both ways, I'd have set you up with Jack a long time ago."

"I've been getting that a lot lately." Andrea glared at Sara, who shrugged in response. "No disrespect, Kay, because I love you for falling in love with the hot mess sitting next to me, but there's nothing about Jack that floats my boat. She's intense and a bit too obnoxious for my taste. Either way, I have zero interest in being set up with her."

"No disrespect taken. Jack is absolutely an obnoxious ass, but she has a heart of gold and she's been my best mate for a very long time."

Andrea looked around the room once more. She didn't see Riley, so she relaxed into the bubbles again. "And yes, Riley really was my first love, my first everything."

"Has she always been into photography?" Kay asked.

Andrea tilted her head back against the side of the hot tub. She had no idea how many photographs Riley had taken of her in her youth. Hundreds. All she knew was that photos of her had been plastered all over Riley's bedroom walls. And back then, she had loved being her focus of attention.

"She was thirteen when she got her first camera. Her parents gave her a thirty-five-millimeter film camera and some dark room equipment for Christmas that year. She carried that thing everywhere she went and always took the most incredible photographs, even back then. You two will be very happy you hired her."

"We're already glad we hired her," Sara said. "And getting to see you squirm is an added bonus. I've never ever seen you care what anyone thinks about how you look. You walk around the locker room in your bra and underwear all the time. You're like a nervous little smitten kitten."

Andrea flicked water at Sara. "Others are coming out, stuff it, sweetie."

"And just so it's said out loud, when you two get married, I'm happy to be your matron of honor."

"Who else is getting married?" Jack asked.

Andrea slid over in the Jacuzzi as others in the wedding party arrived. "No one, Jack. Sara's just being her snarky self."

"Are all three of you buck ass naked in those glorious bubbles?" Jack asked while untying her robe. She draped the robe over a chair and stood at the steps in a tank top and boxer shorts. "Looks like it's my lucky day! Let's see, who to sit next to—"

"You will sit next to me. I've known you long enough to know you can't be trusted when left unsupervised. Oh, and hands will remain out of the water at all times, my little devil." Kay accepted Jack's high five and then handed her a glass of champagne.

Sara leaned over and shoulder-bumped Andrea. "All snarkiness aside. I'm glad you and the photographer found each other again after all these years. I hope it turns out to be a good thing."

"Thanks, hon, me too."

"You know, if it works out, I'll take full credit for fixing you up after all these years." Sara tapped her champagne flute against Andrea's.

"There wasn't a doubt in my mind." Andrea looked over at Sara and smiled just as another few flashes went off. This time Andrea looked up in time to catch Riley's eye. There was that sexy ass half grin and the nod. She raised her eyebrows a few times and winked at Andrea, something she used to do when passing her in the hallway in high school. Andrea returned the wink, just as she had so many years ago. The exchange made her warm and tingly all over. Perhaps this day wouldn't be so bad after all.

CHAPTER EIGHT

The limo was waiting for the group at the main entrance to the lodge. Andrea climbed in next to Sara, and it was quiet for a moment until Jack flopped into the seat across from them.

"I have never, ever, *ever* in my life had so many lovely ladies touching me all over my body and there was not a single orgasm for anyone. Instead, you let them wax and pluck and poke, file and clip parts of me that *no one* is ever going to see! This was not discussed when I agreed to be the best woman, Kiki. I don't for the life of me understand how any of that was supposed to be relaxing. Manicures and pedicures are fucking dumb, and my eyebrows were just fine." Jack rubbed the newly revealed skin on her forehead.

"Sweetie, you had talons for toenails and a serious unibrow. It was getting out of control," Amelia said.

"You're just jealous because I'm the best woman. That's why you made them torture me." Jack opened another compartment between the seats. "Isn't there a bottle of booze anywhere in this glorified station wagon? I need to numb the pain."

"It's almost empty, but you can have what's left." Kay's sister, Tami, passed a silver flask over to Jack.

"Jack, I can't remember a time when you've smelled so delicate and floral and yet I also detect a subtle earthy undertone." Kay inhaled deeply.

"Screw you, Kiki! Like I always say, I'm all leather and no lace. I make no apologies for being a crewcut butch. I ride a Harley, for fuck's sake! I can't tell if it's the massage oil that stinks or the lotion that they slathered all over my feet and hands, but it's a god-awful smell." Jack's face twisted up when she lifted her hands to her nose. "Did you design your entire wedding day to torture me?"

"Oh, so you know what's coming next?" Sara leaned forward in the limo seat.

"No, what?" Jack's face went pale. "Kiki, all you asked me to do was stand next to you and give you the ring. You said nothing about all of this fluffy bullshit!"

Sara's sister, Kelly, began to quietly giggle. The other bridesmaids started giggling too.

Andrea leaned closer to Kelly's ear. "You're so quiet. Are you sure you aren't adopted?"

"Believe me, I have my moments, but today's her day. She deserves it. She's done so much for all of us. Our folks both worked long hours and she stepped up and took care of the four of us, no matter what we needed help with. Since she's been with Kay, she radiates peace and happiness that I've never seen her enjoy before and it's long overdue. Those two are good together. They balance each other."

"You're a great sister. Would you adopt me?" Andrea smiled.

"You've been part of the family for quite some time whether you knew it or not. Sara raves about you all the time, says you're the only reason she made it through nursing school." Kelly squeezed her hand.

"Seriously, ya'll are giggling with these sneaky sideways looks. What's happening next?" Jack's brow was starting to sweat.

"Excuse me, Ms. Martin, the photographer wanted a heads up before you arrived for hair and makeup. Shall I make the call that we'll arrive in fifteen minutes?" The driver came over the intercom. The giggling in the car intensified.

"Thank you, Stacy. Yes, please make the call," Kay said into the intercom.

"Hair and what? Oh, fuck no! I'm out. That's a line I can't cross. Kiki, stop the car. *Seriously, stop the fucking car!*" Jack jumped across the seat and knocked on the divider glass.

"Jack, it's okay. Calm down." Kay grabbed the back of her jeans and pulled her back into her seat.

"Let go of me."

Andrea watched, hoping her irritation at Jack's behavior didn't show. She was always a bit over-the-top, a little too loud, a little too dramatic. She didn't want anything ruining this day, especially the best woman who clearly wasn't onboard with being teased this way.

"Jack, look at me." Kay grabbed her face. "Hair and makeup is for those who want it. We won't make you participate. The four of us are going to get dressed in our suits and have some pictures taken."

"No makeup, you promise!"

"No makeup, no hair stylist for you unless you want to trim the high and tight. I promise, on our friendship."

"I've had enough things trimmed for one day." Jack flopped farther back into the seat.

"I don't know, I still think she should try on the wig. The mullet is making a comeback," Tami said in a deadpan tone.

"Don't make me kick your ass, Tami. I don't care whose sister you are. Kiki, you swear on our friendship, right?"

"I swear."

Andrea felt her eyebrow twitch and looked at her shoes so she didn't give herself away. The idea of Jack threatening to kick someone's ass, even facetiously, was also irksome.

"Okay then. God, you almost gave me a fucking heart attack! All ya'll are assholes and the champagne buzz is completely gone. I need a drink."

"The bar is open!" Kay hit a button and opened a cabinet in the side of the car. She handed a small, unopened bottle of single malt to Jack.

"Now this is more like it! Let me finish this and you can color up my face, and who knows, maybe I'd even wear that mullet wig!"

Andrea leaned over to Sara. "Those two have the strangest friendship I've ever seen. Kay is so polished, and Jack is…a jackass."

"Indeed, but cross one and you'll answer to both. Actually, it would probably be all three of them. Professionally, Kay's this high-profile, posh attorney, always dressed to the nines, but when she needs to blow off a little steam, we leather up, call Jack and Mel, jump on the bikes, and take off. Feeling all that power between your legs is quite the rush. Jack's all bark. She really does have a heart of gold. The three of them have organized quite a few large charity runs that help support the local queer youth center. That's how they all met, young little dykes hanging out at the youth center. Now Jack's on the board and is expanding programs."

"Hard to picture Jack at a board meeting. I wonder how many times the word fuck is in the minutes." Andrea laughed.

She peered out the side window as the car pulled into the parking lot. Riley was supposed to be out there somewhere, but damned if she could spot her. It was all so surreal. She was still reeling from seeing her again, out of the blue, after all of these years. She might as well have brought a fourth suitcase along to hold the guilt she still felt given what happened all those years ago. Still, she desperately wanted to spend some time with Riley, but to what end? Andrea had a career that kept her home. This was the first time she'd traveled alone, ever. She had two children who had school and activities and sports. From what she heard last night, it seemed that Riley spent most of her time traveling all over the country capturing photographs of lesbians in romantic settings. She couldn't imagine Riley ever sleeping alone in any of those big hotel beds. She was sexy and available without any strings or attachments. Why on earth would she sleep alone? Despite all of the warning signs, despite the reality that nothing could come of this chance encounter, she desperately wanted some time with the one person she regretted pushing away so many years ago.

CHAPTER NINE

R iley stood behind the shrubs, well hidden in the shadows surrounding the entryway into the hall. She captured a shot of the limo pulling up and then several shots of the occupants filing out of the car while laughter and conversations continued. These were some of her clients' favorite shots, portraits of smiles and overflowing affection for one another without anyone staring into the camera lens. Andrea looked around while trying to pay attention to whatever Sara was saying, and Riley wondered if she was looking for her.

What she wouldn't give to be at Andrea's side today. It was the first time she wished to be part of the wedding party and not simply the photographer. Riley stepped out of the shadow when Andrea's searching gaze drew close. Their eyes met and there was that incredible smile, dimples and all. The rest of the group remained oblivious of her presence, and Andrea didn't give her away. She gave her a small, private smile before returning to her conversation. The group made their way into the building. Once they were inside, Riley moved into the open.

It was easy to focus on the job while on Kay's side of the building. The banter between the women was light and it was just another wedding shoot. Sara's side of the building was an entirely different story. Riley walked into the room to take a few shots, and then she'd catch a whiff of the perfume Andrea wore to the welcome party. Her knees would get weak and her heart rate would shoot up. She'd take a deep breath and focus on the shots only to catch a glimpse of Andrea having her hair done, sipping on a drink and laughing at something one of the women had said. That smile, those sparkling hazel eyes, and those dimples would steal the breath right out of her lungs. Despite feeling frozen in place, she just had to get the candid shot of Andrea's reflection in the mirror, whether or not she shared it with her client. She made sure to capture plenty of shots of the others, but her all-time favorite subject was sitting just twenty feet away and couldn't be denied.

Kay's group met Riley at the altar and then out on the deck for the posed photographs. Kay was dressed in a white tuxedo with tails, tailored with a touch of feminine flair. The three members of her wedding party each wore black tailored tuxedos, their bowties matched to the colors of Sara's bridesmaids' dresses. Riley had fun with the shoot. Some poses were goofy and others more formal.

Once finished, Riley sent Kay's group to the other room and called out Sara and her wedding party. Sara looked beautiful. Her dark complexion contrasted beautifully against the white gown. She wore her dark brown hair down, allowing the soft waves to cascade across her bare shoulders. The bridesmaids' dresses were each a different color. Sara's sister Kelly wore a deep, dark green and her other sister, Rose, wore an almost midnight blue. While different colors, the dresses were the same cut with an open back and delicate straps. Each woman looked quite elegant. Riley captured shots as they exited the hallway from the dressing rooms, taking care to focus on the subject and blur the log background.

And then, Andrea walked out and stole her attention. The deep, dark burgundy dress hugged her beautiful body in all of the right places. Her hair was up, a new look that Riley hadn't seen before. She wore delicate dangling earrings and a stunning black choker with a garnet pendant teasing the hollow of her throat. Andrea was watching her step, her eyes looking down at the floor. Riley pulled up the camera and took several shots. Andrea stopped to pose where the others had and Riley took a few more shots to complete the series. She looked up, into the camera and Riley reveled in the return of those hazel eyes that seemed to look through the camera lens and directly into her heart. Each expression said something different, and Riley kept engaging the shutter.

"Careful, stud. Drool probably isn't good for the camera," Sara whispered into Riley's ear. "Though, she does look stunning, doesn't she?"

"Stunning doesn't even begin—" Riley looked at Andrea through the viewfinder.

"You heard everything today, didn't you?"

She stopped shooting and pulled the camera away from her eye, though she stared ahead at the now vacant space where Andrea had been. Someone had called her over to the group. "Not everything. I'm sure I missed quite a bit."

"I call bullshit. I saw your shoes, back behind the pedicure chairs. Your legs must be made of steel given the amount of time you crouched back there. I think I turned into a prune just waiting to see if you'd move. Way to hold out and stay on the down low."

Riley looked into Sara's eyes. "I admit this is a first for me. I've never had my personal life cross paths with a job. I wasn't sure what to do. I sat back there wondering if I should stay and get the shots you paid me to capture or should I leave and respect her privacy."

"Once the first few flashes went off, I think she knew that privacy was kinda out the window." Sara smiled. "You made the right call to stay. We do want those shots. Besides, I don't think anyone else noticed, or even knew where to look. I happened to look up when you snuck in. Honestly, there toward the end, I think she was hoping you'd stand up and make yourself known. I could see it in her eyes," Sara said.

"I almost did. Seeing her out of the blue like that yesterday threw me for a loop. We haven't had much time to catch up."

"Threw you for a loop, huh? You're funny. I like that you think you've landed. You're still totally spinning out. I can see it in your eyes. Don't worry, so is she. You two have one hell of a history, and I bet I only got the tip of the iceberg."

Riley looked down at the floor. There wasn't much to say to that, and her history with Andrea was sacred.

"Hey, you two, don't we have shots to get at the altar and on the deck as a group before the guests start to arrive?" Kay walked up behind Sara.

"Absolutely. My apologies. Let's get to it." Riley turned to walk toward the group. A hand tugged on her arm. Riley stopped and turned back.

"I'm sorry if I overstepped. It's a personality flaw." Sara shrugged.

"From what I've seen, you only have her best interests at heart. She's lucky to have you in her life." Riley smiled and then turned back to the group. She'd been glad for the interruption, though. There were things she wanted to say to Andrea, to tell her, but not with a group of people around. Especially clients who expected professionalism.

It wasn't long before the poses were complete at the hall. Kay and Sara made their way to the limo followed by those in the wedding party. Andrea was walking with the group and then turned back and walked up to Riley.

"I was looking forward to seeing you in another suit, but jeans and a flannel look good on you, too," Andrea said.

"I plan to change after this next shoot. No sense ruining good clothes while hiding behind shrubbery." Riley laughed.

"Hadn't thought of that." Andrea smiled. "Could I talk with you for a minute?"

"Would you like to ride with me to the next location?" Riley bent down to pick up a duffel bag but stopped and stood up when she heard footsteps approaching.

"Andrea, come on! Kay and Sara are going to open their gifts from us in the car." Kelly marched across the room toward them, clearly on roundup duty.

Disappointed, Riley still smiled. "I got your note this morning. We're good. Would you save me a dance tonight? I'm done around ten."

"Definite—"

Kelly grabbed Andrea's hand and pulled her toward the waiting limo.

"Go, I'll be right behind you." Riley watched them through the glass doors as they climbed into the car. It was a huge limo. Surely there was room for one more. The car pulled away and she chastised herself. She wasn't part of that group. She was hired staff and she needed to remember her place. Seeing Andrea was a wonderful surprise, but what did it change, really? They still lived in separate parts of the country, in very different lives. This could be a dream, but she'd wake eventually. Riley bent back down and picked up the duffel bag. Maybe she could get a couple of shots of the landscape on her way to the lake. Something to help her feel centered. Just a few more hours and she'd be off the clock.

CHAPTER TEN

The music started to play, and for some reason, Andrea felt a nervous knot develop deep in her stomach. She'd helped Sara plan for this day for so long, and now it was moments away from happening. She watched Kelly and Mel head up the main aisle and then Rose and Tami took their spot in the doorway. She turned to Sara, her eyes welling up a little at how beautiful she looked.

"Don't you dare, 'cause then I'll start. I'll kick your ass if I'm bawling while walking up the aisle," Sara whispered. She had her arm hooked through her father's arm. He beamed with pride.

"Love you, my friend. I'll see you up there, Mrs. Kay Martin." Andrea tucked her arm into Jack's and stood in the doorway.

She drew in a deep breath and then focused on each step while walking up the aisle. For once, Jack was quiet, offering a bit of stability while matching her pace. She looked up in time to catch Riley's eye and the sweetest smile she'd ever seen on her face. All of which quickly disappeared behind the large camera. Riley was dressed in a tailored black suit covering a white shirt open at the collar. She looked sexy as hell, but this wasn't about her. It was about her friends. She focused and smiled at Jack as she let go of her arm. Jack winked at her and took her place next to Kay.

Andrea took her spot next to Rose and then turned to watch Sara walk up the aisle. She was every bit the beautiful, beaming bride. She glanced over and saw the adoration on Kay's face. She longed to feel that kind of love and to have someone look at her the way Kay was looking at Sara right now. She hadn't realized it until that second, but she didn't want to be alone anymore. Sara's father kissed her on the cheek and then kissed Kay on the cheek and welcomed her into the family. Would her father be open to doing that for her someday?

While Kay and Sara were saying their vows, Andrea resisted the urge to turn and look at Riley. She could hear the shutter quietly clicking and knew Riley was focused on capturing this moment for her friends. There were just a few short hours left and then she'd finally get some time with her.

Once the rings were exchanged and the brides shared their first kiss as a married couple, the pace of the afternoon finally slowed down a bit. The wedding party mingled with everyone in the reception area while the row seats were swapped for round tables. Sara and Kay were occupied with close relatives eager to visit with the newlyweds. Andrea took advantage of the few moments of solitude and made her way over to the bar. She ordered two short glasses of whiskey on the rocks and then scanned the room for Riley, finally spotting her by the big windows.

"I thought you might be thirsty." Andrea held up the rocks glass.

"Normally, I wouldn't indulge until after the shoot, but a sip couldn't hurt." Riley lowered the camera and accepted the glass.

"Almost everyone in this room has been drinking since nine this morning. No reason for you to be the only sober one here." Andrea smiled.

"Cheers." Riley held up the glass and tapped it against Andrea's. "You look absolutely beautiful, Andrea. You took my breath away when you walked out of the dressing room."

Andrea could feel her cheeks flush and couldn't stop the smile from spreading across her face. "Thank you. You look quite amazing yourself. Is it horrible of me to wish the afternoon away? I've never looked forward to ten o'clock so much in my life. It's like you're so close and still so far away."

"I'm glad to hear I'm not the only one who feels that way. I'm sorry, one second."

Riley set the whiskey glass on a table and pulled the camera up to her eye. The shutter clicked several times before she lowered it and walked about ten feet away for a few more photos. Andrea turned and looked in the direction of the lens, eager to see what caught Riley's eye. All she saw was a bunch of people surrounding Sara and Kay. She walked up next to Riley and couldn't see anything different.

"It's just a mob of people. What do you see that I don't?" Andrea asked.

"Don't look at the mob. Here, let me have your glass." Riley set it down on an empty table. "Now, take your index finger and your thumb and make an 'L' with each hand. Here, lift them up overlapping the tips of your thumbs so they touch. Straighten your arms up so the box you created is an arm's length away from your eye." Riley moved behind Andrea and guided her arms in the correct position. She leaned into Andrea's back, her lips close to Andrea's ear. "Like this. Oh, perfect example just a little to the left. Now, forget everyone else over there and focus in on Kay and Sara's grandmother. Put them inside of the box. Notice the height difference, see how Kay towers over her but then she crouched down to be at eye level. Kay's in all white and the elder is wearing bright, bold colors, especially in the scarf around her neck. Look at grandma's hands, all knotted and twisted from a lifetime of use. Look at her eyes and how her smile makes them light up and sparkle. See how she's reaching up to cup Kay's face and pulling her over for a kiss on the cheek." Riley had her camera next to Andrea's framed fingers. She pressed the shutter and an image popped up on the screen and then another. The grandmother's hands were gently holding the sides of Kay's face and her lips were pursed and pressed up against Kay's cheek. "When I have the camera at my eye, the noise goes away and these are the moments I look for."

"Oh my God, that's beautiful." Andrea lowered her hands. She stayed still, and Riley's arms slowly lowered on either side of her. Riley's hand rested for a moment on her waist. She could feel Riley's breath on the side of her neck. "I don't want you to move. Could we just stay like this?"

"If I get to be this close to you, then I'd rather you turn around," Riley whispered.

Andrea shivered from head to toe. She slowly turned around and looked up into Riley's eyes. "So, can we stay like this?" She teased the back of Riley's hand with her fingertips.

"I'd love nothing more." Riley stared into her eyes for a moment. "I'm supposed to be working. Soon, okay?"

Andrea nodded and stepped back. "Charge them double for making me wait. Personally, I think they have enough pictures." She picked her whiskey glass up from the table.

Riley smiled at her with that half grin and then ducked back behind the camera and began moving around the room again. Andrea looked at the clock on the wall. Three and a half more hours. The question was, until what?

CHAPTER ELEVEN

As the hours passed, the tender moments became less and less until the silly antics tipped the scale. Jack and Mel had their bow ties undone and the collars of their shirts were open by several buttons. The jackets were long gone. Jack was on the dance floor doing the worm while onlookers clapped to the beat. Riley took a few final shots and then started breaking down her equipment. The happy couple rarely wanted photos of the messier part of the night, where people's inhibitions were drowned in alcohol, love, and sometimes, regrets.

She was almost giddy when the gear was finally loaded into the car. The strong bass from the upbeat song could be felt all the way across the parking lot. Lights flickered and flashed through the windows. She'd never gone back to the after-party of a wedding. She was a contractor, not a friend, and once her job was done, she left. Sure, the occasional woman made her way to Riley's hotel room after the party, but that was their choice and wasn't in view of everyone else. But she'd sensed that Sara and Kay wouldn't mind, given her connection to Andrea, so tonight she'd break her own rules. She shook her head when she realized she was close to skipping her way back into the building. Andrea was still standing between the fireplace and the dance floor looking sexy as ever. Her shoulders swayed along with the music. She smiled when their eyes met. The upbeat song trailed off and the DJ announced that it was time to slow things down. The first few notes of a slow song started to play.

"Excuse me, beautiful, may I have this dance?"

"I'd love nothing more."

Riley smiled and took Andrea's hand, leading her out to the dance floor. Before the first chorus, Andrea nuzzled in close, and her head dropped down to rest on Riley's shoulder. The warmth of her breath felt amazing on her neck. Andrea's arms wrapped around her shoulders and Riley slid her hand from Andrea's waist around to the bare skin of her lower back. They still fit perfectly together. Andrea stepped in closer, so close that Riley could feel Andrea push into her when she inhaled deeply. They swayed rhythmically to the music. She wasn't even sure their feet were moving, but their bodies were definitely connected. This was a moment in time that Riley wanted on film, a moment she wished would never end. Words weren't exchanged. There would be time to talk later. She simply wanted to treasure the way this felt. Treasure the way Andrea nestled into her neck and the way Andrea's thumb was gently stroking the hair at the base of her skull. She had missed holding her in her arms. She'd missed feeling her breath on her skin. There were so many people on the dance floor that a second slow song started.

"Another dance?" Andrea whispered into Riley's ear. "It feels so good to hold you again."

"I'm not going anywhere." Riley pulled her in closer and held on tightly. It might be a mistake. It might lead to getting her heart broken again, although that was jumping the gun. But she'd treasure this moment forever.

Andrea leaned into Riley with all of her body. Her hip and thigh pressed between Riley's legs. The years melted away and it was just the two of them again, still captivated by one another, in a world of their own. The giddy happiness from her teenage years took over. The feelings were so strong that they kept a tight hold on her heart all those years, even if she hadn't realized it. Riley inhaled deeply cherishing the smell of Andrea's perfume. It was like an intoxicating drug. The way Andrea's body felt up against hers took her breath away. Everything else disappeared, none of it mattered, the past, Andrea's parents, Scott and the years they'd lost, all of it simply ceased to exist. It was finally just the two of them, on this one night, dancing to this unforgettable love song. All too soon, the song ended, and the tempo of a fast song forced them to break away from each other. Andrea stepped back, her hand resting on Riley's chest and she looked as disappointed as Riley felt. It warmed her heart.

Riley wasn't ready to let go just yet. "Come on, kick up your heels. You used to love to dance. Dance with me."

Andrea accepted Riley's hand and twirled in close. There was that amazing laughter and those dimples again, such an incredible treat. Her eyes lit up like sparkling diamonds. They had learned how to do a fun swing dance in gym class ages ago and loved practicing it, mostly because they could hold each other for a moment when they would spin in close. Riley dropped into the steps and Andrea fell into perfect rhythm. It was fantastic. The upbeat tempo of the song was the exact timing needed for the steps and the spins. Riley couldn't stop smiling, it was like a dream come true. They danced for a few more songs, a two-step and then just some good old-fashioned, silly wedding dancing. It was an evening that could have gone on forever. The next song started and as soon as the first few notes played Andrea squealed out with excitement.

"Sara, I have to find Sara! We dance to this at work to blow off steam!" She grabbed Riley's hand and pulled her across the dance floor until they were standing next to the brides.

"Hips." Sara pointed to Andrea.

"Don't." Andrea pointed back to Sara.

"Lie." Sara spun up against her bride.

Sara started to dance, seducing Kay with a series of hip flicks and pelvic thrusts as she spun around and explored her bride's body. And then, Sara motioned to Andrea who performed a similar dance up against Riley. She revealed moves that Riley had never seen before. The high-heeled shoes were quickly shed and her hips became liquid, rocking from side to side with seaworthy fluidity. Riley couldn't take her eyes off of her goddess, completely mesmerized by her movements. She finally snapped out of the trance and joined Andrea in a body melding dance of seduction. The rest of the dance floor disappeared. Her focus was transfixed on the hazel eyes making love to her with each seductive glance.

Riley's jacket was pushed off her shoulders and down her arms and then her suspenders became a means of beckoning when Andrea grabbed onto them and pulled her in close. Riley was putty in her hands, helpless against her spell. And then, just as the song trailed off, Andrea finished with a spectacular series of hip rocks and pelvic thrusts before collapsing into Riley's arms.

"You two are fucking hot together!" Sara said, somewhat breathless.

"Not as hot as you two!" Andrea hugged her friend.

Another song started to play. Kay tapped on her shoulder. "I think my wife needs me. Have fun, you two," Sara said and then spun into Kay's arms.

"Could we get some air, just for a moment? I think the whiskey might have caught up with me." Andrea stepped back into her shoes.

"Come with me, I know just the spot." Riley wrapped her arm around Andrea's waist and guided her out to the deck overlooking the lake.

"Oh, this is perfect, thank you." Andrea leaned up against the railing and drew in a deep breath of the crisp evening air.

"Are you okay here for a moment?" Riley asked. Andrea nodded and smiled. "I'll be right back."

Riley ran up to the bar and asked for two glasses of water then made her way back out to the deck. Andrea was facing away from her, staring out across the landscape. Stars sparkled high in the sky and reflected beautifully in the still lake just over Andrea's right shoulder. She resisted the urge to run for her camera and took a mental picture instead.

"This should help." Riley handed Andrea a glass of water.

"How I've missed you. You're still the same kind, caring woman, aren't you?" Andrea leaned her head on Riley's shoulder.

Was she? "I think we've both probably changed over the years. No one stays the same." It wasn't romantic, maybe, but it was true.

Andrea visibly shivered after a drink of water. The temperature had likely fallen at least twenty degrees when the sun had dipped below the horizon. Riley took off her suit jacket and draped it over Andrea's shoulders. Andrea's eyes closed and a smile touched her lips when she tucked her arms into the sleeves of the jacket and snuggled into the warmth. Riley would freeze for hours in order to see that smile again.

"Thank you, but now you'll be cold," Andrea said.

"I'm wearing a long sleeve shirt, not a knockout gorgeous dress. I'll be fine."

"Listen, they're playing another slow song. Will you dance with me?"

Riley took the empty water glass from Andrea's hand and set it on the railing. She wrapped her arms around her and pulled her in close. Instead of tucking her head into Riley's shoulder as she had done earlier, Andrea just stared up into her eyes. Her hands moved slowly up Riley's arms and then up the sides of her neck, over her ears and into her hair. The sensation of Andrea's touch was almost too much. Riley felt Andrea's hands pull her head forward ever so slightly, and it was all the encouragement she needed.

She leaned down and kissed Andrea's cheek, and then that spot at the corner of her mouth where whipped cream used to catch after a sip of hot cocoa, and then she kissed her fully on the lips. Andrea's lips parted slightly, and the tip of her tongue teased Riley's upper lip. Self-control melted away as their tongues became reacquainted in a deep and passionate kiss. Riley's hands dropped onto Andrea's hips and then she set out on a path of exploration up the sides of her waist. Breathless, Andrea broke the magical kiss. She looked up into Riley's eyes, her fingers still buried in Riley's hair.

"Sweetheart, can we head back to the hotel?" Andrea asked, "I need some time with you."

Riley looked down into seductive hazel eyes. The power they still held over her was undeniable. The dizziness she felt, along with the weakness in her knees, couldn't be blamed on alcohol since she'd had very little to drink. No, the culprit of her state of being was snuggled up in her arms, pressing into her with each breath. There was no doubt that she wanted to go back to the hotel room too. More than anything, she wanted to help Andrea out of that dress, but then what? Was Andrea just another single member of the wedding party who needed relief after a day bathed in romance?

Not that she minded offering that relief to any number of women over the years, but Andi was different. Andi possessed the key to her heart and the risk of being hurt all over again was very real. She drew in a deep breath, immersing her senses in the fragrance of Andrea's perfume. The regret she'd feel if she denied herself the chance to experience an evening alone with Andrea far outweighed the possibility of being hurt again. She wrapped her arm around Andrea's waist and led her to the car.

CHAPTER TWELVE

Andrea's mind and body were buzzing, and it wasn't entirely due to the whiskey. Riley's hand was resting on her lower back beneath the suit jacket as they walked to the elevator together. It had already been such an electric evening. She knew they needed to talk, but really, she wanted nothing more than to feel Riley make love to her.

"What floor are you on?" Andrea asked, pressing the button for the third floor.

"Fourth. Room four ten." Riley smiled.

"My room's closer." Andrea leaned into Riley's body.

The elevator chimed and the doors opened.

"Lead the way." Riley grabbed the handle of her equipment tote and then she felt Riley's free hand lift the back of the suit jacket. Her heart rate shot up the moment those fingers touched the bare skin on her back.

Shivers ran up and down her spine and then throughout her core as she swiped her door card. The green light appeared, and the door clicked open. Andrea led the way into her room. She closed her eyes for a brief second trying to control her heart rate while searching for the light switch. Riley Canon, her Riley, was standing directly behind her. She'd never considered the possibility. It had been so long ago and she'd buried those fierce feelings away so deeply. Though it took no more than a moment in time for it all to bubble back to the surface. The lights clicked on and the room door clicked closed behind her.

The suit jacket was lifted off her shoulders and her body erupted into a series of fiery shivers. Hands were on her hips and then lips on the back of her neck. Andrea drew in a sharp breath. Now, she was hot, so hot, with a need to be touched everywhere all at once.

"Oh yes," she whispered.

Riley's hands teased her with delicate touches up her sides and then along the outline of her breasts. It felt amazing to be touched like that again. Sweet, tender touches that made her feel savored. She slowly turned around and stared into Riley's eyes. Eyes that seemed to be drinking her in and memorizing her every feature. It felt as if Riley was touching her everywhere she looked and it caused another round of shivers to erupt.

Riley cupped her face in her hands. She leaned in close and then the sweet sensation of Riley's kiss melted her entire being into a puddle. It was everything she'd dreamed about over the last decade. Delicate touches trailed down her neck for a brief moment before guiding the shoulder straps of her dress down her arms. *Yes, please, take it off.* She didn't break the kiss to actually speak the words. Riley didn't need words, apparently the deep throated moan was enough. The dress slid down over her bare breasts and then was guided over her hips before it fell to the floor. Riley's hands explored up her legs and onto her hips and then her ass. She felt her lace panties slide down her legs and her body shivered with desire.

"I need you." Andrea's voice was a breathless whisper.

Riley silently guided her to the edge of the bed. Andrea stood there, in the dim lamplight, completely exposed. Riley seemed oblivious to the stretch marks and the extra pounds from carrying two children. Instead, she seemed to admire everything about Andrea, every flaw, every scar. Her touch was so delicate, and Andrea had never seen that look in her eyes before. It was a wanting, a longing, a desire and then there was so much more. Riley reached behind Andrea and threw the covers back before guiding her down onto the bed. The sheets were cool, but not cool enough to calm the heat coursing throughout her body. Riley had way too many clothes on. Andrea held her palm against her stomach, stopping her from lowering herself.

"I need to feel you too. I need to feel all of you." Andrea reached for Riley's shirt and set on a course of unfastening. She stood up and leaned forward, capturing Riley's earlobe ever so gently with her teeth and then sucked it into her mouth. Riley leaned her head back and moaned. Andrea slid the suspenders off her shoulders and then reached for the button of her dress slacks. Two clips and a zipper later, they finally slid down around her ankles. Riley shed the rest of her clothes quickly and stood there, completely naked, staring into Andrea's eyes. Long gone was the lanky teenager. Riley had certainly filled out over the years. Her arms and shoulders had definition, probably from lugging around all of the photography equipment and suitcases. Her breasts were more than tiny bumps with nipples, now they were a plump handful of heaven. She still had a slight waist, but her hips were slightly fuller and her legs muscular. She was sexier than Andrea had envisioned when pleasing herself over the years. Andrea sat on the edge of the bed and then slid into the center. She patted the side of the bed.

"Andi, you're so beautiful."

"Come here."

Her breathless plea was met with a hungry kiss. Riley knelt next to her. A hand on Andrea's knee, and then her thigh, her hip, her waist and then circling her breast.

"Oh, please don't stop." Everything felt alive, she tingled everywhere Riley touched.

The deep, passionate kiss was something so familiar and yet so new. She could have climaxed given enough time to savor that kiss alone, but then Riley's hands cupped completely around her breasts, and then her fingertips pinched and teased her nipples. Riley seemed to remember exactly what she needed, exactly what she loved. Andrea explored Riley's back with her hands and then reached down lower and cupped her ass. Her skin was so silky smooth. Everything about being with Riley was so completely different than it was with anyone else.

"Oh, yes." Andrea managed between gasps. She wanted to ask to feel what they'd never finished but didn't want to bring up that night from so long ago. She didn't want to spoil the moment.

Riley seemed to know exactly what Andrea needed. She pulled away from the kiss and moved to her earlobe and then kisses and nibbles trailed down her neck. It felt so good to be touched like this, as if Riley was exploring her body in an effort to become reacquainted. This wasn't the hesitant, unsure exploration of teenagers. This was a woman who knew what she was doing and exactly how to do it. Andrea leaned her head back into the pillow when Riley's hands cupped her breasts again and then her lips encased one of her nipples. Teeth grazed across her hardened nipple and then disappeared for a moment before her lips surrounded the other nipple. It felt amazing to once again be the complete focus of her attention. Andrea pulled her arms up above her head and held onto the iron bars of the headboard. A long time ago, she had loved being Riley's focus of desire, and after fifteen years, it seemed that her determination to please hadn't changed.

Riley's hands slid down her waist and then her lips explored Andrea's stomach. Riley worked her way down Andrea's body with hot, melting kisses and nibbles. Suddenly, her lips were teasing and nibbling a trail up her inner thigh as she worked her arms under Andrea's thighs. Her legs were gently pulled farther apart and hot breath teased her just before Riley's tongue tenderly offered a touch of pressure where she needed it most.

"Oh, yeah." Andrea's grip tightened on the headboard.

Riley sucked her clit between her lips. The sweet sensation of gentle suction was everything she remembered from that night so long ago. There were no words to describe how amazing it felt. Others had tried to please her orally, but it was never like this. It never felt the way this felt. Riley pulled back a bit and then, just as Andrea thought she was going to pull away completely, she drew her back in and it seemed as if it were deeper and more intense each time, the sensation overwhelming. Just when she thought she'd tip over the edge, Riley slowed down and teased her tenderly with her tongue again.

She kissed all along her inner thigh and then she swept that talented tongue up between Andrea's legs again and into that sweet, sweet wet spot. She felt Riley take her in her mouth again and then

Riley was inside her too, and the pressure seemed to come from everywhere and she pushed into it with needful thrusts.

"Oh, Riley. don't stop—" Suddenly, she needed all the air she could claim.

She could faintly hear herself calling out, crying out, begging Riley not to stop, begging her to go faster, deeper, anything to keep the sensation from ending. Andrea let go of the headboard and buried her fingers in Riley's hair, completely consumed by tsunami-sized waves of ecstasy. She couldn't speak, couldn't breathe. She held her legs as far open as she could and still have a bit of leverage to push herself into the pleasing pressure that Riley offered. She wanted to feel everything for as long as it would last and then all of a sudden it was too much. Too much electricity, too much movement. She clamped her legs around Riley's head and held her as still as possible while she convulsed wildly inside. She felt Riley's mouth match her waves of climax and she seemed to come over and over again with quick, jerky shudders. Her muscles felt as if they had turned to liquid and it was all she could do to let her limbs collapse as she tried to catch her breath.

Riley kissed her inner thigh and then her hip and then that damp spot between her breasts before she pulled herself all the way up and was staring into Andrea's eyes. She leaned down and kissed her with fierce passion, wrapping her arms around Andrea and holding her tightly. She managed to lift her arms up too and wrapped them around Riley's back. She trailed one hand down to Riley's hip and then pushed it between them. She needed to touch her, needed to feel her again. Riley gasped and then moaned when Andrea slid her hand between them and felt how wet she was for her. She brought her knees up and straddled Andrea's hips. She looked up into Riley's eyes and felt her hips thrust forward onto her hand. She twisted her wrist and pushed the palm of her hand up against Riley while gliding two fingers inside. Riley started rocking her hips with more urgency.

"Oh, yeah, that's it, come for me, sweetheart. I want to feel you," Andrea whispered.

She lifted her free hand and teased Riley's breasts and nipples, switching from one to the other. Riley moaned and her pace picked up. She leaned forward and rolled over onto her side. She reached between Andrea's legs and entered her again too. Their legs were tangled together and they were thrusting into each other while moaning and crying out. Andrea couldn't believe she could climax again so soon after the last one, but all of a sudden, she was consumed with wave after wave of orgasm. Riley was right there with her, shuddering and quivering in her arms. It was such an incredible feeling. Why had she ever let this go? Why had she ever let Riley go? Why had she let so many years pass without trying to find her?

No one else had ever made her feel this incredible. She caressed Riley's back, enjoying how soft her skin was. She had no idea how much she'd missed her all these years. She only had herself to blame. The reality of it all, especially after such a magical evening, hit her hard and tears started to spill over. She became completely overcome with emotion.

She curled up in Riley's arms and sobbed. She couldn't stop, couldn't control the overwhelming feelings of guilt and loss that had been locked up for far too long. They were mixed with the beauty of what had just happened between them, a bittersweet reminder of all she'd given up. She didn't fully understand why it was hitting her at this very moment; all she knew was that she couldn't stop.

CHAPTER THIRTEEN

Riley stared at the ceiling, trying to settle the anxiety welling up from within. Andrea had cried for so long that she cried herself to sleep. She tried to comfort her, hoping she could collect herself and explain what had upset her, but words never came. Did she regret the evening they had shared? Had she simply been swept up in the roiling waves of romance and alcohol? She'd once dreamt about a life with Andi. Had the memories from her naive teenage days put too much romance into this unplanned reunion? What did she think was going to happen? Did she think that if they made love, it would heal all the old hurts and they'd live happily ever after? Like that would ever happen. No, it seemed there was too much water beneath that proverbial bridge. Riley blinked back the emotion that threatened to take over. The questions were coming much faster than acceptable answers.

The longer Riley lay there, the more her mind chattered, the more she felt like she shouldn't be there. She carefully slid her arm out from around Andrea's shoulder. Andrea shifted and rolled over on her side. Riley climbed out of the bed carefully and got dressed as quietly as she could. She looked over at Andrea one last time before grabbing her jacket and the handle of her rolling equipment tote. She held the door as it closed and was grateful for the almost silent click when it latched.

This was too much like a walk of shame. Lights flickered in the ceiling above her while she waited for a ride to the floor above. The elevator chimed out its arrival with such gusto in the stillness of the night that it caused her to jump. She stepped in and held the door for a second, hoping she'd hear Andrea call out for her once she realized her absence. Nothing. She let the doors close and made her way back to the loneliness of her own hotel room.

She looked at the bed, knowing she needed some sleep, but she was too keyed up. No, sleep wasn't what she needed. She needed answers. She needed to understand. She shook her head. Was it worth it? Were those couple of hours of bliss worth this feeling of emptiness? At this very moment, she wasn't so sure. Riley walked over to the desk and grabbed the unopened pint of Jack next to her laptop. The small water glasses were upside down on a tray by the coffee pot. She pulled the wrapping off of a glass and then twisted the cap off of the whiskey. She looked at the glass and then at the pint. *Fuck it.* The glass stayed on the tray and she simply tipped up the bottle. How could such an amazing evening turn into something so confusing so quickly?

She picked up her suit jacket off the back of the chair and caught a whiff of Andrea's perfume. She held the coat close to her nose and inhaled deeply. This new fragrance was already a fixation. Her heart flip flopped in her chest. She hung up the jacket and took another strong swig of whiskey before replacing the cap. The liquid was warm as it slid down, but it did little to untie the knot in her stomach.

The sun was starting to peek above the horizon. Riley sat in the chair at the small table and watched the day come to life. Birds started to flutter about, and squirrels came out of nests located high up in the treetops. She sat there replaying the entire evening in her mind over and over again. She was completely baffled. One moment they were tangled up in the sheets climaxing together and the next Andrea just broke down. Riley thought she'd heard her say she was sorry a couple of times, but sorry for what? Sorry for inviting her in? Sorry for starting something that had no future? It was true, their lives were so incredibly different. Why did she lower that camera? Riley rolled her eyes, knowing damn well there was no way she wouldn't have lowered that camera, allowing Andi to see her without her buffer. The issue was that she'd let her guard down and felt the fool for doing so. The hurt from all those years ago was creeping back into her heart. Andi had pushed her away.

They were supposed to go to college together, start their own life away from Andi's parents. They were so close to their goal, too, but then came Scott and the pregnancy. Everything was ruined. Andi had picked everyone and everything except her. Back then it had all been so devastating and it had taken a long time to recover. Which was precisely why she remained single, why she never let anyone close. This kind of hurt was all-consuming. Opening up and letting her guard down hurt more than she remembered.

It was almost seven thirty in the morning, too late or too early to try to sleep. Riley took a steaming hot shower and then made a small pot of coffee. She pulled out her laptop and the container of disks from the events over the last couple of days. She sat down with a cup of coffee and allowed herself to get lost in the project of downloading and organizing the photographs, something she always loved to do. There were so many shots of Andi. Candid moments that captured the very essence of her being. She wasn't ready to deal with them but couldn't delete them either. She created a special folder on the desktop and copied the Andi shots to that location. Once the welcome party photos were downloaded and saved into the folder, Riley looked for the series at the bar. That first moment they had spotted each other was magical. The photographs were everything she'd hoped for, the emotions of the moment shining through. Maybe she was overreacting. Maybe there was an explanation. She couldn't just give up, could she? She added the final thirty-three shots into the Andi folder and then made sure to back up all of the files to her cloud account. Lost in thought, she sipped on her coffee while waiting for the entire wedding project to upload. Her phone buzzed in her pocket and she opened the text message.

OMG, New Mexico shoot is one for the books. Shit you not, a huge rattlesnake made a surprise appearance and then one of the bridesmaids tripped on her own dress on the way up the aisle. Total belly flop! Tits popped out! No pasties! Check it out!

A three-photo series arrived a few seconds later. Sure enough, the bridesmaid landed her swan dive directly on her small bouquet. Riley's heart ached for the woman given the shocked horror on her face. Her breasts had popped free from the top of the dress in the last shot and the expression of everyone around her was the most powerful photo of the series. Hopefully, she hadn't hurt herself and could someday laugh at the memory, because these photos would never be shared beyond this text. Riley had a hard rule on that one. But that wasn't to say photos from people who'd been taking their own shots wouldn't make it into the cybersphere. Sometimes, she wasn't so sure that social media was a positive invention.

Her phone buzzed again. *Beat that one, Chumly!*

Riley browsed to the cloud account and downloaded the shot of Andrea in her maid of honor gown. The slight tilt of her head and the way the makeup made her eyes sparkle. It was a breathtaking shot, simply incredible, definitely one for the wall. Andrea's hair was up, but she knew Jodie would recognize her.

I see your falling bridesmaid, exposed breasts and all, and raise you a one in a million chance encounter with the maid of honor. I have a few new photos for the wall. She hit send with the photo attached.

Silence. Silence for what seemed like an eternity. The last of the files uploaded from her laptop before a response finally buzzed in.

Is that who I think it is?

You stared at her on my wall all through college. It's exactly who you think it is.

Silence again. Riley kept the camera disks from the two days of events as additional backup and carefully slid them back into the protective case. She labeled it and put the sealed case in her laptop bag before refilling her cup of coffee. Her phone started ringing on the table.

"Got tired of texting, eh?" Riley leaned back in the chair.

"I know I begged to take the New Mexico job, but I would have given anything to see your face when you first saw her. So, Andi's there? In Alaska?"

"Yup, she's here." Riley could only imagine what her face must have looked like when she first spotted her.

"Holy shit! Have you two talked? Is she still with what's-his-face?"

"No, they're divorced. Get this, she has two kids, both girls."

"It had to be weird seeing her again after all this time, especially given how things ended. How are you doing?"

Riley took a deep breath. How was she doing? Completely consumed in a whirlwind of emotion, that's how. No doubt, it was weird to see her out of the blue like that. It was also incredible to be with Andi again, in every sense of the word, but then she needed to understand what had happened last night. What had she been thinking? Why had she been so foolish? Her arguments to pursue the evening made more sense when staring into those seductive hazel eyes. And it was absolutely wonderful, all of it, until it wasn't. She was spinning out.

"Umm, hello—"

"Sorry, Jodes, it's too much to explain over the phone. I'll be okay."

"Yeah, sure. If you say so. You forget that I know you. The tone of your voice says otherwise. What happened?"

"We reconnected and it was fun and unbelievable and then something happened. I don't know what I was thinking. I'm not sure I want to get into it right now." Riley swallowed the emotion. She wasn't ready for Jodie to know everything, but somehow, she knew that Jodie already had a good grasp on the bulk of it.

"Ah, Chumly, I've heard this record before and if I remember, it skips...a lot. Remind me, how does it go again? She's the one your heart can't let go of and all that shit? It took a lot to pull you out of that hole and what, two days for you to jump right back in with both feet?" The disappointment in Jodie's voice could be felt across the miles.

"Trumps the hell out of your rattlesnake. I win." Riley looked out the window.

"It doesn't sound like you won anything. Sounds like you're neck deep in quicksand. Do you want to talk?"

"I don't know what to say. I don't even know what happened. I think I just need some sleep." Riley leaned back in the chair and ran her fingers through her hair.

"I'm headed to the airport soon. Do you want me to change my flight and head your way?" Jodie asked. "I could be your backbone if you need one. I'd need to borrow a coat, but we'd figure it out."

"Ha ha, very funny." Riley shook her head.

"Seriously, I'm there if you need me."

"You were so excited to get out of this trip and that's when you were just going to be here for the two-day event. Now, you're offering to hang out and rough it with me in the Alaskan landscape? Did you forget that you hate it when nature gets all over you?" Riley laughed. "Thank you for the offer. I'm good."

"I call bullshit, but I'm here if you need anything. Be cautious, okay? It's probably already too late. Please try to remember how it ended last time around. I know you've known her for a lifetime and all that, but it was also a lifetime ago. She might not be the same person you remember."

"She's still my sweet Andi. I doubt her parents are going to ban me from her life again. I also doubt that she'll go out with Scott and end up pregnant." Riley closed her eyes and shook her head at the insanity of it all. She definitely needed a good night's sleep. It would all make more sense then. "Shit, Jodes, you're right. Same record and it still skips. I don't even know how it could possibly work. I don't do relationships. I don't do kids, and our lives are so completely different."

"Finally, some reason and logic!"

Riley sat there looking out the window. She had no idea what to say to that one.

"Gotta go, Jodes. I'll catch up with you later. Thanks for… well, just thanks."

"Watch out for the bears. See ya on the flip side, Chumly."

Riley disconnected the call and picked up her coffee cup. It hadn't always been like this with Andi. It hadn't always been complicated. The complications had only really happened at the same time as the grand finale. What she treasured was the lifetime of memories that were amazing and wonderful, until they weren't, and everything changed. Was there too much history between them to get past the past? Even if they could, it didn't mean there was any hope of a future.

CHAPTER FOURTEEN

Andrea rolled over and reached across the bed. She explored the mattress for the warmth of Riley's body but found nothing more than cold sheets. She opened her eyes as much as she could against the harsh daylight. The pillow had a dent in it but no Riley. Her head was pounding from either the whiskey or the sobbing, probably a little of both. She slowly sat up and looked around her hotel room then leaned to the side and looked down at the floor. Riley's clothes were gone. Disappointment washed over her. She climbed out of bed and walked into the bathroom. Her hair was a tangled mess, half pinned up and sticking out in every direction. Makeup was smeared and streaked all over her face. She was still wearing the choker necklace and only one of the two earrings. *Well, aren't you a glorious sight.*

Her phone started ringing and she ran for it, hoping it was Riley. The caller ID dashed her hopes.

"Good morning to you, Mrs. Kay Martin," Andrea said, hoping her voice didn't sound as disappointed as she felt.

"Good morning to you, *Andi*. Don't think I didn't catch that the photographer calls you *Andi* and the way you two danced together, whoa, totally smokin' hot. So, details are needed. Did you do the nasty?"

"Aren't you supposed to be on your honeymoon consuming large volumes of both Kay and alcohol? Why on earth are you calling me?" Andrea pulled her robe on and flopped down onto the bed.

"Kay's driving Jack and Mel to the airport and I have to meet my family before they take off, too, but I just had to call you quick. Come on, don't keep me in suspense."

"We enjoyed a lovely evening together," Andrea said.

"Sweetie, I don't have much time, spill it! Did you fuck the photographer?"

"Sometimes you can be so crude. She came back to my room and—"

"And you tipped off the top rail and finally came! Yahoo! Did you get the orgasm of your dreams? Ya know, the one your parents never let you finish? Is my best friend a lesbian now? Are you going to see her again?" Sara asked.

"Sara, it was everything I remembered and so much more, magical even and then—"

"And then what? Do I need to seek and destroy a certain photographer? I will forsake my wedding photos and kick her ass if she—"

"God no, you're so overprotective!" Andrea looked out the window. "Besides, it's my ass you need to kick, not hers. She was kind and gentle and amazing. I don't know what came over me but afterward, while we were lying there in amazing afterglow bliss, I lost it. I broke down like a blubbering idiot and couldn't get a grip. Seriously, like eyes leaking, snot dripping, big time sobbing. I think I cried myself to sleep."

"What on earth was that about? Did something upset you?" Sara asked.

"Nothing specific, nothing that I can put my finger on, other than the fact that it's all so overwhelming. I flew out to a remote corner of Alaska to watch my best friend get married and then bumped into the one person that I used to daydream about marrying someday! I mean, who does that happen to? You know I've been wrestling lately, feeling like I'm so busy being a mom and a nurse that I forgot what it was like to be Andrea."

"Or *Andi*. I think you should be Andi, she's a blast."

"Sara, it's too late to be Andi. I lost that chance. If you could have seen her eyes the day I told her I was pregnant…I hurt her so deeply. I closed and locked the door on that part of my life. Besides, you know I'm bi, but it's nothing I've ever discussed with the girls. What would they think if their mom came home and announced she wanted to be with a certain female photographer?"

"The girls could give a shit who you're with as long as you're happy. I'd bet our friendship on that, and the photographer definitely makes you happy. You rock her world too. Honey, I've seen the way she looks at you, and trust me, if that door's locked, then she's begging you for the key. In fact, I'm willing to bet that she's already picked the fucking lock and has the door propped wide open hoping you'll sashay your fine ass through it and right into her arms!"

"Ha! If only. Sara, I asked her how I could fix it all, how to make it right and she told me that there was no way to make things right." Andrea took a deep breath.

"When did she say that?"

"The last time I saw her."

"The last time you saw her? Like, fifteen years ago? *That* last time you saw her? Excuse me, can we hold the drama for just a moment, please? Okay, so now that I've had time to noodle on the back story a bit, I'll share my opinion with you whether you want to hear it or not, and I say this with the utmost love. *So fucking what*? You got caught having sex in your childhood bedroom. Who hasn't? So what if you had sex again with Scott a few months later? Again, who hasn't? So what if you got knocked up and had a kid? Shit happens, get over it. We have all done questionable things at one point or another. Stop trying to make up for it by being so perfect all the time. You don't have to keep proving you'll do better. You've already done some pretty amazing things. It's time to move on! Sweetie, if you could have seen yourself last night. Seriously, in all the years we've been friends, I've never seen you more carefree and comfortable. Sure, you and I joke around and laugh, but I've never seen you laugh like you did last night with Riley. You have the most amazing smile when you're with her, and watching you two dance together, I mean, come on, serious sizzle! If the woman that I saw last night is Andi, then I think Andrea needs to spend a little more time with her and chill the fuck out."

No one on earth could monologue like Sara when she was on a role, and there was no point in trying to interrupt. Still, her logic made sense. "Why on earth did you go into nursing? You should have been a psychologist."

"I'm too fucking blunt to be a psychologist. You should know that." Sara laughed. "Sweetie, your girls are amazing, and they want nothing more than to see you happy, and from where I stand, Riley is what makes you happy. Go, move forth and be happy."

"Not so fast, my friend. Maybe I was no more than a notch in her bedpost, not that I resisted. Anyway, she's single and travels all over the country for a living, you said so yourself. She's the most sought-after lesbian photographer ever, and she has her pick of women wherever she goes. Our lives are so completely different. How could it possibly work? Oh, and let's not forget that she was never a fan of kids. Anyway, before I consider a future, I have to see if Riley even wants to talk to me again." Andrea twisted the robe tie in her free hand.

"Why wouldn't she want to talk to you?" Sara asked.

"She was gone when I woke up." This time the disappointment came through.

"Did you ever figure out what room she's in?"

"Yes. She told me last night in the elevator. "

"Go talk to her. See how she's feeling, spend some time together. Explain whatever it is you have to explain and then move on! Shit, I'm late. Sweetie, I've gotta run. Are you okay?" Sara asked.

"I'm fine. Go, give Kay my love and have an amazing honeymoon," Andrea said.

"I'll call and check in with you when I can. I love you, sweets!" The elevator chime sounded in the background.

"I love you too."

After a long hot shower and a few ibuprofen, Andrea hung up her dress in the wardrobe bag and slipped into a pair of jeans and a blouse. She applied a little makeup and left her hair down and slightly damp. She looked in the mirror and decided that she finally looked presentable enough to knock on Riley's hotel door. Sara was right, they needed to talk if Riley was open to it. She tucked her key card into her back pocket and took the stairs two at a time.

Andrea knocked on door four ten. "Riley, are you awake?"

Silence. No footsteps, no television playing. She knocked again.

"Riley?" She waited a few moments. "Riley, can we please talk?"

She stood in the hallway, her heart pounding. What should she do next? Was Riley asleep? Maybe she had an early flight and was already gone. Her heart sank. *No, please don't be gone.* She knocked one more time.

CHAPTER FIFTEEN

Persistent knocking at the door jarred Riley awake. She must have dozed off sitting at the small table. Her neck was stiff, and her left arm was completely numb. The knocking at the door started again. Was that Andrea's voice? Riley stood up, still in a sleep daze, and made her way across the room. She opened the door and stood there staring for a second. If this was a dream, she didn't want to wake up. Andrea stood outside her hotel room in jeans and a peach-colored blouse with enough buttons undone that she could see a hint of cleavage. Her hair had been up for the wedding, and while she looked sexy as hell last night, there was something about seeing her with her hair down, dressed like this, that made Riley weak in the knees. This look, this person was Andi, her Andi. The shoulder-length hair was full and thick with a soft natural wave to it. She blinked a few more times when a huge yawn took hold and she turned away slightly.

"Did I wake you?" Andrea asked.

"I thought I was drinking a cup of coffee." Riley rubbed her eyes. "But I must have dozed off between sips."

"Did you get any sleep last night?"

Another yawn stole her words, so Riley shook her head. She was starting to feel the effects too. Perhaps whiskey and coffee weren't the best choices for breakfast.

"Go get some sleep. We can talk later." Andrea turned to leave.

Riley reached out and touched her arm, "No, please don't go. Come in. I'm glad you're here. I was worried about you."

Andrea turned back. Something in her eyes said she understood. She smiled and stepped into the room.

"About last night, I owe you an explanation and an apology." Andrea looked down at the floor, her hands in her pockets, her weight shifting back and forth.

Everything about her looked hesitant, as if she was nervous to say whatever it was that she wanted to say. The look in her eyes was a familiar one. Riley last saw it fifteen years ago when Andrea told her she was pregnant with Scott's baby. She braced herself for the blow. She knew what was coming and it was suddenly too much. Everything she remembered about the two of them together had always been incredible and amazing, and then all of a sudden, a switch was flipped, and she was told that she had to turn all of those unbelievable feelings off. It took her a long time to let go and move on. Well, she thought she had moved on. She thought the feelings had been extinguished, but it took nothing more than the sound of her voice to reignite that flame into the same strong torch that burned so long ago. And yet, here she stood, once again, wondering when the other shoe would drop. Riley waited for the words to come. Andrea just stood there, shifting from side to side and chewing on the inside of her cheek. The silence was deafening. Enough of this, time to rip off the Band-Aid.

"Look, Andi, you don't owe me anything. I get it, it happens." Riley walked past Andrea and opened the closet. She pulled out an empty suitcase and flung it onto the bed.

"What are you doing? Do you have to leave already?" Andrea stepped closer.

"I'm not good at tiptoeing. That's not who we've ever been with each other." Riley stepped past her again and opened a dresser drawer. She grabbed an armload of clothes and made her way back toward the suitcase. "You have regrets about last night. It's okay. I get it. I'll tap out and let you enjoy your vacation. I can handle being nothing more than your after-party relief."

"My after-party what? Seriously? It seems to me it's the other way around. You were the one who disappeared in the middle of the night."

"I don't tend to stay where I'm not wanted." Riley threw the clothes into the suitcase. She walked back over to the dresser and pulled the clothes out of another drawer.

"God damnit, stop packing!" Andrea yanked the clothes out of Riley's arm. She turned back to the dresser and shoved them into the drawer. Riley flinched when the dresser drawer slammed shut. "You're hurt, you're pissed, I get it, but you don't get to run off this time. We're talking through this, damnit. Yes, I have regrets, a fucking boatload of regrets, but not about being with you last night. Are you the only one that gets to be hurt and pissed off about what happened? It didn't just happen to you!"

Riley looked up at the ceiling and blinked back the tears that threatened to spill over. "Let's be crystal clear. *I* didn't run off last time. You pushed me away. You told me to leave. We were supposed to go together. There was room in the car for you. You baled on me, not the other way around."

"Believe me, I know that, but it doesn't mean that it didn't hurt to see you go. You were my whole world and just when I needed you the most, you were gone."

"Oh, no. Don't put that on me. I was there for you. I begged you to choose me, but you didn't. Was I really supposed to stay and watch you get married and have kids with Scott? Hard pass, I can't stand the guy. But I was easy enough to find if you really did want me back. To this day, my parents still have the same phone number they've had all through our childhood. There was *always* a way to get ahold of me. All you had to do was say the word and I would have been there. You were the one who disappeared, not me." Riley walked over to the window and looked outside. She focused on a stand of trees against the blue sky and blinked back the emotion. It wasn't helping. She turned back to Andrea. "Every letter I wrote to you was marked return to sender. You disappeared and I had no way to find you. Phone numbers changed. I even went to your parents' house after college. Imagine my surprise to find out that they had sold the house and moved to Florida. At least I tried to find you. If you missed me, if you needed me, why didn't you reach out? You never even tried."

Andrea flinched, and her eyes were watery again. "I didn't know you wrote. I never knew you tried. All this time I thought you hated me. I thought you left and never looked back. Every day, for the longest time, I'd ask if I'd gotten any mail or phone calls, and they said there was nothing for me. They told me to focus on Scott and the baby. Good ol' Mom and Dad, I should have known." Andrea looked down at the floor. Slowly, she brought her gaze back to Riley. "Besides, at the time I was too ashamed. What was I supposed to say? 'Hi, how are you? Oh, hey, I got married at the courthouse today. The baby's due in a couple of months. And guess what, I finally moved out of my parents' house and now I live with Scott in his parents' basement. I work part-time at the grocery store while he goes to community college. All of my goals have been realized. Isn't life fucking grand!'"

"Seriously? You lived in Scott's parents' basement? Did you at least get to keep that cool pinball machine that was down there?" Riley took a deep breath and let her shoulders relax. Getting it all out there was a good thing.

"I beat the shit out of that pinball machine. Took all of my frustrations out on that thing. I probably still hold the high score." Andrea shook her head, and a faint smile touched her lips. "Riley, that last day that I saw you out by our apple tree, when I told you about Scott and the baby, it was all the strength I could muster to push you away so you would go to school. For being such a shy and quiet kid, you were quite confident and strong inside, something I wasn't, especially when it came to standing up to my parents. I always admired that about you." Andrea stepped closer but kept her hands at her side. "The regret I feel? I regret that I blindly accepted my parents' 'punishment' for finding us together in bed that night. I regret that I didn't try to talk to them and explain how I felt about you. I didn't know *how* to talk to them back then." Andrea sighed and sat on the edge of the bed, her hands folded between her knees.

"But if we're being completely honest here, I knew in my heart that if I reached out and if I got the chance to hear your voice, even if just for a second, I'd crumble and beg you to come back to me. Without a doubt, I knew you'd be there, all I had to do was ask. I missed you more than you'll ever know." Andrea reached over and tugged on Riley's hand. Riley sat down next to her with a leg bent up on the bed so that she was facing Andrea.

"I can't tell you how many nights I cried myself to sleep out of loneliness. It really hurt, like physically ached, but nothing about my life back then was fair to you. I couldn't ask you to stay and watch me figure out parenthood and life with Scott."

"But you could have figured out parenthood and life with me," Riley said quietly. "I told you that."

"Oh, sweetheart, to have the chance to make different choices. You don't know how much I thought about that. There are so many what ifs and maybes, but I knew I needed my parents' help, and I knew I wouldn't have their help or support if I defied them to be with you. I was a child having a child and I didn't know the first thing about what to do." Andrea twisted sideways on the bed, so she was facing Riley. She reached over and traced the bones on the back of Riley's hand.

"Could you and I have figured it all out? Maybe, but it also could have torn us completely apart and made things worse for everyone involved. I thought about all of the options until I made myself sick. In the end, I made the best choice I could at the time, right or wrong." She pulled her hand back into her lap. Riley missed the contact instantly.

"It wasn't an easy road to travel, and yet I can't imagine my life without my girls. They're my entire world. I have accepted what happened. I took responsibility and did the best I could. I don't regret any of the hard stuff with Scott because I was blessed with my two beautiful children, but I *do* regret how much I hurt you in the process."

Riley sat there and let Andrea's words sink in. She lifted her hand and wiped away a tear that trailed down Andrea's cheek. She couldn't begin to image what it had been like for her back then. At the time, she'd been so wrapped up in her own hurt that she never considered how difficult it had been for Andrea. How scary the unknown must have been.

"I'm sorry about everything. I know that those two words don't undo the hurt and pain that I caused you, but I am sincerely sorry.

Can you ever forgive me?" Andrea's voice pulled her from her thoughts.

The room blurred with fresh tears. Her emotions felt like they'd been raked over the coals. "Can I ask you something?"

Andrea nodded. "Anything."

"If you didn't regret being with me last night, then what happened to upset you so much?"

"The emotion surprised me as much as it did you. I think it was a combination of things, but most of all, I think the dam simply gave way. It was a release of everything I've held inside all these years. The guilt, the hurt, the shame, and most of all, the realization of what we lost." Andrea leaned closer and reached up to cup Riley's face in her hands. "It hit me how much I've missed my lifelong best friend, Riley Canon. Sweetheart, last night was incredible, more than incredible. Everything about it. Spending time with you and just being us again, the dancing, the laughter, and then coming back here and being together. Being able to touch you and feel you touch me. God, no one else has ever made me feel the way you do." Andrea stared into her eyes. "When do you have to fly out?"

"I'm in Alaska for the entire week. It's a photographer's paradise." She rolled her eyes knowing damn well that the camera would stay in the tote if there was a chance to have some time with Andi.

"I only have a few more days. I fly out on Thursday morning." Andrea reached for Riley's hands. "Look, I'm not naive. I know that we've gone down our own paths and live completely different lives. That said, I'm not ready to say good-bye either, not when I've just found you again. So, in the spirit of not tiptoeing, would you consider spending some of your vacation time with me? Let me into your world and show me what your life is like? Give me a chance to earn back your friendship? The ball's in your court. You've more than earned that right. I accept anything you decide, though, I'm hoping that maybe you'd show me how to use the new camera that I brought."

Riley could feel the smile spread across her face. She drew in a deep breath and exhaled slowly. It was true, their lives were completely different, but seriously, what she wouldn't give for a little more time. "Well, I don't know, that's asking a lot. It really depends entirely on what kind of camera. I do have standards."

Andrea pulled her closer. She looked up and a smile touched her lips. "I've seen your gear, I guarantee it's the wrong kind. I'll buy whatever it takes to win your friendship back."

"My friendship, huh?" Riley raised her eyebrows. "Friends don't do what we did last night, but I suppose I could refrain."

"Just shot myself in the foot, didn't I?" Andrea smiled. "I'm asking for time to get to know you again. I never said there were activities I was unwilling to repeat. We're adults and we are on vacation."

"I think that's called friends with benefits. What happens in Alaska, stays in Alaska?"

"No labels, no rules, no hiding. Just Riley and Andi on a three-day adventure. Is that okay?"

"Definitely okay. Come here. I'm sure we can work something out." She held her arms open and Andrea leaned into the embrace. "I've missed you."

"I've missed you too."

"I have reservations north of here tonight. If you want to see what my life is like, you can join me? Or I can cancel and stay down here."

"I'd rather cancel the two-hour tour that I had scheduled. I would love to join you, on one condition."

"Name it."

"If we're in the same room and especially if we're in the same bed, then I expect you to be there, in my arms, when I wake up in the morning."

"I think that can be arranged."

Riley sat there with Andrea wrapped up in her arms. The chance to spend some time together. She'd take it. Without a doubt she'd take it. Andrea had missed her too. She'd felt the loss. Riley knew they both needed time to heal, time to get to know each other again, but this was a wonderful start.

Chapter Sixteen

"Where are we going again?" Andrea asked once Riley was sitting behind the wheel.

"North of here. It's an adventure." She started the car.

"You're really not going to tell me?"

"Nope." Riley turned out onto the main road.

"And you promise that we won't sleep outside."

"I promise to honor all your requests. We will not sleep outside. I will not let you freeze to death. I will make sure you get home to your girls in one piece. Andi, trust me, you're going to enjoy this. If we get there and you don't like it, I promise to bring you back to the resort and we'll go on the day trips."

Riley was being elusive, and Andrea wasn't sure how she felt about it. The unknown surprise of the trip was exciting, but giving up control was just a little unsettling. Maybe Sara was right and she just needed to let go and have a little fun. She leaned back in her seat and adjusted the seat belt so it wasn't quite so tight.

"Alaska must have some serious long and dark winters because that's the third billboard sign for an adult toy store that I've seen since we got on this road." Riley laughed. "I guess they need a little something to pass the time."

"Do you remember when we found that vibrator in your mom's drawer? It was still in the box and everything. That was a fun weekend!" Andrea laughed.

"Ha! I think we both lost our virginity to that thing. It was indeed a fun weekend. I had to cut so many pieces of packing tape before I got the seal back on the box just right." Riley shook her head and chuckled.

Sara's voice popped into Andrea's head saying how she thought Andi was more fun. Another billboard went by. Hell, maybe it was time to be a little bold.

"Have you played with toys since?" Andrea asked. Her face grew hot the moment she asked the question.

Riley grinned but kept her eyes on the road. "I've been with women who've enjoyed them. I'm open. You?"

Andrea fanned her face and tried to suppress the nervous giggle. "I've thought about getting something, but the girls are into everything and I remember how we were. I know I'd always wonder if they had found it."

"They make lock boxes." Riley laughed.

She kept her focus on the trees zooming by at sixty miles per hour out the side window. Another billboard went by. Andrea felt silly for even bringing it up. What Riley must think of her. The blinker sounded in the quiet car and they were exiting the highway.

"What are you doing?" Andrea's stomach was full of nervous butterflies.

"There's a toy store just off this exit. Are you up for an adventure?" Riley asked.

"Shit." She giggled. "I think I am."

The store was right off the exit. Andrea looked around the parking lot and didn't see another car anywhere. She turned back to the building and saw a small neon sign in the window blinking OPEN in alternating colors. She picked up her purse and followed Riley up to the entrance. A bell sounded when they walked into the store. It was the longest chime she'd ever heard.

"Is that 'Lady Marmalade'?" Andrea cocked her head to listen.

"I think it is." Riley smiled.

"I'll be right with youuuu." A male voice with a feminine flair called out from the back room.

"I can't believe we really stopped! Sara's always going on and on about all the different toys she and Kay use, but I've never been in a toy store. I had no idea what to expect." Andrea kept spinning around taking in all of the displays. "It's not as seedy as I expected."

"What did you expect? Live demonstrations?" Riley held a studded leather harness in front of her hips. "Maybe this is what you have in mind?"

"That looks scary and a little dangerous." Andrea laughed. "I don't know. Maybe something we can play with or something you can wear or hold. I really have no idea."

"That leaves lots of options available to you, honey. Strap-on toys are over here in this corner. Handhelds are right in front of you on your left, and if it's beads or clips, they're on that small island display back behind you. We have batteries too, should you want anything with a little buzz."

Andrea turned toward the voice. A gorgeous queen easily six and a half feet tall stood behind the counter in full drag. The tall blond hair reminded her of a Dolly Parton wig, with ringlets in front of her ears. Her makeup was absolutely impeccable.

"Miss Charlotte at your service," she said.

"Nice to meet you, Miss Charlotte," Andrea said.

"May I say, you look picture perfect, like you're ready for a photoshoot," Riley said.

"Flattery will get you everywhere." Miss Charlotte batted her hand in the air before covering her mouth and batting her long dark eyelashes. "You gals give me a shout if you have any questions."

"Will do, thank you, Miss Charlotte." Riley turned back to Andrea.

"You used to be so shy and now you seem so comfortable around people, even in a toy store. Another thing to adore about you." Andrea looked up into Riley's eyes, that now had the slightest lines showing at the edges.

"I'm sure there are things about both of us that have changed a bit in fifteen years. I had to learn to be more social when I opened the studio. There was no buffer between me and the clients."

"I like this socially confident side of you." Andrea turned her attention back to the toys. She made her way over to the wall of strap-on toys. "What do you think of trying something like this with me?"

"How on earth do you pick a size?" Riley asked.

Andrea looked up at the wall of unlimited options. Indeed, how on earth did you pick a size? Dildos displayed in clear plastic windows offered a range of shapes and sizes. Some were long and slender while others were short and quite stout. There were also some with multiple offshoots of different sizes from a single base. Andrea wasn't quite ready for that.

"I certainly don't mean to get all up in your business, but too small will be a lackluster disappointment and too big could add more pain than pleasure. Let me ask you something, sugar, how many of your stud's fingers do you enjoy?" Miss Charlotte asked as she walked up the aisle.

Andrea ignored the uncomfortable question and instead admired her tall stiletto heels. Her gate was as graceful as any model.

"Don't be embarrassed, darlin'," she said, looking at Andrea. "Get what's going to make you scream out in pleasure, not pain. Well, unless you're into that."

Andrea felt the color flush her cheeks, still she avoided answering. "I was admiring your shoes. They are stunning."

"Aww, you definitely know the way to a queen's heart." Miss Charlotte smiled.

Andrea looked between Riley and Miss Charlotte. Time to woman up and answer the questions. "I'm definitely not into pain." Andrea turned to Riley. "How many—" She squeezed her eyes shut knowing she was turning scarlet red. "Did you use last night?"

"Three." Riley laughed.

"How about depth? Did the three fingers go deep enough?" Miss Charlotte asked with a serious expression, not much different than a doctor might ask the same question.

Andrea inhaled a sharp breath. She'd never in her life had anyone ask questions like this. Her heart pounded in her chest and she could feel the heat rise in her cheeks again. Sara's ability to simply speak her mind inspired Andrea to answer.

"If I'm honest, I'd love to feel that deeper, much deeper." Andrea looked over to Riley for a reaction. She was difficult to read with that half-ass grin on her face.

"Show me your fingers, stud." Miss Charlotte held out her hand.

Riley's face finally flushed when she held her hand out for Miss Charlotte. Andera couldn't help but giggle. This was probably the best person who could have worked today. Miss Charlotte wrapped her hand around Riley's first three fingers.

"Oh, nice, very, very nice."

Andrea couldn't hold the giggle in any longer, so she bit her bottom lip in an effort to maintain composure. She was a nervous giggler, and she couldn't think of a more awkward moment. Riley looked at her with raised eyebrows.

"Okay, for you two, I'd go with the purple prince." Miss Charlotte pulled a box off the shelf. "It's got the girth you crave and hopefully gives you the depth you're looking for without being too intense. Nice firmness, but also a bit of flex for the fun positions. The harness is easy on, easy off, yet it tightens up nicely to offer good support. Plus, there's an added bonus for which ever one of you wears it. When you try it, you'll know what I mean."

Andrea accepted the box. She looked at the purple prince through the small plastic window. She knew her expression had to be a good one because she could hear Riley snickering.

"Does anything else interest you?" Riley asked. Andrea swatted at her arm.

Miss Charlotte handed Andrea another box.

"Lube. You may not need it, but you don't want to be without if you do. Trust me on this one, darlin'." She winked.

"I think this is a perfect starting point." Andrea held the purple prince in one hand and the lube in the other. She knew she was all kinds of red. She could feel the heat in her cheeks.

"Thank you for taking the time to help us today. Given that it's an adult toy store, it's got to be the classiest one I've ever seen. The way items are displayed, the colors are quite artistic, and it's super clean. Is it yours?" Riley asked looking around the store.

"It is! My website is taking off too. I'm hoping this palace makes me enough money to pursue my real dream. You see, I belong on a stage. It's my callin'." Miss Charlotte twirled and then bowed.

"What is it that you want to do on stage?" Andrea asked.

"Sing, dance, strut, perform. I shine when I'm on stage! I want people to know Miss Charlotte like they know RuPaul!"

"Are you online? You could create your own Miss Charlotte channel. Share videos of you doing your thing, sort of like a virtual audition. I have a photography channel with tutorials, and it picks up quite a bit of traffic. The site brings me a fair amount of business too. Maybe you could do that in the meantime, show off your stuff to the world through the web. You can use anything from a high-tech camera or a simple high-definition webcam."

"That sounds intriguing! Though our internet out here isn't quite what they have in the lower forty-eight. It gets better all the time though." Miss Charlotte walked toward the cash register. She stopped halfway up the aisle and then spun back around looking at Riley. "Did you say you're a photographer?"

"I did. I am. What's up?"

"Well, speaking of virtual auditions, there's this drag show of drag shows happening in January in New York City. Honey, I belong in this show! Entries are due by midnight tonight, but I'm having a hell of a time getting a picture to turn out. I've been trying all day. No matter what I do, I look like a washed-out ghost. Any ideas?"

Andrea looked over at Riley who was looking up at the lighting in the room. She could see the gears turning. She stepped up next to her and leaned in close to her ear.

"She's been so helpful. What do you think of spending a bit of time here to help her?" Andrea asked.

Riley looked at her and nodded slightly. "It wouldn't take long. The entry photo is the big first impression and you're right, she's been great."

"I'd be your helper." Andrea leaned into her.

"Let's do it." Riley smiled

"Miss Charlotte, we'd like to help. You're in great hands."

"Are you two on vacation?" Miss Charlotte asked. "I don't want to take you away from your trip."

"It's an hour, two at most, and it would be an honor to shoot you. Let me grab some gear out of the car."

Andrea followed Riley to the door. She looked down and realized she was still carrying the purple prince and the lube. She looked around for a place to set the items down.

"Looks like you already have your hands full." Riley smiled. "I've got it. My gear is just behind my seat in the car."

Riley returned with the equipment tote and her camera bag. She released the clasps holding the lid in place.

"Girl, are you just haulin' all of that equipment around with you?" Miss Charlotte fanned her face.

"This was a working trip. I shot a wedding over the last couple of days, so yeah, I just happen to have everything we need for a professional shoot. Now, if you'd be so kind as to show me what you want to wear, that way I know what lighting and setups to use." Riley looked up, smiling.

Miss Charlotte squealed so loudly that it hurt Andrea's ears. She took off for the back room almost at a full run, stiletto heels and all, shrieking in delight the entire way. She returned with an armload of clothes, feathery boas in several colors along with various boots and shoes.

Riley lifted a tray out and pulled out what looked like a bag of folded up sheets and then grabbed some type of tripod.

"These are the flash stands that I used at the reception hall last night." Riley handed one to Andrea. She watched Riley lock in the feet and then extend the pole and repeated the steps.

"Now this one is much like the poles used for tents. It has elastic inside the tubing and snaps together to form a long pole. We'll slip the pole into the loops for the black backdrop, hang it up on the flash stand, and viola, we have a studio to shoot in."

"Well, isn't that crafty. Look, the wall of dildos has disappeared!" Andrea stepped back, admiring the setup.

"Miss Charlotte, if we could shut off these first three banks of overhead lights, I think we'll be all set."

Andrea stood behind Riley and watched her work. She kept looking at the tiny images on the back of the camera and shaking her head.

"What's wrong?"

"They don't pop. Something's missing. Miss Charlotte, do you happen to have a step stool and a fan?" Riley looked up.

Without a question or comment, Miss Charlotte leapt into action. She disappeared into the backroom and returned a few minutes later with a long extension cord, two types of fans, and a sturdy six-foot ladder.

"Perfect! Now, I'd like you to pick out the outfit that makes you the envy of every queen. Let's get you a spot on that show."

Miss Charlotte squealed once again and ran for the back room. She returned wearing a full-length black evening gown, fitted on the lower half with a slit up the front showing off long muscular legs in fishnet stockings. The top of the dress showed a lot of flair along with a decent amount of cleavage. She was carrying several new feather boas in various bright and bold colors. Her blue eyes were complemented with a dark smoky gray shadow. Riley and Andrea both reached for the deep purple boa at the same time. They looked at each other and smiled.

"I was going to suggest that one too. It's unanimous!" Miss Charlotte clapped.

Riley looked through the viewfinder and shook her head.

"Andi, can you drop that side of the backdrop? She's disappearing into the background. I have an idea."

She rummaged through the bag of backdrops. "Ah-ha! This is exactly what we're missing. How about we put you on Times Square?"

Andrea helped hang the new background. The new scene made all the difference. Brilliantly colored city lights complemented her gown perfectly. Miss Charlotte clapped and brushed away fake tears. Riley had such a talent for this. Andrea watched in awe as Riley had Miss Charlotte say specific words to get the expressions she was looking for. In some of the shots, she used the fan for effect which added a fun element.

"That should do it. Let me play with these on the laptop for a moment. I want to make sure you're happy with the outcome before we break everything down." Riley pulled a disk out of the camera.

Less than a half hour later and the entire photo shoot was ready for Miss Charlotte to review. She screamed, squealed, and cheered enthusiastically while reviewing the shots.

"I can't thank you two enough! These photos are amazing! Who knew I looked that fucking hot! So much better than anything

I could have dreamt of! How much do I owe you?" Miss Charlotte asked.

"Our pleasure. You don't owe us a thing. Perhaps you'd like to pick out a few favorites and let me publish them to my website, if you're open to it? That, and maybe invite us to one of your shows someday. I'd love to see you on stage!" Riley handed her a card. "Thank you for letting us take over your store for a couple of hours. It was a lot of fun."

"Would you come to New York if I'm chosen?" Miss Charlotte asked.

"Oh my God, that would be a blast!" The thought of going to a drag show in New York with Riley was almost too much to handle. Could something so wonderful be possible?

Riley handed Miss Charlotte a memory stick of the images. "I have them saved in different sizes. Some sites have an upload size requirement. Please let us know if you're chosen, okay?"

"I'll definitely let you know. I can't thank you both enough. Here's some serious swag, including that purple prince, all on the house. Thank you again for everything! My contact info is in there too." Miss Charlotte bent down to hug Andrea and Riley. "I expect to see you both in New York!"

Andrea hugged Miss Charlotte one last time and then held the door open for Riley and her traveling equipment totes. She looked down at the swag bag of toys. Never before had anything like this happened to her. It hadn't even fazed Riley. She suddenly felt like the shy and quiet one, whereas Riley seemed to be bold and daring. She looked over the roof of the car into Riley's smiling eyes and wondered how else she had changed over the years.

Chapter Seventeen

The hotel attendant set the last of the luggage down. Riley slipped a few bills into his hand and then locked the door behind him. The two-room suite was everything she'd hoped it would be.

"Is this the room you had reserved for yourself?" Andrea asked from the other room.

Riley walked through the double doors into the bedroom. She found Andrea sitting on the edge of a deep Jacuzzi tub. The bedroom was huge with French doors that led out to a balcony. She couldn't have dreamt up a more perfect room for the next few days.

"I might have called for an upgrade while you were packing up your room." Riley smiled.

Andrea closed the drain and turned on the water. She looked up with a mischievous expression on her face and began to unbutton her blouse. "Care to join me?"

Riley wasted no time stripping down and nearly tripped out of her pants when she stopped to ogle Andrea's beautiful body as she bent to check the water.

Andrea flicked a switch and the jets kicked in. She lowered herself into the water and sat between Riley's legs and then leaned back into her arms.

"It doesn't get much better than this," Riley whispered into Andrea's ear.

"Hmmm, no, it certainly does not," Andrea said. She caressed Riley's knee beneath the water.

"I think we need to add a tub like this to the dream house." Riley leaned her head back on the neck rest.

"That's right! Our dream house, we had it all drawn up. Three bedrooms, two bathrooms and we even had a darkroom for your photography. God, I haven't thought about that in years. We were going to live on a lake with a wooden dock and have a canoe or kayaks. If we add a tub like this to the dream house, it has to be in our bedroom. I'm not sharing it with anyone but you." Andrea nuzzled in a little closer.

"Our bedroom, I like the sound of that," Riley said. She had to remember that this was three days of fun, nothing more. Andi's life was in Wisconsin with kids, and Riley lived a nomadic existence with a business she adored and a lifestyle that suited her almost perfectly, with no obligations to be home at a certain time or for any event. Still, she could enjoy everything about the three days. She was gently teasing Andrea's skin with her fingertips. Riley leaned forward and kissed Andrea's neck.

"Hmmm, that feels nice." Andrea tilted her head to the side.

Riley lifted Andrea up in the water a bit so she was sitting on her lap instead of between her legs. She trailed kisses down Andrea's back and caressed her skin beneath the water. Before she could explore any more, Andrea slipped off of her lap and made her way to the far end of the tub. She straddled Riley's shins and lifted herself out of the water while reaching for something outside of the tub.

"You have the sexiest ass," Riley said.

Andrea turned back and smiled before lowering herself back into the water. She lifted one of Riley's ankles, sliding something beneath it and did the same thing with the other leg. Her eyes held a mischievous glint as she reached behind her back and pulled her harness up Riley's legs.

"Would you hold yourself up for a second?" Riley asked

"I think I could manage that." Andrea bit down on her bottom lip and winked.

She planted each hand firmly on the sides of the tub and leaned back. Her expression grew more mischievous, more seductive.

Long, sexy legs came up out of the water. She draped the back of her knees over Riley's shoulders.

"Like this?" Andrea lifted her hips up, almost out of the water.

"Uh-huh, and I'm supposed to focus on getting the straps lined up right?"

Riley cupped Andrea's ass in her hands and lifted her out of the water. She leaned forward and teased her with her tongue.

"Oh, that feels so good." She lifted her hips completely out of the water, holding onto the sides to keep her head from going under.

Riley took her time, teasing and exploring until Andrea began to quiver all over.

"Sweetheart, wait, I'm not strong enough to enjoy this and hold myself up. My arms—" Andrea started giggling. "Hurry. I'm going to fall."

Riley pulled away and quickly slid the harness in place. She pulled on the side straps and tightened the fit before she moved her hands to help support Andrea. Still giggling, Andrea pulled her legs back into the water and straddled Riley's lap. She leaned forward until her forehead was up against Riley's.

"Everything is still so fun and easy with you," Andrea said and then stared deeply into Riley's eyes before leaning in for a kiss.

There was a tug on the harness and then Andrea shifted in the water. Riley watched the expression on her face change, admiring her ability to say so much without uttering a single word. The look in her eyes morphed from playful to seductive. The pressure she felt as the purple prince slid inside of Andrea was indescribable. There was something about this harness that made it feel as if it was really part of her body. Andrea moaned and the tip of her tongue touched her top lip and then her head tilted back. What Riley wouldn't have done for a photo of that exact pose.

Andrea pulled back and then pushed into her again, driving away any thoughts of photos or anything else. Riley leaned against the back of the tub and lifted her hips to match Andrea's need. Her breasts dipped in and out of the water with each thrust. Riley wanted to catch the water droplets with her tongue as they dripped off her nipples, but she was moving too fast. She could feel something thumping against the back of the tub each time Andrea thrust forward. She reached down and realized Andrea's knees were slamming into the back of the tub.

"Andi, your knees, let's move to the bed." Riley was so close it was hard to get the words out.

"I don't care, sweetheart, I'm so close. Please don't stop." Andrea leaned down and cupped Riley's face in her hands.

Riley slid farther into the tub which increased the pressure from the harness on her clit. Every time Andrea pushed into her, it brought her closer, yet she tried to wait. It was so much more incredible when they came together. She lifted her hips into Andrea again and it was all she needed to tip over the edge. In a loud, vocal explosion, Andrea came with Riley while water splashed over the edge of the tub, onto the floor. Andrea collapsed forward into Riley's arms, shifting her hips in tiny circles.

"Next time, I get to wear the purple prince," Andrea whispered into Riley's ear.

"I don't know about that. I love the way fucking you feels," Riley said, her chin barely out of the water.

"Let's move to the bed, sweetheart. I'm not done with you yet," Andrea said.

Riley's eyes were heavy. She hadn't slept for far too long, and that orgasm had wiped her out. She looked up into seductive hazel eyes and decided that she could sleep some other time. Andrea lifted herself up off of the purple prince and stepped out of the tub. Riley missed her the moment she stepped away. She stood and slid her way across the tiled floor to the warmth of the bed and Andrea's waiting arms.

CHAPTER EIGHTEEN

It was already starting to get dark outside. Andrea was curled up contently in Riley's arms savoring in the grand finale orgasmic afterglow. This seemed like a perfect way to start spending more time together. She snuggled in closer enjoying the sound of Riley's heartbeat.

"Riley?"

"Hmmm?"

"How did Candid Photography come to be?" Andrea rolled over on top of her and looked into her eyes.

"Why do you ask about the studio?" Riley's eyes remained closed. She sounded sleepy.

"I may have looked you up on the web while I was supposed to be packing up my hotel room earlier. Is it true that photographing a favorite subject back home gave you the concept of candid photography? And hiding in the shadows to get shots of unsuspecting people, isn't that called stalking? But for you, it's, umm how did they put it, award winning photography, eh?" Andrea watched Riley's face for a reaction.

Riley opened her eyes. The trademark half grin appeared on her face. "You were on my bio page."

"I was on your bio page. Clicked on the link to the article too and read it and then reread it several times. Nice head shot of you, by the way. That shirt was always one of my favorites. Let me see if I can remember how the article goes. 'Amateur photographer

Riley Canon was awarded Best Series on Film, Best Portrait on Film, Most Emotion in a Shot, and Best Golden Hour Shot as a first semester freshman, beating out over eight hundred submissions of mostly junior and senior level students. All of Canon's submissions were from a single roll of film taken the evening before she left her hometown to attend Webster University. Her award-winning shots can be seen on display in the Student Commons Room. Because the *Gazette* was unable to obtain consent from Canon's favorite subject, the photographs could not be published in the paper. Congratulations to Riley Canon on this outstanding achievement.' Well, it reads something like that anyway. The black-and-white shot of our tree in the article was pretty incredible too."

"You read that quite a few times to remember all of that detail." Riley wrapped her arms around Andrea and flipped her over onto her back so that she was on top. "I won a one-year scholarship for that roll of film. My parents were pretty stoked about that part."

"You used to take pictures of me all the time. I don't remember seeing anything on your wall that I didn't recognize. When did you start lurking in the shadows?"

"After that night at your house, when we weren't allowed to see each other. I'd catch you every so often, when you didn't know I was around. Those are some of my favorite photographs of you. The roll that won the awards was that last day by the apple tree." Riley brushed a strand of hair out of Andrea's eyes.

"Do you still have the prints? Can I see them some day?"

"I'm starving. Are you hungry? Let's order room service."

Andrea was confused by the change of subject, but she was indeed starving. She thought back and realized she hadn't eaten much of anything all day.

"I could eat. How about a cheeseburger with bacon and French fries? No, wait, onion rings? Oh, and an ice-cold beer. Doesn't that sound heavenly?"

"It does sound pretty good. Let me make a quick phone call and then I want to show you something."

Riley climbed out of the bed and ordered a variety of food and a six-pack of beer. Andrea snuggled into the covers and wondered how her girls were doing. The last time she'd checked in with them was just before the wedding. They knew she was enjoying some adult time, but it didn't stop her from feeling guilty for not calling every day. She looked over at the clock and added the three-hour time difference. It was already too late to call tonight. She'd check in with them tomorrow.

Riley returned with her laptop. Andrea propped up a few pillows and snuggled up close. A password and a few clicks opened a folder with several subfolders. Riley selected all of the images in a specific subfolder and clicked "open slideshow." Andrea's breath caught. She recognized her teenage self, and the location, but certainly hadn't posed for the shot. She was leaning forward, looking off to the side. Her hair glistened in the sun as it cascaded down to frame her face, and her eyelashes seemed to glow, even the irises of her hazel eyes seemed to pop every color. The detail was incredible. Tiny glowing dust particles floated in the air around her head. It was a profile shot from her shoulders up. Her lips were slightly parted. The woods behind her were filled with deep, dark shadows.

"This shot won the best golden hour. That last day, I arrived early but you were already there. I stayed back in the woods and watched you for a moment. I was completely captivated by what I saw and had to see if I could capture that image on film. I took several shots before I stepped on a stick and you looked my way. I caught that moment too." Riley clicked on the next photo. "Now, this one won the most emotion in a shot."

"Oh, I do remember this one." Andrea reached up and touched the screen. "You had just given me that beautiful bracelet. I know the camera was between us, but I was totally looking at you. I was a whirlwind of emotions at that moment. I knew what I had to do, I knew what I had come there to say, but my God how I adored you. I'd missed you so much. I treasured the way you treated me, the way you spoiled me rotten and cherished me. But that day I knew my words would break your heart. I knew it because mine was already broken. One evening turned my entire world upside down and I had to confess that truth to you. I see the emotion on my face in that photograph and I feel sorry for her."

"I see all of it. The love. The adoration. The guilt. The fear, everything. It's still one of the most powerful photographs I've ever taken." Riley clicked to the next photo.

"When did you take this one?" Andrea stared at it, trying to remember it.

"When the stick snapped and you caught me lurking in the woods. It was the moment you realized it was me, and you gave me that smile that totally lights up my world. The dimples show up when you're that happy. This one won best portrait because you weren't totally looking at the camera. I somehow caught it just as you recognized me, but you weren't posing for a photo. Your smile says it all."

"You can see every strand of hair on my head, every eyelash. The sun was so bright. Look how small my pupils are."

"Okay, now this next one is a thumbnail series of the entire roll of film, front to back. It won best series."

Riley clicked on the next photo and the screen filled with each small photo from the entire roll of film, twelve images in all. Andrea was the subject in every single photo. There were a few of her side profile, one of her looking into the woods, others when she realized it was Riley in the woods and then the few around the bracelet. Andrea studied each shot and admired Riley's talent.

"Can I ask you something?" Andrea looked up.

"Anything."

"What did you see in the Jacuzzi at the hotel that made you take a picture?"

"Ah, the Jacuzzi. That's already a new favorite." Riley backed out of the folder and opened a different one. She scanned the thumbnails and then clicked on a shot. "Here it is. The three of you were talking about something or another. What caught my eye was how Kay was looking at Sara, how Sara was laughing and how you were watching the two of them with such a tender smile and sparkling eyes. Each of you holding a flute of champagne. The soft steam rising up from the bubbling water made the shot completely irresistible and worth being outed by the flash."

"Now I understand." Andrea looked at the photograph. "I can't believe it. This is what Kay was talking about. These shots. You captured the emotion of that moment perfectly. They are going to be absolutely thrilled. Seeing examples on your site is one thing, but I know these people, I know their hearts and you captured all of it, their essence, their love for each other, with the click of a button."

"Sara's right about one thing, they probably deserve a discount because there are as many shots of you as there are of their weekend. I used twice the number of disks as I have on any other job." Riley smiled.

"Oh, so you heard us, eh?"

She winced. "Andi, I had a job—"

"Shut up. I know. It's okay. Could I see what you captured this weekend?"

A knock on the hotel room door interrupted the conversation. "Room service."

Riley backed out of the folder and opened a different one. "Here, start here and I'll get the food."

Andrea clicked through the moments of the weekend. Shots of Kay and Sara in the lobby of the hotel greeting guests. A photo of Kay and Sara in the bar with Cat setting drinks on the table. Sara was blushing at something Cat had said, and Kay was belly laughing. Andrea could only imagine the comments needed to get Sara to turn that shade of red. She kept clicking through the images. Shots of Kay and Sara at the welcome party playing Connect Four and Jenga. Shots of her turning away from the bar in that cute black cocktail dress. *Wow, who knew I looked that hot? Definitely hot mom.* A funny thought occurred to her as she clicked through the photographs marveling at the emotion in each captured moment. If things worked out, if they were ever to have a ceremony… Who would capture their special day? Who else could capture the emotion of their day in a way that could possibly compare to this? Andrea shook her head and a sadness washed over her. She needed to stop thinking like that. There wouldn't be a special day for them. Their lives were too different, and she wasn't about to ask Riley to give up her glamorous life to do soccer games and ballet lessons. Andrea had been so wrapped up in being a mom and nurse she'd forgotten how to be anything else. She couldn't possibly expect Riley to take on that kind of existence and give up her dream life. She needed to accept these next few days for what it was and then just enjoy the fact that she had Riley's friendship back in her life. It had to be enough.

CHAPTER NINETEEN

The ringer on the room phone pulled Riley out of a deep sleep. She stumbled over to the desk and picked up the receiver.

"Hello." She rubbed at her eyes.

"Yes, hello, Ms. Canon, this is Monica at the front desk. You asked to receive a call if the lights were active. You certainly timed this trip perfectly. It's a new moon and the lights are on full display right now."

"Thank you so much for calling. I really appreciate the heads up." Riley's heart skipped a beat. The moment she'd been waiting for. The need for sleep evaporated instantly. The northern lights were active. "Andi, wake up."

"What is it? What's wrong?" Andrea rolled over and sat up.

"Nothing's wrong. Would you get up and get dressed? Bathing suit first and then warm clothes."

"Seriously, Riley? It's the middle of the night. Come back to bed." Andrea flopped backward on the bed.

Riley turned off the small lamp and opened the blackout curtains covering the window. The room filled with a green glow.

"Andi, look." Riley stood there mesmerized.

"Oh my, it's so beautiful. I wondered if I'd get to see that." Andrea got up and stood next to Riley looking out the window.

"I know it was a long day, but by chance are you up for an adventure?" Riley had looked forward to this moment for as long as she could remember. It had always been a dream and now she was going to get to share it with Andrea.

"Suits first? Well, alrighty, let's do this." Andrea kissed Riley's cheek and moved into action.

Riley too dressed quickly, mentally making a note of everything she needed to have with her. She couldn't get outside quickly enough.

The parking lot was already full of people eager to witness the aurora borealis in all its brilliant glory. Bright green and blue with hints of pink and purple floated above, shifting and weaving in a fluid rhythm. It was as if a fluorescent box of crayons had been tossed up into the sky and then exploded into thousands of glistening and glowing pieces swirling high above her head. The Cree people, indigenous to Canada, call the northern lights the Dance of the Spirits. It certainly looked like an ancestral spiritual dance to her. She'd read everything she could get her hands on about this magical phenomenon and how to enjoy the experience from this specific location. From her research, Riley knew the path she sought was off to the left at the end of the parking lot. She kept a tight grip on the rolling tote with one hand and reached for Andrea's hand with the other.

"Come on, let's go this way. I have the perfect setting. I'm so excited."

The path was a couple hundred feet long and opened up into a clearing surrounded by tall pines. A hint of steam rose into the cool night air at the end of the path.

"What is this place?" Andrea wrapped her arm around Riley's waist.

"It's a hot spring. I was going to show you tomorrow, but now works even better. May I take a photo of you in the water beneath the northern lights before others start to get the same idea?" Riley asked.

Without a word, Andrea began to strip down to her swimsuit. Riley opened the tote and set up three tripods. She mounted a camera body on each and then fit two with wide-angle lenses and one with a portrait lens. Finally, she connected a wireless shutter remote to the camera with the portrait lens and took a few test shots. Her heart was hammering in her chest. The images on the display screen were flawless. The steam was calm enough not to interfere with the shot. Absolute perfection.

"Riley, strip down and get in here. The water is unbelievable. It's like getting to take a steaming hot bath beneath a nighttime rainbow." Andrea leaned back in the water.

"Just one second. Can you go over by that rock and look at me?" Riley stood behind the camera. Andrea came into the viewfinder. "Okay, right there is perfect. I can see you, the trees, and the lights. Now, hold very still. Any movement will blur in the photo." She took the shot. "Beautiful! Wait right there for me? I'm coming in."

Riley stripped down to her bathing suit and set one of the other two cameras to high resolution video and the last on a timer scheduled to take a photo of the landscape and sky every minute until it ran out of disk space. She checked each display screen and was giddy with what was being captured. She dipped into the hot water holding the remote for the portrait lens camera which was still fixed on Andrea. The sky continued to swirl brilliant shades of green, pink, purple, and blue. It was everything Riley had dreamed of. She made her way to Andrea and kissed her beneath the northern lights. She took a few more posed shots and then tucked the remote into the top of her suit just above her left breast. She reached between her breasts and pulled out a small flask of whiskey.

"Care for a nip?" Riley unscrewed the cap and offered Andrea the bottle.

"You sneaky little devil, don't mind if I do." She tipped up the flask and then passed it back to Riley. "Is this what your life is like? You go on a job for a few days in some remote place and then go on countless adventures in search of incredible natural wonders?"

"Typically, I schedule a day or two for sightseeing after a job, but this trip is an exception to the rule. Alaska is a bucket list trip. I was hoping for two weeks out here, but I just couldn't free up that much time on my calendar. I'm ecstatic that the timing lined up perfectly with the phase of the new moon so I could have a chance to see this light show with my own eyes. I've dreamt of this trip for years. I've always been completely fascinated by the northern lights. I'm just so happy that you're here too."

Riley squatted down in the steaming water and pulled Andrea onto her lap. She was enjoying watching Andrea experience the light show. Her eyes were darting all over the place trying to take it all in. The sky above was incredible. She pulled out the remote and took a few more shots of the two of them watching the lights together. She hoped they turned out as well as that first one of Andrea alone had. No matter what, she had an amazing memory to look back on.

"Not to sound dumb, but what does the phase of the moon have to do with anything?" Andrea asked.

"The lights are best seen when the skies are cloudless and there's no moonlight. The moon would dilute the colors in the aurora. Right now, the moon won't rise for a few more hours so the sky is at its darkest, allowing the northern lights to be as brilliant and colorful as they are." Riley's cheeks hurt from smiling.

"This is the most magical thing I've ever seen."

"I'm so happy you're here. I'm so thrilled to have you back in my life."

The lights were beginning to fade, slowly returning them to the moonless starlit night. It was still quite beautiful. Riley took one last photo before the glow was completely gone.

"Would you like to stay out here a little longer or go back inside?" Riley leaned forward and kissed Andrea's neck.

"Can we sit here together for just a bit longer?" Andrea asked, still looking up into the night sky. Hits of color still popped here and there in the sky.

Their short time together had been one amazing experience after another. Riley watched Andrea watch the sky and wondered how a simple friendship could work after a week like this. It had to, there was no other option. Andrea had two children and lived a life consumed with work and her children's events. Riley lived and worked all over the country. She rarely spent any time in her loft. It was a place to land and swap out gear and clothing before she flew off again. There wasn't time for kids or even a partner who wanted, and deserved, more than a fleeting night here and there. She squeezed her eyes shut and counted to three before she allowed them to open again. She needed to stop thinking and enjoy this time while she had it.

CHAPTER TWENTY

The water lapped gently on the side of the canoe in the slow-moving current. Andrea dipped the paddle opposite Riley's stroke in an attempt to keep the canoe from zigzagging upstream. Yellows and golds glistened from the treetops. The fall colors were stunning, out in full force on this beautiful sunny day.

"This was a great idea. I can't remember the last time I've been canoeing. It's so peaceful out here, way better than running up and down the road in the car looking for wildlife." Riley still had her camera with her, of course, but it hadn't taken any begging to get her on this trip.

"Thanks for going along with it. I saw it in the brochure and was thrilled that they were still renting them out." Andrea twisted in her seat and watched Riley paddle for a moment. She looked like the perfect outdoors gal with her Henley shirt and heavyweight flannel. Andrea snuggled a little deeper into the flannel she was wearing. She'd snagged it from Riley's suitcase. It matched her blouse perfectly and might have to go home with her as a souvenir of their time together. The thought made her ache, and she pushed it away.

"Do you remember paddling our asses off trying to go upstream from the lake your family used to vacation at? Your folks would find something that they forgot to pick up at the store and send us on our way. It would take us a good hour or so to get to that little corner store and all of ten minutes to get back to the lake." Riley was smiling and shaking her head.

"I hadn't thought about that in years! It was so much work getting upstream, especially after a good rain when the current was running hard. We'd paddle like crazy and get a few feet forward and then stop for a break and end up losing all of our progress and more." Andrea laughed.

"Good thing this current is fairly calm. We can get upstream before our arms catch on to what we're doing. The slow float back will be an easy cruise."

"Riley, look up there, on that tree branch. Is that a bald eagle?" Andrea whispered. "Oh, wait, there's two."

"Would you look at that," Riley said from behind her. Andrea heard the crinkle of the waterproof bag.

"My word, they are magnificent birds."

A half-eaten fish slipped off the branch and splashed into the water. Andrea could hear the shutter from Riley's camera. She was so busy enjoying the experience that she hadn't even thought to reach for her own camera. Good thing she had a personal photographer to get her vacation shots for her.

The closer eagle spread its wings and took flight, soaring directly over their heads. The second eagle followed suit. She could hardly believe her eyes. Eagles nested in Wisconsin, but they were always brown dots with white heads on the far side of the river. She'd never seen one this close. It was an unbelievable experience. They continued to paddle upriver in silence. Andrea noticed some movement up ahead. She drew in a sharp breath while trying not to squeal. A large bull moose was standing belly-deep in the water eating greenery from the edge. Shutter sounds could be heard from behind her again. Of course, Riley saw it. The moose looked up, chewing on the green snacks and made no effort to move. Andrea kept paddling, giving the moose lots of space, so Riley could keep taking pictures. Another amazing experience.

"This is so much better than what I had scheduled. Right now, I would have been crammed into a tour bus trying to see out of a tiny side window sitting next to some stranger." Andrea looked back into Riley's smiling eyes.

"I, for one, am very grateful for the upgrade. An intelligent, beautiful woman in a canoe on the river with abundant wildlife.

Who could ask for anything more?" Riley dipped the paddle into the water.

Andrea was grateful for the upgrade too, though she had to keep herself in check. She'd missed Riley so much over the years, and while this was amazing, it was a bubble, a moment in time that would end. Still, in spite of that harsh reality, she couldn't recall when she felt more comfortable or more relaxed with anyone else, ever.

"You mentioned that this was a bucket list trip. What else is on your bucket list?" Andrea tucked her paddle next to her seat. She carefully turned around to face Riley.

"There aren't many places left, but I'd like to do a few trips over again as a real vacation." Riley kept paddling.

"What do you mean? Didn't you say you plan mini vacations on every trip?" Andrea wanted to move to the center of the canoe, closer to Riley, but she didn't want to capsize the tiny vessel into the frigid river water, so she stopped shifting and stayed in her seat.

"I do and I guess you could call them mini vacations. I thoroughly enjoyed shooting in Hawaii and Maine, oh, and Vermont in the fall was breathtaking, but I would love to go back and share the experience with someone special instead of it being just me and my camera." Riley looked at Andrea, and there seemed to be unasked questions there. She shifted the paddle to the other side of the canoe. "What's on your bucket list?"

"I don't know that I even have a bucket list yet. I have to get the girls through school and college and then off living their own lives before I think about anything like that," Andrea said. And there it was. The acknowledgement of how different their lives were, what expectations were waiting back home. She focused on the colors around them.

"Ah, come on, there must be something on your list, some sort of dream vacation. Where have you always wanted to take the girls? Or is the dream vacation an adult only experience? Overseas? Anything?" Riley shifted the paddle to the other side of the canoe and kept paddling.

Andrea replayed the question in her mind and realized that she hadn't even considered a vacation with the kids other than a weekend at a water park up in the Dells. Where would she like to go on a real vacation? There was always too much going on for a vacation.

"Honestly, I've never thought about it. Let me get back to you on that one. Let's go the opposite direction. What's a day off look like for you? Do you stay in your sweats all day and binge watch something on Netflix?" She couldn't even picture it.

"I'd pretty much have to be deathly sick to do that." Riley laughed. "A typical day off for me includes catching up on laundry, a little house cleaning, bills to pay, always a trip to the dry cleaners, and maybe some grocery shopping."

"Holy shit, you just became a little bit human," Andrea said.

Riley tapped the paddle into the water splashing a spray of water toward the front of the canoe.

"Hey, watch it! You're going to get me wet." Andrea laughed.

"What do you mean a little bit human? I'm human."

"For some reason, I figured you had a housekeeper or something since you're on the road all the time. I never pictured you doing laundry or cleaning house. Your life sounds way too glamourous for that. Though, I should know better, given how clean your room always was. Everything in its place. Come to think of it, you're the only person I know who unpacks in a hotel room. I mean really? Who uses the dresser at a hotel? It's called 'living out of your suitcase' for a reason." Andrea winked and smiled.

"Ouch! Don't make me splash you with water again!" Riley had that half grin on her face. "I'm still me, Andi. It's easier to find stuff if it's put away properly. Besides, I can't show up to appointments in wrinkled clothes."

"Fair enough, so, what do you wear when you clean house?" She wanted an idea of what Riley looked like when she was relaxing at home to take with her when this trip ended.

"Jeans and a T-shirt, or if it's summer I wear shorts and a T-shirt. What do you wear when you clean house?"

"Yoga pants and a comfy shirt. What's your least favorite house cleaning task?"

"Dusting. It's pointless because it just comes back the next day. Yours?"

"Laundry. It never ends in my world. Sometimes, I think the girls change their clothes several times a day just so I don't get bored. It's maddening." Andrea laughed.

"Do they help you with stuff? Do they have chores?" Riley asked.

"Yeah, they help and have chores, but their version of a folded towel is much different from mine. Oh, here's a question. What's in your grocery cart when you go shopping?"

"I'm not home much so maybe a few cans of soup. Once in a blue moon I'll get hungry for eggs and buy a half dozen, but I've had them go bad, so I don't buy them often. Sometimes I buy stuff for a nice salad, and then I'll have to fly out the next day. By the time I come home a week later my fridge is a slimy science project, so I tend to order salads out. I do have a tiny gas grill on the balcony and will pick up a single chicken breast or a small steak to cook for a home meal. What's in your grocery cart?"

What a contrast, and it made Andrea a little sad to think of the meals for one and empty fridge Riley always came home to. "I think you mean carts. There's no single grocery cart in my world. I have two teenagers and all of their friends to feed at any given time so, I shop with at least two grocery carts."

"Andi, do your girls still believe in Santa? Slowly turn around." Riley rested the paddle in her lap and reached into the waterproof bag. She aimed the camera beyond Andrea and took several pictures.

"Santa, no, not for years," Andrea whispered while carefully pivoting in her seat. "Holy shit, is that a reindeer?"

Riley adjusted the lens. "Yep, I think the tag says Comet."

Andrea looked over her shoulder. Riley took a couple of shots before lowering the camera. That half grin appeared with the brightest smiling eyes. *God, she's adorable.*

They floated slowly, silently, down the river, with Riley occasionally taking shots. Andrea couldn't help but think of the differences in their lives. "Riley, would you tell me about your last relationship? What worked, what didn't, what you might have liked to have been different?"

"Really? Why? Tell me about yours?" Riley said, looking at the shore.

"I've dated some, after the divorce, but only on weekends that Scott had the kids."

"Why only when Scott has the kids?" Riley asked.

"I guess I wanted it to be serious before I'd let anyone meet the girls. I don't want them meeting someone if it wasn't going to work out," Andrea said

"Did anyone ever get to meet the girls?" Riley asked.

"No."

"What happened? Why nothing serious?"

"A variety of reasons. The feelings didn't click, or it was too much effort to have a simple conversation. The big tell was that I never caught myself daydreaming about a future. Also, the couple that got to meet Sara didn't pass the Sara test and then, most importantly, no one totally rocked my world. Serious deal breaker right there." Andrea looked into Riley's eyes. Riley totally rocked her world, but this was friendship with some fun. Nothing could come of it. "Your turn, tell me about your last serious relationship. What worked, what didn't, what you might have liked to have been different?"

Riley seemed to sit there forever, paddling upstream, looking at everything and nothing at the same time. Her lips opened and then closed twice without words. Andrea watched and waited.

"There's this little authentic Mexican food place down the block from the studio. I've developed an addiction to really good Mexican food, in case that's the next question. Her parents had immigrated from Mexico and started the little café when she was just a kid. She grew up in that building and knew everything about the business." Riley continued to paddle, looking lost in thought.

"What was her name?" Andrea watched Riley's expression, but she'd shut down.

"Maria." Riley looked at the paddle.

Andrea wanted to ask several more questions. Was she pretty? What was she like? Did you love her? She decided to remain quiet and let Riley talk.

"I used to walk over and pick up to-go orders at first. We'd stand at the counter and talk about anything and everything until the food was totally cold and soggy. Then, I started walking down there for lunch or dinner anytime I wasn't traveling. I'd stay and eat there, and sometimes I'd take my laptop down and work from there. Maria would grab a beer and join me when it was slow. Eventually, I got the courage to ask her out."

"Where did you go on your first date?" Andrea asked. It hurt in a strange way to hear the details, but she did want to know.

"I have got to ask better questions. I did not get this kind of information on your dates." Riley smiled. "During a conversation early on she let it slip that Italian was her favorite food, so I took her to a nice Italian restaurant."

"What did she order? This is important information."

"She ordered your favorite, chicken piccata with capers."

"I love that you remember. It's still a favorite. What did you order?"

"Really? I went to an Italian restaurant Andi, what did I order?"

"You ordered chicken parmesan? That's still your favorite? Seriously? Okay, did you order wine or a cocktail?"

"We ordered wine that night."

"If you could pick only one, wine or whiskey?" Andrea asked.

"Whiskey. Have you seen me drinking wine at all this week? You?"

"Oh, sweetheart, I'm all in a whiskey girl. You should know that by now." Andrea smiled. "How long were you two together?"

Riley looked up, her eyes meeting Andrea's. "We were together for over a year. It was about the same time that the studio really took off. My travels caused quite a few arguments. I reached out to Jodie to see if she would consider flying out to help. It took the pressure off for a bit, but the jobs were just pouring in. Before I knew it, Jodie and I were both on the road more often than not. When I was home, I spent my time finalizing shoots, catching up on email and inquires, booking flights, reserving hotels, confirming jobs, buying supplies, and trying to keep up with everything. She grew tired of waiting for me to get caught up. It was quite the recipe for disaster."

"So, that's what you meant when you said that you travel too much to be with anyone?" Her heart sank and it hurt to breathe.

Riley nodded. "One day I came home from a job and the keys I'd given her were sitting on the kitchen table next to a note. She asked me to let her know when my life settled down and I was ready for a relationship. I knew my life wouldn't settle down anytime soon, or at least I secretly hoped not if I wanted my business to succeed. After a couple of months, I finally figured out a rhythm and had a little more time. I went down to talk to her, and she was in a booth chatting up another dyke with an addiction to Mexican food. I ducked out before she noticed me. Jodie bumps into her every so often. She's in a relationship and says she's happy."

"Do you miss her?"

"Once upon a time, I thought she was someone who could have made me happy, but that was quite a few years ago. But it was a good lesson. My life is my work, and I can't promise to be the person someone depends on. And I guess I've been fine with that over the years." She seemed to shake off the weight of the memories. "Somehow the stars lined up and gave me a chance to sit in a boat with you while we enjoy the Alaskan landscape together. Can we be done talking about exes?" Riley held the paddle in her lap and looked at Andrea expectantly. The canoe twisted in the current.

Andrea watched as Riley squared up the boat. She cut the paddle such that they were flowing with the current, back to the resort. She wasn't ready to go back quite yet because that would mean they only had one day left before her flight home. She wasn't ready for their time to end.

CHAPTER TWENTY-ONE

Was it possible to look peaceful and sexy at the same time? Only Andrea could look this amazing while sound asleep. It was cute how she slept with three pillows. One for her head, one to wrap her arms around and one beneath a bent knee. The sheet covered her bare hips. Her torso and legs were exposed in the early morning sunlight. Riley adjusted the settings on the camera and took a few shots from different angles. She zoomed in a bit and took another of her from the shoulders up. She couldn't resist capturing her sleeping beauty.

"Don't think I don't hear the click, click, click of that camera. Sweetheart, some things are for your eyes only." Andrea rolled over onto her back and yawned.

Riley snapped one more shot and then set the camera on the table before climbing into the bed. Andrea rolled over and snuggled into her arms.

"Did you ever think in a million years that we'd find each other again?" Andrea asked. She trailed her finger up Riley's arm.

"I keep thinking I'm going to wake up and it will all have been a dream and yet, here you are, right next to me when my eyes opened this morning. Like a gift I get to enjoy over and over again." Riley kissed the top of her head. "Being with you feels amazing. Your touch is electric."

"Do you remember when it all clicked that we were more than the best of friends?"

"I not only remember the exact moment that we admitted it to each other, but also the way my body felt that evening and all that night. I used to listen to girls talk in class about how some guy made them feel all tingly. How their eyes would glass over and a stupid grin would spread across their face. I never understood what they were talking about because I certainly never felt like that. Until that night on the couch sharing that bowl of popcorn. My world tipped off its axis that night."

"That night also started unedited. You're the only one in this world I can be one hundred percent unedited with. I remember you saying, 'Nope, stop overthinking it. Be unedited, Andi. Say exactly what's on your mind. You can fix the words that don't work later.'" Andrea chuckled.

"Was that supposed to be my voice? Because I sound like someone's dad." Riley laughed. "I haven't had unedited with anyone else either. I remember every single detail of how unedited came to be."

"Yeah, tell me what you remember. I'll decide if you're right."

"We were freshman in high school. It was a Friday night after a home football game and we were at my parents' house down in the basement watching a movie. It was chilly down there, and we were sitting next to each other on the couch sharing a blanket. Mom had made us popcorn. We both reached in the bowl at the same time, like we had done a million times before, except this time when our fingers touched, you pulled your hand away superfast. You looked at me, stared really hard, for quite some time." Riley ran her finger down Andera's forearm and smiled when the goose bumps erupted.

"That's when I knew you felt it too. The zing. I craved your touch, craved the zing I'd feel all through my body. The look in your eyes told your secret, but when I asked you what you were feeling, you said hungry and grabbed for a handful of popcorn. I moved the bowl and asked you again. I could see that you were thinking, trying to come up with the words. That's when I asked you to just say what you feel." Riley smiled and rolled her shoulders.

"You looked at me and then smiled before you said, 'It tingles, when I touch you, it tingles everywhere…and I mean *everywhere*.'

And I said, 'for me, it's more of a zing. It zings everywhere,' and you smiled that sweet, bashful smile. It was the first time we held hands, under the blanket, beneath the bowl of popcorn. We reached into the bowl with our other hand at the same time, on purpose, for the rest of the night and took forever finding a single piece of popcorn just so our fingers could touch for a bit longer. Or at least, that's how I remember it."

"Hmmm, that's a wonderful trip down memory lane. I remember lying in bed with you later that night and you held your arms open for me. I had nervous butterflies in my stomach, but it felt so good to curl up against your body. It wasn't too long after that when we shared our first kiss, beneath the apple tree. Our freshman year was definitely a year full of firsts for us."

Riley closed her eyes. Movie reels played in her mind of the time they shared before everything fell apart. The memories were bittersweet. They were talking about a time that they could never get back. So much had changed since then, but she couldn't resist the chance to hear more.

"What's your favorite memory of us?" Riley asked.

"There are so many, I don't know if I could pick just one. Everything we did together was always so much fun. I treasured going camping with your family, especially after we figured out how we felt for one another. Your parents would retire early to the camper and let us have some time out by the campfire. I still think of those nights whenever I smell a campfire burning. The way it felt to be snuggled up in your arms. When the fire was down to a few smoldering coals, we'd cover it up with that metal plate that your dad made and then go to our tent."

Riley could imagine the smile on Andrea's face because she could hear it in her voice.

"I loved that we'd get to have our own tent. Those were some pretty great memories. The kisses and the tender touches that would last for hours and hours. You were so good at staying quiet when you came and it was so hard for me, and then afterward, we'd talk and giggle until all hours at night. I loved it when it was cold and we'd zip our sleeping bags together so we could snuggle up inside.

Oh, do you remember walking through the woods in the fall? We walked up to the school and cut through the woods to the back of the apple orchard. We'd get a cup of hot cider and a cider doughnut before walking back home. It would take us all day to get there and back. Hand in hand we walked both ways and talked the entire time. Okay, your turn. What are some of your favorite memories?" Andrea nuzzled in closer.

The memories were fun to think about, but suddenly, they reminded Riley of what would never be. Everything changed. The relationship ended and they'd parted ways. Their lives had gone down different paths. Why were they wasting precious minutes talking about experiences long gone?

"How much time before we have to be ready?" Andrea seemed to sense Riley's shift in mood.

"It's our vacation, there's no timeline. We decide." Riley smiled faintly.

"So, there's time to see if my touch still gives you the zings?" Andrea pushed herself up and straddled Riley.

"There's always time for a little zing." Riley pulled the sheet away. It didn't matter what sightseeing option they were missing if it meant they could spend the morning in bed making love. She wanted to experience everything they could now because it wouldn't be long before their time was up and this fantasy world would be confronted by harsh reality. They had one day left before Andrea went back to her life. One day before Riley would be all alone once again.

CHAPTER TWENTY-TWO

Andrea sat in the passenger seat looking out the side window. It was almost dark outside. She heard the blinker click on and knew they were close. This was the last stop on their list. The grand finale scenic tour. That said, the building didn't look like much from the outside. It was a large white building with impressions on the siding to make it look like a giant igloo. Riley assured her that she'd enjoy it, but at the moment she was melting beneath the several layers of clothing that Riley insisted she wear to stay warm.

Andrea knew she was just tired and a little crabby, so she kept it to herself that the car felt like a fucking sauna. She'd spent much of the night tossing and turning, trying to find a solution when there wasn't one.

Riley pulled into a parking spot and shut off the car. Andrea stuffed her hands into her gloves and picked up her camera. Time to buck up and pretend like she was having fun, when really, she just wanted to spend her last evening in Alaska in bed making love and memorizing every inch of Riley's body. She shook her head and silently scolded herself. It wasn't like she'd been denied. They hadn't slept much that was for sure, but then that wasn't why she was crabby either. She knew why she was crabby. Their time together was coming to an end and she wasn't ready for it to be over. She wasn't ready to trade this in for her mundane life of work and cooking and groceries and taxi service. Riley's life was filled with travel and adventures, and she couldn't but be envious. She'd had so many first-time experiences on this trip. Her first time soaking in a natural hot spring, hell, first time making love in a hot spring. Oh, and the glorious northern lights, another first, and probably the only time she'd get to see that brilliant display.

It had been an incredible few days, with enough time together to fall into the semblance of a routine too, just like a normal couple. Even that was magical. Sitting side by side on the couch, legs tangled up on the ottoman, sipping on a cocktail in the evening while sorting through photographs and chatting freely about the day's experiences. Everything about their short time together was amazing, and she wasn't ready to let it go. Riley had been up-front with her. She'd been honest that her life didn't have room for a relationship. The problem was that Andrea had a feeling they'd be perfect together, and she wanted a chance to find out if she was right. Maybe, just maybe, what they had could alter the plans and routines they'd created for themselves.

"Are you okay?" Riley stood outside her open car door looking at her.

"Are you sure we're at the right place? This doesn't look like a museum." Andrea draped her camera strap over her neck when she climbed out of the car. The thick gloves made it hard to hang on to anything.

"This is the right place. Do you want to skip it?" Riley's expression was full of concern.

"No, I'd like to go inside. I really am looking forward to seeing this. What I'm not looking forward to is the first morning that I don't get to wake up in your arms." Andrea was mad at herself for saying it out loud. She'd meant to keep the serious stuff to herself, so the trip wasn't ruined.

"Believe me, I understand completely." Riley held her arm up, and Andrea tucked hers inside it.

While the outside of the building was lackluster at best, the inside was completely breathtaking from the moment she stepped in the door. Suddenly, she understood why Riley had suggested the layers of clothing. It was cold, absolutely frigid. So cold that she could see her own breath. The building, all of it, even the artwork was glistening and glowing, the lighting shifting between the different colors of the northern lights. Greens morphed to purple, to pink and then to a blue to green again. Everything in the building was created out of ice. Crystal clear ice etched perfectly for depth and dimension. About ten feet inside the doorway were two life-sized knights, jousting on horseback, made entirely of ice. The sculpture was huge with unbelievable detail. Andrea heard the shutter clicking on Riley's camera and remembered that she was carrying one too. She couldn't even turn it on with the bulky gloves. She seriously needed an attitude adjustment. If she were one of her girls, she'd be sitting in the car until that frown was turned upside down. The thought made her smile.

"Andi, look this way." Riley had the camera at her eye and kept taking pictures.

Andrea wanted a picture on her camera of the two of them. Time to stop being a sourpuss. She looked around and spotted another couple looking around too.

"Excuse me, I'd be happy to take a photo of the two of you by the knights." Andrea pulled off her gloves and tucked them into her pocket.

"Oh, would you?" The woman's eyes lit up.

Andrea accepted their camera and the short tutorial from the gentleman. She framed the couple and took a few pictures.

"Would you like us to take a photo of you two?" the man asked while accepting his camera back.

"I'd love that, thank you." Andrea handed her camera over. "Riley, come here. They're going to take our picture."

Andrea didn't care that she looked like an abominable snowwoman. She wrapped her arm around Riley's waist and snuggled in close for the photograph. There would be tons of pictures of her, but few of the two of them together.

She led Riley to the next sculpture, an ice rose. It was stunning and glowed a deep fuchsia pink. Even the railing to keep people away from the artwork was carved from ice and reflected the changing lights brilliantly. They continued their way through the museum, enjoying the exhibits.

"Are you thirsty?" Riley asked as they walked away from an extremely detailed polar bear sculpture.

"What do you have in mind?" Andrea tucked her arm into Riley's. She was starting to feel just a little bit better.

"They offer an appletini at the end of the tour, in a martini glass made completely out of ice. You know I need a picture of you sipping on one of those." Riley smiled.

"I'm in, lead the way, sweetheart." Andrea leaned into Riley's body. She needed to be present and make the most of every precious minute they had left.

Soon, she stood at the ice bar next to Riley sipping on her frozen appletini.

Riley turned to face her on the ice stool. "So much going on behind your eyes tonight. A penny for your thoughts?"

Andrea's chest tightened up. Riley had always known when something was going on inside, and apparently no amount of time could change that. She stared into her appletini wondering if she even fully understood what was swirling around in her mind.

"What's next?" Andrea looked up. "Where do we go from here?"

"Back to the hotel—"

"That's not what I mean. You and I, where do we go from here?" Andrea reached for Riley's gloved hand. "Do we go back to being just friends? I know you said you don't do relationships, but I want more than just a friendship with you, even though I know how hard it will be."

"I've been thinking about that, and what we have doesn't have to end with this trip. What if we keep things as they are, but let it extend beyond Alaska? Our friendship is the base with no labels, no rules, no hiding, just like you said. We could plan another get away like this. You pick a place, anywhere you'd like to go. I'll block out a few days, maybe even a week once in a while. We can get away from it all and spend some more time together just like this."

"And that's enough for you? A weekend of sex and exploration a couple of times a year? Sounds to me like every day in the life of Riley." Andrea squeezed her eyes shut and bit on her lower lip. "Shit, I'm sorry. I don't mean to lash out at you, but I can't just take off like you do. This week was a once in fifteen years event. I have a job and two children to think about." Andrea stared at her empty appletini ice vessel.

"I could come up and see you when I have lighter weeks. You got to spend some time in my world, let me into yours."

"I'm afraid to let you spend any time in my world. I don't know how I could ever compete with this," Andrea whispered.

"Why would you need to compete with this? Enjoy it. Experience it. There's no competition." Riley squeezed Andrea's hand.

"You don't understand. Our lives are so different that they're on the edge of incompatible and it scares me. You live this exciting life, full of adventure and travel. You have people who call you in the middle of the night to tell you about an amazing experience that's waiting for you outside. Me, I wear Hello Kitty scrubs and dole out meds, take vitals, and get puked on. I speed-grocery shop while one or both of my kids are at any given sports practice so I can maybe get to see them at a game. I spend my evenings doing laundry and cooking and helping with homework until I collapse on the couch or in bed. How on earth can my boring existence compete with your adventurous life?" Andrea exhaled loudly and turned to look at Riley. "Don't suppose I can have a second appletini thingy?"

Riley got the bartender's attention and ordered a second drink for Andrea. Once the glass was filled, she took Andrea's hands in hers. "So, let time with me be your escape, your place to unwind and relax. Seriously, your life sounds anything but boring, just a different kind of adventure. Andi, there's no competition. Why can't we just enjoy some time in both worlds? You asked what's next and I'm offering ideas. What do you see when you think of what's next?"

Could she admit it out loud? Admit that she was tired of being alone. Admit that she knew she wanted more, wanted a relationship.

Wanted a chance at something Riley had made clear she wasn't able to give.

"I don't know. I worry that our time together was a mistake and we're both just going to end up hurt all over again. It seems we want different things, and you have no idea how opposite our worlds are. Oh, and if that's not enough, let's not forget that you were never a big fan of children." Andrea tipped up the appletini and drained the entire drink.

"Can I meet them?" Riley asked quietly.

"Who?" Andrea stared at her empty glass. Appletinis were tiny dumb drinks. What she wouldn't give for a double of whiskey.

"Your girls. Can I meet them? I've never been a kid person, but maybe we'll get along fine."

"Maybe you won't, and you'll turn tail and run." She wished she could break the ice martini glass.

"So, it's better to hedge your bets and not let me into that part of your life at all?" Riley's expression closed and she let go of Andrea's hands.

"I'm sorry, Riley. None of this is coming out right, and all I want to do is curl up in your arms." Andrea stood up. "Can we go back to the hotel? My flight leaves early and I need to pack."

Andrea didn't wait for Riley to answer. She turned and made her way through the ice museum toward the exit. That hadn't gone at all like she'd hoped, and once again it was all her own doing. Why couldn't she get out of her own way? She wanted more with Riley, more of this, and she felt so selfish for feeling that way. She loved her girls. She missed them tremendously, but she couldn't shake the feeling that this could have been her life if she had just skipped that stupid party and not gotten pregnant. That thought alone created so much guilt it made her physically ill. She was standing at the passenger door when Riley came out carrying both cameras. She must have left hers on the ice bar. God, she was an emotional basket case. Once again, Riley had been nothing but kind and she was falling apart at the seams.

❖

This felt a bit too much like déjà vu. Riley was in bed, staring up at the ceiling, trying to settle the anxiety that welled up from within. Andrea stirred restlessly next to her, a cavernous void between them in the king-sized bed. It seemed that sleep would be elusive tonight, as her mind wouldn't stop rehashing the events from earlier. The light fun that they had shared over the past few days had been replaced with tension and sadness. Questions were met with one-word answers. It wasn't who they were with each other. The tiptoeing had returned with a vengeance. Riley couldn't take the silence any longer.

"Are you still awake?" she whispered.

"Yeah," Andrea said softly.

She was on her side, facing away. Riley rolled over on her side and stared at the dark, shadowy outline of Andrea's head on the pillow. She reached up and touched her hair. The texture was like silk sliding through her fingers.

"Do you really feel like our time together these past few days was a mistake?" Riley's heart ached and she had to know the answer.

"No, I know it wasn't a mistake. Honestly, it's been an experience I'll treasure forever. No matter what the future holds, I got to share so many firsts with you." Andrea rolled over to face her. She moved closer and held her arms out.

"They were firsts for me too. It felt so good to share them with you." Riley scootched down in the bed and snuggled into Andrea's arms. She wrapped her arm around Andrea's waist and listened to the beat of her heart. It was soothing. "I don't want to let you go. Can Alaska be our new secret spot? Our place to go when we just need some time alone with each other?"

"Alaska seems a bit out of the way. How about something closer, like Rockford? It's exactly halfway between our houses. I might have already mapped a route. Theoretically."

"That would work if I was ever home." Riley caressed the skin on Andrea's stomach.

"Is there room for me in your world?" Emotion was heavy in Andrea's voice.

Absolutely there was room for Andi in her world, but it was so much more than that. Riley wasn't so sure there was room for her in Andi's world, what with her career, the girls, the schedule for sports and activities. Riley's travel schedule wasn't the only obstacle that they faced. It just added a complexity that she didn't have a solution for.

"We'll figure something out. If these past few days have shown me anything, it's that I still care deeply for you." Riley squeezed her arm tighter around Andrea's waist.

"Do you think you'd ever want something more than a few days away once in a while?" Andrea's chest froze at the end of the question. Was she holding her breath?

"Sweet Andi, I don't know how to answer that. I want to say yes. I want to tell you that I'm all in, but the truth is, we're in uncharted territory and there's still so much that we don't know about each other as adults. I've never spent time around kids. I don't know what your world is like, but I'd like the chance to find out. I'd like the chance to see where this could go, to see if we can find some kind of rhythm between our two worlds. Having you back has shown me how much I missed you." Riley traced her finger along the edge of the sheet where it met the skin on Andrea's stomach. She slowly let out the held breath and drew in another.

"At least it's not definite no," Andrea whispered.

"It's definitely not a no." Riley lifted her head and looked into Andrea's eyes. There was just enough light to see her blink back the emotion.

"Promise me we'll find time to see each other. Even if it's some time here and there?"

"I promise that I'm just as eager as you to spend more time together." Riley caressed her cheek with her thumb. "I'm going to miss having you with me every minute of the day. I want you to know that."

"Oh, sweetheart, I'm going to miss you too. Will you call me?" Andrea was playing with the hair at the base of Riley's skull, and it was like a relaxing sedative.

"Absolutely, probably more than you'd like. Will you call me? Can we keep an open mind and see what the future holds? Can I take you out on a real date? Doesn't that sound like fun?"

"I'd like that. It'll give me something to look forward to." Andrea sounded tired.

Riley's eyes were heavy too and the alarm would sound in just a few short hours. The beat of Andrea's heart was lulling her to sleep. It wasn't over. It wasn't good-bye. They were going to see each other again and that was good enough for now.

Chapter Twenty-three

R iley returned to the hotel after taking Andrea to the airport. It felt empty. The cozy, homey feeling that they had created over the past few days was lost when Andrea and her three suitcases disappeared. Their tiny oasis became a bleak and empty hotel room once again. Without Andi, this trip was no longer an adventure. Riley picked up her phone and canceled her flight for Sunday, rescheduling for a flight later that morning.

She worked on fine-tuning the photos from Sara and Kay's wedding throughout the flight home. It felt good to get back into her routine for a moment. It kept her mind busy, even when candid shots of Andi popped up in every other image. This was still work and she could get lost in it. When the final shots were uploaded for Sara and Kay to review, she sent off a few emails, and checked the studio's schedule among other tasks that had been neglected throughout the week.

"Good afternoon, passengers. This is your captain speaking. I'd like to welcome you to Chicago O'Hare—"

Riley blocked out the rest, since she could recite the spiel in her sleep. She sat in her seat and waited for the plane to unload, uninterested in joining the line of people jostling to get off as quickly as possible. She looked at her watch and knew Andrea should be home by now. A quick touch of a button and the phone was off airplane mode.

Hope you had a safe flight. I miss you. Call when you can. She typed and tapped send.

She had no missed calls, no missed texts. Some exciting and glamorous life. She hadn't missed the look of pity in Andrea's eyes when she'd described the meals for one and her empty fridge. She'd had no problem with her bachelor existence, but going back to her place now made her feel hollow inside. She picked up the camera case and her briefcase and then joined the others in the tiny aisle down the center of the aircraft. Her phone chimed just as she stepped off the gangway and entered the airport terminal.

What adventure did you go on today after I left? Is it too late to come back? I miss you too. Andrea added a heart and a kiss emoji to the end of the text.

Riley's heart flipped-flopped. Part of her had been terrified she'd never hear from Andi again, that she'd simply disappear like she had fifteen years ago. She stepped off to the side, out of the flow of travelers and sat on a bench. *Today's adventure was a flight back to Chicago. It wasn't the same without you. I can be in Madison in about three hours. I'm not due back until Sunday.* She held her breath, hoping her unsubtle hint for an invitation wouldn't be ignored.

Dots flickered and then disappeared and then flickered again and then disappeared again. Finally, a response popped up on the screen. *I wish. Not yet, okay? I have the girls.*

The girls. She'd never spent much time around kids, let alone teenagers. Fourteen and twelve, so that meant *at least* six years before the girls wouldn't dominate every moment of Andrea's time. It took a special kind of person to have children and she knew herself well enough to know that she was not that person. Or, at least, she hadn't been. But people changed, right? She sat there wondering where Andrea would like to escape to on their next jaunt of adult only time. The question would be a good excuse to hear her voice.

Can I call? Riley typed. Once again, the dots blinked in and out.

Not now, okay? The girls are catching me up on their week and I'm trying to get things ready for school and work tomorrow. They will be going to bed soon. I'll call then.

Understood. I'm available this weekend if you would like some company. Doesn't have to be overnight.

It seemed to take forever for any dots to appear this time. Riley watched the phone and waited for so long that she started to feel foolish for staring at the unchanging screen. She reread her text and realized she hadn't asked a question. No question, no response required. She really needed to get a grip. Maybe she should have just stayed in Alaska. Kept to her life, her plans, to being alone. She lifted the phone to tuck it away and it began to ring. Andi's name popped up on the screen.

"Hey, you," Riley said.

"I'm hiding in the bathroom for two seconds of alone time. Does it make me a bad mom that I just want to go back to our little hideaway in Alaska and stay there forever?"

"I don't think anything could make you a bad mom. It's good to hear your voice. I miss you." Riley leaned back into the seat, relief masking the confusion and warning voices in her head.

"I miss you too." The line went quiet for a moment. "I want to see you, but I need to talk with the girls before you come up. I could come down and spend next weekend with you?"

"I think I'm in Connecticut next weekend. I fly back on Sunday night. Maybe I could get a flight out at midnight Saturday after the reception."

"Could Jodie take the job?"

"No, she took on both schedules so I could be out through Sunday. Let's see, today's Thursday, right? She flies out tomorrow afternoon for a shoot in Maine and then she'll be in California for a midweek wedding, and then she's in Oregon next weekend." Riley shook her head. Jodie had taken on a lot so she could have a week off in Alaska. They really needed another photographer. "I fly out Tuesday for a shoot in upstate New York and then on to Connecticut on Thursday, and I'll be home on Sunday."

"So, this is what we have to look forward to? Schedules that don't mesh at all. We come home and there's no time for a chance at anything." Andrea's sigh seemed to echo over the distance between them.

Thoughts of arguments with Maria flashed in her mind. She'd said the same thing to Riley over and over again until she'd finally given up and walked away. It had always been the same complaint, there was never any time for them to be together. Riley closed her eyes and could see the set of keys sitting on top of the note on the table. She'd made no effort to change things back then, she'd just gone deeper into the needs of the studio. Maybe it was time for things to change.

"We haven't even had a chance. Let me see what's on the calendar. We'll figure something out, Andi." She squeezed her eyes shut and pinched the bridge of her nose.

Silence. She could hear Andrea breathing, so she knew the connection hadn't been lost.

"You're free through Sunday, eh? How do you feel about pizza and arcade games? You said you wanted to meet the girls, spend some time in my world. I'll try to figure out how to approach the issue of us with them before we get there."

Relief made her dizzy. "I could do pizza and arcade games. When?"

"Saturday? I'll text you a time and address. It's too soon for overnight, okay?"

"Day trip, no problem." Riley sat there smiling.

"I should go. The girls were right in the middle of a story and I totally ditched them. I'll call you later, okay? I miss you."

"Saturday's a date."

"You can call it a date, but you still owe me a real date."

"Deal, I'll still owe you a real date. Call anytime. I miss you too." Riley tucked her phone into her jacket pocket. In a day and a half, she'd get to see Andi again. Was she prolonging the inevitable? Would Andi grow weary of her schedule, too? Weary of a lack of commitment, the lack of a label. Maybe another photographer could free up some time, help lighten the load, but it wouldn't give Andrea any reassurance. That was a problem for another day. Right now, she had to figure out how to free up some time in her schedule.

The studio was dark and quiet by the time she pulled into the rear parking lot. Riley left her equipment tote and cameras in the office and then carried her suitcases up the stairs to her loft. She slid the loft door open and tossed her keys onto the kitchen table next to a pile of mail. The thought of leaving her suitcases until morning was tempting, but she decided to just go ahead and unpack. Her internal clock was off anyway given the three-hour time difference. Riley clicked on the overhead light and at the same time, swung the larger suitcase up onto the bed. An ear-piercing shriek caused Riley to jump back against the wall, her heart hammering wildly in her chest.

"What the actual fuck?" Jodie popped up from beneath the covers. "Riley? It's not Sunday already, is it? Ah, shit, you came home early."

"Jesus, you have pierced nipples? I can't un-see that, Jodes." Riley spun around to face the wall. "What are you doing in my bed? Is there something wrong with your place?"

"Well, about that. I couldn't justify the spend. It was almost two thousand dollars a month to live there, and seriously, I was *never, ever* there. If I was in town, I crashed here half of the time so, I gave it up almost a year ago. You said I was always welcome and you're on the road all the time. I sort of claimed squatters' rights. You weren't supposed to be home until Sunday, and I would have disappeared before then." Jodie tapped Riley on the shoulder. "You can turn around now. I'm dressed."

"Well, I knew you crashed on the couch sometimes, but I didn't realize you had completely moved in."

"That couch is uncomfortable as hell. One night I tried your bed and it's like sleeping on a fluffy cloud. You never use it, so I thought what the hell. I make sure to wash the sheets before you get home."

"Where's all of your stuff?"

"I took over the big hall closet. It was empty except for a few boxes. I moved the boxes into your closet and put all of my stuff there, and you've never even noticed. The furniture at my place came with the house except for my good office chair. I put that at my desk downstairs. Goes to show how much you look around. My shit has been here all year and you never noticed." Jodie grabbed her pillow. "I'm sorry, Riley. I should have talked with you about the fact that you had a roommate, whether you wanted one or not. Let me get a blanket, I'll take the couch."

"Hang on, Jodes, go ahead and keep the bed tonight. I'm sorry that I came home early. It's been an intense week, and at this point I—" Riley sat on the edge of the bed. "Honestly, I'm glad you're here."

"What happened? Why'd you cut your trip short? You've been talking about going to Alaska for almost as long as I've known you. Did Andi break your heart again?" Jodie flopped down next to Riley.

"No, Andi didn't break my heart. She flew out early this morning and it wasn't the same without her there. We saw most everything on the list anyway. Hey, since you're awake, are you up for a drink?"

"Yeah, why not. My boss is cool if I'm a little late to work." Jodie followed Riley out to the living room. "I'm sorry I secretly moved in with you."

Riley finally looked around and saw a few things that weren't hers. How long had they been there? "I can't believe I didn't notice. Am I so self-absorbed that I've become oblivious to everything? That I don't even notice when someone is living in my house? Jesus Christ."

"Riley, you're not self-absorbed at all, you're a workaholic. There's a difference. The studio is your life. It comes before anything or anyone."

Riley made them each a drink and handed Jodie a glass. "Do you still like the work?"

"Are you going to fire me for moving in with you? If so, then maybe this should be a triple." Jodie flopped down on the couch.

"Jodes, I'm being serious. Do you still like the travel and the work?" Riley sat in the recliner. The whiskey was smooth and warm. She closed her eyes and enjoyed the way the first sip felt on her throat.

"Yeah, I do. Sometimes I forget what state I'm in or what day of the week it is, but I do like the work. It's rewarding when the clients rave about what we capture." Jodie spun around and lay on her side on the couch. She propped her head up with one arm and held her drink in her free hand. "Why do you ask? How about you?"

"Would you rather shoot or run the office?" Riley asked.

"Shoot, always shoot, the office stuff sucks balls." Jodie grimaced.

"Do I pay you enough?" Riley leaned back in her chair and flipped up the leg support.

"Yes, you pay better than any studio that's tried to steal me. You offer great benefits, match my retirement contributions, reimburse my travel expenses. You spoil me rotten. I'm sorry I squatted in your place. Like I said, I felt like I was throwing away two grand a month and I hate wasting money, and I knew you weren't using this place hardly at all. I took your advice a couple of years ago and started a brokerage account if that makes you feel any better. You were right, it adds up quick. What's going on? You're starting to freak me out a bit."

She started laying out the questions that had been bouncing around in her head after the conversation with Andi. "Does the location of the studio matter to you? Do we even need a studio? Do you ever sit at your desk downstairs? I do most of my edits on the airplane, I hardly ever use my desk. What if I made sure you had a place to live? I could buy a house big enough to share."

Jodie laughed. "Can I have your bed in my new room? What do I have to lose? I don't even have my own apartment. I'm a fucking nomad, Riley. It's not like I'm anywhere long enough to have any friends other than you. Do we need a studio? I think we'd have a lot more studio work if there was someone *at* the studio. How much business do we turn away because we're both on the road? Now, are you going to tell me what's going on?"

"You're right. We do turn away quite a bit of work because there's no photographer available." Riley took the last sip of the whiskey. "Jodes, I looked at the calendar for the foreseeable future and we're booked solid. Neither of us get more than a day off here and there, sometimes not even that. We're both running six to seven days a week. I'm noodling the idea of adding a photographer. What do you think?" Riley's ice clanked against the side of the empty glass.

"I think you could add four with our skills and we'd still have to decline work. We've been running like this for years, and now you're looking at the calendar with concern?" Jodie stood and held her hand out for Riley's empty glass. "Another?"

"Please."

"Looking at our schedules, worried about days off. Wondering about our location. Are you going to talk to me about Alaska and what's going on with Andi? Can I assume that she's what prompted this sudden interest in our work-life balance?" Jodie asked over her shoulder on the way to the kitchen.

"It wasn't all Andi. I was actually thinking about Maria and how my schedule was always such an issue."

"Maria? Casa Grande Maria? Wow, that's a way back. What made you think about her? She's married now, by the way."

"Andi asked me about my last serious relationship and what went wrong. Hence, Maria." Riley accepted the refreshed glass. "Thank you."

"I remember sitting downstairs at my desk right after I started working here. You two would be upstairs arguing for what seemed like hours, or at least until Maria slammed the door and stormed off. The studio was the mistress who took up all of your time. She used to tell me that she was tired of sharing, but she never seemed to get that you were starting your own business, and that's the kind of commitment it takes. Honestly, I thought she was kind of a shit for not supporting you more. Jesus, how many years ago was that? She was your last serious relationship? I guess so. I haven't seen anyone around since then." Jodie sat at the end of the couch facing Riley and pulled her legs up beneath her.

"Relationships seemed like too much trouble and not worth the effort. No different than you. We've each had our occasional bed warmers while away, but neither of us are around here long enough for anything more." Riley smiled faintly. "I'm sorry it took so long for me to see what our schedule was doing to our lives."

"Our schedules aren't that bad."

"Not that bad? Apparently, they were bad enough for you to give up your place and move into mine without me even noticing." Riley smiled and shook her head.

"Point taken. Ah, I see, now the puzzle pieces are falling into place. You're thinking about something more with Andi, but you have no time, and you don't want it to end up like you and Maria. And now the business is where you wanted it to be." Jodie cocked her head to the side and raised her eyebrows expectantly.

"You're a little slow on the uptake."

"I was sleeping until someone threw a suitcase on me."

"Yeah, sorry about that, but in my defense, I didn't know anyone was sleeping in my bed, Goldilocks." Riley took a sip of whiskey. "Honestly, I don't know what this is with Andi or what it could be, but I guarantee it will be nothing if I can't free up a little bit of time every once in a while. The only thing Maria and I argued about was time and it's still the one thing I don't have to give."

"It would be nice to travel a little less. Don't get me wrong, I love my work, but the schedule can be daunting."

That was exactly the confirmation she needed to hear. "So, let's hire another photographer or two and take some pressure off. Even if nothing comes of this thing with Andi, we deserve a little breathing room, don't we? Maybe you can meet someone who appreciates pierced nipples." Riley laughed and wiggled her eyebrows.

"You're a jerk. Did anyone ever tell you that jet lag makes you snarky? And I'll have you know, plenty of women like pierced nipples."

Riley laughed. Jodie had always been such a great friend. She was grateful to have her in her life. She sipped her whiskey and considered what the future held. Those few days with Andi showed her just how lonely her life had become, even when she had someone sharing her hotel bed. It wasn't the same kind of connection. It had become nothing more than sex, a way to pass the time, but time with Andi, even the sex was so much more than that. It was tenderness and touches. It was being on the edge but waiting because it was even better for both of them when they came together. It was the conversations and being present with each other and knowing when something was wrong. Her life was awesome, no doubt about it. But it was lacking depth and emotion, and Andi had shown her that was exactly what she needed most now.

CHAPTER TWENTY-FOUR

A ndrea sat at a table and watched the door. She'd arrived over forty-five minutes early, and only ten minutes in, the girls were already nit-picking at each other. This was going to be a long day. What was she thinking, agreeing to let Riley spend the day with the girls, at an arcade, of all places? Talk about stimulation overload. What was it they said about ripping off the Band-Aid? She'd either stay or take off running, and it would be better to know now. Wouldn't it? She thought about their time together just a few days ago. Maybe it would be better to keep the two worlds separate, to keep it in the beautiful bubble they'd developed in Alaska. Olivia threw a piece of paper or something at Sydney. Maybe Riley's initial suggestion about making time for just the two of them wasn't so bad after all. What if Riley and the girls didn't get along? Before Andrea had a chance to change her mind, a large truck pulled in with Illinois plates. It had to be her. Only Riley would also be half an hour early.

"Who are we waiting for again?" Olivia asked.

"Her name is Riley and she's a friend from when I was younger that I just found again." Andrea hadn't explained everything just yet. She still hadn't figured out how to approach it so quickly after returning from Alaska. How did you tell your kids something like this? She was sure that at some point the right words would come.

"I already like this friend. Usually, your friends like to eat lunch at boring places where we have to be quiet. Does she have kids too? Is she bringing friends for us?" Olivia asked.

"Liv, we get to eat pizza and play games. Who cares! Can you stop with the questions and just be happy that we're with Mom and get to have some fun and we're not bored out of our minds at Dad's house?" Sydney rolled her eyes.

"Girls, please behave. I want the day to be enjoyable for everyone, okay?" Andrea chewed on her lower lip.

Her heart skipped a beat when Riley climbed down out of the truck. She couldn't look any more adorable in her jeans, a Bears football jersey, and hiking boots that looked like the pair she'd worn in Alaska. Of course, she had that trusty camera draped across her body too. Andrea looked over to Sydney in her Packers jersey and then back to Riley as she walked toward the entrance. Hopefully, the rivalry stayed with the football teams. It was going to be fine, it had to be. The giddy jitters had her heels bouncing on the floor and her fingers tapping the tabletop. She stood up and waved the moment Riley stepped through the doors.

Riley waved back. She had that sexy half grin on her face and did the eyebrow raise and wink thing as she approached the table. Andrea couldn't stop smiling. She winked back.

"Somehow, I knew you'd be early. You're always early." Riley stood at the edge of the table.

Andrea pulled her into a hug. It had only been a day and a half since she'd last seen her, but it felt like another fifteen years had passed. Riley smelled so good. That same sexy scent from the wedding made her swoon. She had to find out what it was. All she knew was that when she smelled that scent, her body reacted with the memory of Riley's hands exploring anywhere they wanted. She shivered and stepped back.

"Girls, I'd like you to meet Riley. Riley, this is my younger daughter, Olivia, and this one is my elder daughter, Sydney."

"You can call me Liv, everybody does." Olivia held out her hand.

Riley shook her hand. "It's very nice to meet you, Liv."

"Bears fan, huh? Or was it laundry day and that's all you had left in the drawer? Maybe we'll win you a Packers jersey so you can retire that nasty old thing." Sydney's smile was genuine, and she tilted her head in that way she understood something others didn't.

"Ouch, dagger to my heart right off the bat!" Riley covered her heart with her hand and leaned back. "Hey, aren't the Bears playing the mighty cheese heads tomorrow afternoon? Are you going to watch the game?"

"Definitely, I always watch, especially when they can stomp all over the little bear cubs." Sydney giggled. "We win you a different shirt today and you can come over and watch it with me."

"Ouch, you're killing me!" Riley laughed. "It's very nice to meet you both. I hear you two can show me how these games work."

"How about some lunch first, then games?" Andrea asked.

"Mom, we've been waiting forever. How about some games first and then lunch?" Sydney turned to face Andrea.

"I wonder if you're going to be a lawyer when you grow up? You already negotiate like one. All right, a few games first." Andrea smiled and winked at Riley.

"I was secretly hoping we could play games first too. So, do we need a bucket full of quarters or what?" Riley asked.

"No, silly! You buy a card and we swipe it to play the games." Oliva grabbed Riley's hand. "Come on, this way."

"Liv, I already have the cards." Andrea held up three cards.

"Princess Adventures first." Olivia held her hand out for a card.

"Liv, air hockey. We agreed in the car." Sydney held her hand out.

"Yeah, but air hockey is dumb. You always hit my fingers with the puck."

"So, what I'm hearing from you two is that I need to keep the cards and we eat lunch first or maybe, if you can't get along, we should simply go home?" Andrea looked from one girl to the other. "Come on, you promised."

"Sorry, Mom. We'll sort it out," Sydney said.

"Yeah, sorry, Mom." Olivia stuffed her hands into the front pockets of her pink jeans.

Andrea was tempted to hand each kid a card and tell them to come back when they were starving, but that wouldn't help Riley get to know them. She'd never felt more selfish, but what she wouldn't give for some alone time.

"All right, let's try this again. You two lead the way." Andrea stood next to Riley, close enough to catch a whiff of that scent again. Oh, she had it bad.

The girls led them into a room of bright flashing lights, loud music, bells, whistles, and spinning disco balls hanging from the ceiling. Every game screamed for attention with a different melody begging to be played. Riley was looking around the room and then adjusted settings on her camera. Andrea wanted to grab her hand and go make out in the bathroom or maybe break in the back seat of that big ol' truck out in the parking lot.

"It's good to see you. I'm having a hard time keeping my hands to myself," Andrea whispered in her ear.

Riley leaned close. "I know what you mean. I'm doing my best to behave."

Andrea could feel her breath on her ear and she shivered with a rush of desire. *Get a grip. You're not in high school.*

"Liv, would you like to play the princess game with me and we'll let Riley and Syd smash each other's fingers with air hockey?" Andrea shoulder bumped Riley.

"Yeah, that would be awesome." Olivia jumped up and down in place.

"You're going down!" Sydney accepted a game card from Andrea.

"Oh, you think so, cheesy McCheese Head? I've been known to be pretty good at air hockey." Riley swung the camera around to her back. "Bring it!"

Andrea lost three games in a row to Olivia, mostly because she was too busy watching Riley play. She and Sydney were a good match, tied at two games apiece. They moved on after Sydney won the tiebreaker game. Andrea was sure that Riley had thrown the final game on purpose and the thought alone made her smile. So far, so good. Everyone was getting along very well. The girls begged to go on a virtual reality ride around a dinosaur park. The four of them climbed up onto the platform and sat in the seats. There were lots of squeals and screams as dinosaurs tried to derail the scenic cart, snapping at the group with razor sharp teeth. Andrea reached over and held Riley's hand for a few minutes. It was like they were a little family. Happiness filled her heart, and she didn't want the ride, or the feeling, to end. It was becoming clearer by the moment that she wanted more. She wanted something that Riley had told her she couldn't give. Maybe she would change her mind if she enjoyed the day with the girls and saw that having kids around could be fun.

"Hey, Sydney, why don't you and Olivia climb up on those motorcycles and let me take your picture," Riley said.

Andrea helped Olivia up on a street racing motorcycle and then scanned the card so the girls could race. She could hear the shutter clicking and couldn't resist resting her hand on the small of Riley's back. This felt right. Nothing else had ever felt more right. She decided at that moment to talk with the girls later that evening about her feelings for Riley.

"Why do you use that kind of camera and not a phone like everyone else?"

Sydney pulled Andrea out of her thoughts. The game had ended and the girls were standing in front of them. She let her hand slide down from Riley's back.

"Well, phone pictures are fine for some things, but this camera lets me decide on a bunch of different settings that most phones don't know how to do. And I can pick different lenses to use based on what I'm shooting," Riley said.

"What do you mean?"

"Let's do an experiment. How about we take the same picture with your mom's phone and with my camera. Why don't the three of you stand over there by the motorcycles."

Riley held up Andrea's phone and took a photograph and then lifted her camera to her eye and took another photograph. Sydney darted toward Riley the moment the shutter clicked. The two of them seemed like kindred spirits. Andrea shook her head.

"The first thing I want you to do is to look over where you were standing. Pay attention to the colors, the flashing lights. Notice what the screen looks like on the game right there." Riley held up the phone and opened the photo app. "Now, look at this, compared to real life. You see, with the phone, the settings aren't designed to recognize the dark and the flashing lights. Also, the auto flash kicked on and your faces are sort of bleached out and look grainy. All three of you have red Dracula eyes too. The bright colors flashing in the room are muted and dull, and the screen on the game behind you is all washed out. You can't see the racetrack at all."

Riley handed Andrea her phone and then lifted her camera. She clicked a button and the display screen on the back of the camera came to life. Andrea opened the photo app on the phone and looked at Riley's camera. The images were as different as night and day. Andrea was still amazed at her talent.

"Here, I didn't use a flash. Because of this, the bright colors that you see with your eyes are also on my screen. There's a decent amount of light coming from the dining room to illuminate your faces, so your skin is almost the correct color, but see here how your hair glows with the greens, reds, and blues that are surrounding you? The clarity and focus are different too." Riley touched the screen and it zoomed in closer. "Look at how clear your eyes are and how Olivia's freckles show up. That kind of detail isn't in the photo on the phone."

"How do you know how to do that?" Sydney asked, staring avidly at the picture on the camera.

"Well, you know how your mom is a nurse and she went to college to learn how to be a nurse? I'm a photographer. I went to college to learn how to do this."

"She was a photographer long before she went to college." The photographs of herself plastered all over Riley's walls popped into her mind.

"Mom, I want to be a photographer when I grow up!" Sydney said. "Can I try a picture with your camera?"

Panic leapt into Andrea's chest. "Syd, not today. That camera probably costs more than our car."

"I tell you what. I only brought this one camera today and it's for work, but I have another one that I'll bring up next time. It's the camera that I learned how to take pictures with. I'll show you some tricks. How's that sound?" Riley smiled.

"That sounds cool!" Sydney's face lit up with excitement.

"Will you bring me a camera, too?" Olivia asked.

"She has to copy everything I do." Sydney rolled her eyes.

"Do not!" Olivia stomped her foot. "I can want to take pictures too."

"Girls, enough," Andrea said. "It's time for lunch."

The pizza buffet offered everyone their favorite. Andrea set her plate and drink on the table before sliding into the booth next to Riley. She tapped Riley's leg with her knee and gave her a wink when she looked up.

"Riley, where are your kids? How many kids do you have?" Olivia asked.

Riley pulled the pizza away from her mouth without taking a bite, her eyes wide. "I don't have any children."

"Why don't you have any kids? Don't you like kids?" she asked.

"I don't dislike kids. I just don't have any of my own."

"Where's your husband?" Olivia cocked her head a bit.

"I don't have a husband," Riley said around a mouthful of pizza.

"How about a boyfriend?" she asked, her brows furrowed.

Andrea thought of stopping the line of questioning, but Riley might as well get to know Olivia for the inquisitive child that she was.

"Nope, no boyfriend." Riley smiled.

"Even I have a boyfriend. His name is Marcus. He sits behind me in class. Don't you like boys?" Olivia asked.

"I don't dislike boys, I've just never had a boyfriend." Riley took a bite of pizza and shot a puzzled glance at Andrea.

"Never? Like *never ever, ever*? But you're old, like my mom!"

Andrea picked up her orange pop and sucked in a long sip. Awkward wasn't exactly the word. Mortifying, maybe.

Sydney twisted in her seat to face Olivia. "Oh my God, Livy, sometimes you can be so dense. Come on, Mom hasn't stopped talking about Riley since she got back! Riley doesn't have a boyfriend because she wants mom to be her girlfriend! Not everyone likes boys! I don't like boys like that, either. I'm with Mom and Riley. I'd rather have a girlfriend!"

Andrea began choking on the soda. The mouthful of orange pop shot directly up into her sinuses at the same time it dove down her throat and into her lungs. The burn was instant, and the bubbles made her eyes water. She snorted, coughed, and sneezed simultaneously. She franticly reached for napkins in a hopeless effort to contain the bubbly liquid streaming from her.

When she looked up, Sydney and Olivia had orange pop dripping down their faces. It was everywhere. Orange pop covered their shirts and their plates of food. Thankfully, no one was sitting in the booth behind them because they certainly would have gotten a shower too. Riley was no help, since she was laughing too hard to speak. Tears were streaming down her face. Sydney's face was bright red. Her eyes were as big as saucers. She blinked and orange pop dropped off her eye lashes. Andrea took in the sight of her children and burst into laughter while still coughing, sputtering, and gasping for air. She pulled handfuls of napkins out of the dispenser and offered them across the table. Olivia looked at the napkins and then looked into Andrea's eyes.

"What just happened?" Orange pop continued to drip off her chin.

Andrea couldn't speak yet and looked at Riley, who finally gasped in a regular breath and stopped laughing long enough to start wiping up the table.

"Hey, I know of a store close by that sells Bears jerseys. I could get one for each of you," Riley said, while shaking pop from a piece of pizza.

"Ouch, dagger right through my heart!" Sydney started to push Olivia out of the booth. "Come on, Livy, let's go clean up in the bathroom. We've got Mom spit all over us."

"Girls, I am so sorry," Andrea said between fits of laughter. "Thanks for helping, Syd."

Sydney leaned back across the table and tapped Riley on the arm. Riley turned toward her and then knuckle-bumped Syd before she slid the rest of the way out of the booth and led Liv toward the bathroom.

"Did you just knuckle-bump my daughter?" Andrea shook her head. Definitely kindred spirits.

"She looked like she could use an ally." Riley dabbed Andrea's chin with a napkin.

She leaned into Riley. "What the fuck just happened? Did Syd just come out to us?"

"Well, I don't think she'll have any issues accepting us, and she'll certainly remember the day she came out to you." Riley bit her lip, trying not to laugh. "Haven't stopped talking about me since you got home, huh?"

"Apparently not. I don't even know what to say! Sara called and wanted details on our three days together. I didn't think the girls were listening. Fuck me! Was I really just outed by my lesbian daughter? Can she even know that about herself this early?" Andrea asked.

"Really, Andi? How old were we when we shared our first big kiss beneath our tree? Thirteen, maybe fourteen? Sydney's fourteen. I think she knows who she is."

"Holy shit, my babies are growing up." Andrea stopped cleaning up the table and turned to Riley. "Are you going to watch the football game tomorrow?"

"I'll probably have it on, why?" Riley asked.

"Do you know if it's the early game or the later one?"

"I think it starts at noon."

"Would it be rotten of me to invite the three of us down for the game? Today's not enough and it's too soon to have you stay the night, but I'm more than happy to make the trip down tomorrow if it means I get more time with you." She bit her lip. Was she moving too quickly? The girls seemed to have taken to Riley right away, so was there any point in moving slowly?

"That would be fantastic! I'll pick up some food when I get home tonight. Come over anytime."

Andrea collected the pop-covered plates of pizza and walked toward the garbage cans. Everything was so easy and fun with Riley, even this unexpected moment. The girls certainly seemed to get along with her great. Syd felt comfortable enough around Riley to come out. Why hadn't she said anything to Andrea before today? Did her inability to talk to the girls about her sexuality keep Syd from feeling like she could open up? Everything was up in the air at the moment, and it had Andrea a little off balance. She looked over to Riley and savored the rush of affection that she felt throughout her body. Would the girls get too attached if they tried for something more? Andrea certainly wanted to try for more but worried the girls would get hurt if things didn't work out, which she stupidly hadn't even considered before. What if Riley didn't want a life tied down by children and her brick-and-mortar job at the hospital? It was all such a risk. Maybe it would all become clearer with a bit more time.

Chapter Twenty-five

R iley climbed up into her truck and sat behind the wheel. She'd walked Andrea and the girls to her car. It was difficult to share a quick hug and wave good-bye. What she wouldn't have given for a little something more than a concealed peck on the side of the neck when they hugged. It was difficult to hit the affection brakes after their week in Alaska. There was a time and place for everything, and she didn't need the kids to feel uncomfortable.

The afternoon spent together at the arcade had been light and fun. Much better than she'd expected. The girls had such different personalities. Olivia seemed to go on full speed at all times, consumed with questions and thoughts about anything and everything. Sydney was much more laid-back but keenly aware of everything that happened around her. It didn't seem like there was much she missed. The way her eyes darted around showed how much she paid attention to every little thing. Not to mention she'd figured out the relationship between her and Andi practically within seconds.

She started her truck and backed out of the parking space. Just as she was turning out onto the interstate heading south, her phone rang. Riley glanced at the display screen on the dashboard and smiled. She pressed a button on the steering wheel and connected the call.

"Hey, Mom, this is a nice surprise. How are you? How's Dad?"

"Hi, honey. We're doing pretty well. Are you home? I called to see how your trip went. I kept expecting to see posts with pictures on Facebook, but your page has been eerily quiet. Is everything okay?"

"Everything's fine, Mom. I just haven't had any time to post yet." Riley checked her mirror and changed lanes.

"Where are you? It sounds like you're in a cave."

"It's road noise. I'm on the expressway, heading home from Wisconsin." Riley set the cruise control and kept pace with the flow of traffic.

"Well, call me when you get home. You shouldn't talk and drive."

"My truck is linked to my phone so it's hands-free. No different than if you were sitting next to me and we were chatting. It's okay if I talk and drive, if the road noise isn't too annoying." It was nice to have someone to talk to. It would help her get away from the thoughts constantly swirling in her head.

"Honey, did I get the dates wrong? Wasn't this week your Alaska trip? What on earth are you doing in Wisconsin?"

Riley wasn't sure where to start. It was all such a whirlwind. Then again, if anyone could help her sort it out, it was her mom.

"No, you didn't get the dates wrong, but I did come back a few days early. Do you remember Andi?" Riley asked.

"I certainly do. I always had a soft spot for her. You two were my girls. I still think of her every so often." Her mom had bragged throughout Riley's childhood that she had two daughters and only had to give birth to one. She too had felt the loss of Andi in their lives.

"I drove up to Wisconsin to have lunch with her and her two daughters today," Riley said. Saying it out loud sounded surreal.

"You don't say. How'd all that come about?"

"You're never going to believe this, but she was the maid of honor in the wedding I shot in Alaska. It was the most bizarre thing, to pick up on her voice at an event in the middle of nowhere. I'm still trying to make sense of it all. We spent the three days after the wedding exploring Alaska together."

"That would explain your digital silence and why you didn't call to let me know you were home safe. You two were always in your own little world when you were together. Did you take some time to heal old wounds?" The question lacked any judgement.

"We've talked. I think there's better understanding between us. We both had such a skewed perception about what the other was feeling back then. She's spent all these years thinking I walked away and never looked back. She thought I hated her."

"I recall hearing something very similar from your lips back then about her. Misunderstandings have destroyed many a relationship. That's why open and honest communication is so important. What do you hope comes of this, as if I need to ask?"

"Something, everything and yet, I'm not sure. It was just the two of us for those last few days in Alaska and we still have such an amazing connection. Everything clicked like no time had passed at all. The complications are starting to pop up now that we're home. My schedule at the studio dominates my time. She's a mom, which is weird to see, and has a pretty demanding life three hours north in Wisconsin." Riley drew in a deep breath and let it out slowly.

"I take it she's no longer with that fella who graduated with you two. Is she single?"

"Yeah, she's single. They've been divorced for some time. He's remarried now." Riley looked at the screen on the dashboard almost expecting to see her mom's face. She'd have to make time to see them in person soon. She tapped the steering wheel and looked back up to the road.

"Mom, if it were anyone else, I'd look at the big picture and consider all of the reasons why it wouldn't be worth the effort. If it were anyone else, I wouldn't think twice about walking away, but it's not anyone else, it's Andi and it feels so great to be with her again. She has this effect on me that I can't explain, and I can't seem to get enough. I don't know how I could ever walk away a second time."

"You two have always had such a bond. If your lives don't blend, you always have your friendship to keep the connection alive." Her mom had a way of seeing the silver lining in any situation.

"I thought about that, too, but I tell ya, I don't think I could stand to see her with anyone else." It felt good to admit that. She'd never said it out loud before.

"Honey, give it time. See if what you consider complications aren't actually blessings. Your world is so meticulously planned. Even as a child, everything had to be just right and in its place. It's okay for life to be a little messy. You can't plan out every little thing."

"It's worked well so far." Riley tried to quelch her defensiveness.

"Has it really? Seems to me like you've been lonely for a good long time."

"Mom, I've been busy with work. There's a lot on my plate. I have a very successful business to run, and it's taken a lot to get it to where it is today." It sounded like a feeble excuse, even to her. Her mom was quiet for a moment. Riley stared ahead at the road and waited for what was coming.

"Honey, I couldn't be prouder of all that you've accomplished. No doubt you have a successful business, but at what cost to you and your happiness? You dove into it all to stop the hurt from so long ago. And before you say anything, I know you enjoy your work, but, honey, that isn't all there is to life." Her mom sighed. "Or maybe that is all you want from life. Who knows. It's a question only you can answer. If I can put my two cents in, I'd be okay with being a grandma to a couple of girls. No matter what you decide, I love you and I'm here for you."

"I love you too, Mom. I'll post some pictures soon. Thanks, you've given me a lot to think about."

"Drive safe, honey, call anytime. Good-bye now."

Riley disconnected the call.

Had she fallen into a safe groove of perpetually packed schedules and tight deadlines to keep from taking any risks? Was everything designed to protect her heart? Was that really why the studio came before anything or anyone?

"Incoming SMS, say 'read it' or 'ignore.'" The truck speakers interrupted her thoughts.

"Read it."

"I wanted so much to invite you back to the house, but given Sydney's confession today, I thought she might want some time to talk. I miss you. It was wonderful to see you. Can't wait until tomorrow." Andi's words flooded the sound system.

Riley smiled inside and out. Andrea was worth the risk. She was worth the time to see if this could work. She replayed the message twice more before turning on the radio and enjoying the rest of her ride home.

CHAPTER TWENTY-SIX

"Now, remember to say please and thank you. Keep your hands in your pockets and no fighting." Andrea looked at her daughters before they got out of the car.

"Mom, we heard you. You've been saying the same thing for hours!" Sydney climbed out of the car and stretched.

The building looked like an old brick warehouse. Windows on both stories were twice as tall as they were wide. Additional bricks created an arched flange above each window that gave the tall structure nice character. It was a building she'd expect to see in a black-and-white photo from the early nineteen hundreds. Leave it to Riley to give this incredible architecture new life. A bell jingled as the front door was pushed open from the inside. A sign reading Candid Photography hung above the door.

"Hey, you made it! How was the drive down?" Riley walked outside and pulled Andrea into a hug. She stepped back and turned to the girls. "Long time, no see."

"This is how far you drove yesterday to have pizza with us? You must really like my mom." Sydney offered a fist bump. Riley returned the gesture and smiled.

"Please tell me that you don't have any orange pop. Mom's grounded from orange pop for at least a week." Olivia crossed her arms and looked at them pointedly.

"I have all sorts of fun treats, and hopefully none your mom will spit on any of us. Come on inside. It's cold out here." Riley held the glass door open. When everyone was inside, she turned the deadbolt.

"Why did you lock us in?" Olivia asked.

"Because the studio isn't open. I don't want strangers trying to steal all of the hot wings," Riley said.

"Why do you live at your work? I thought you flew on airplanes for your work?" Olivia asked.

"All good questions." Riley looked at Andrea.

Andrea shrugged and smiled. She enjoyed seeing how Riley interacted with the girls.

"Most of the time, I fly on airplanes for my work, but sometimes people come here to have pictures taken. The downstairs is the photography studio and my house is upstairs, but you have to come through the studio to get to the stairs that lead up to my house. I don't have a separate entrance from the outside."

"Can we see the studio?" Sydney asked.

"Absolutely." Riley turned to the left and flipped a panel of switches.

Prints hung in almost every open space that Andrea could see. One by one, banks of lights turned on and bathed the large open space in a soft golden glow. Spotlights highlighted several large prints and other collages of smaller prints. Several of the walls were painted bright and bold colors that seemed to frame the canvas prints. As always, Andrea was in awe, and the girls looked similarly impressed.

"Come this way," Riley said. "This is where we actually take the pictures."

Riley led them into a large open room off to the side. There were lights and silver umbrellas all around the perimeter of the space.

"Why is there so much stuff? Where are the cameras?" Sydney asked.

"All of this stuff allows for options. If we're taking pictures of a baby in a basket, then we need different things than if we're taking pictures of you with your softball stuff or Liv in her dance costume. If you come over to this side, you'll see what I mean."

Andrea was just as curious as the girls. She followed them over to where Riley was standing. Riley opened a cabinet in the back of the room and pulled out a camera on a tripod. She set it up on some taped marks on the floor.

"Okay, come look through the camera and you'll see how little space is actually needed to take a picture."

Once Sydney and Olivia had looked through the viewfinder, Andrea took her turn. She could see the top of the stool and the gray background behind the stool and that was all.

"What are the umbrellas for? Does it rain in here?" Olivia asked.

"The umbrellas are for light, not rain. They focus light where I need it so there aren't any harsh shadows. See, if we put your mom on the stool, look at how half of her face is hidden in the dark because of how the light is hanging from the ceiling. If I click on these lights and these over here, now she's lit up perfectly with no shadows." Riley stood behind the girls as each looked through the camera again. "Here, this button takes a picture. Go for it."

"Really?" Sydney's face lit up. She stood behind the camera and pressed the button. "How do I see what it looks like?"

"Press this button and it will show up on the screen."

Sydney pressed the button and a photo of Andrea showed up on the small screen.

"Wow, that's so cool."

"Let's let Olivia take one, too, okay?" Riley lowered the tripod for Olivia's height.

"Mom, you have to smile," Olivia said from behind the camera.

Andrea looked into the camera and smiled. She stood once she heard the shutter click and looked at the wall behind Riley and the girls. Her breath caught.

"Is there a light switch for that wall?" Andrea asked.

Riley turned to see what Andrea was pointing at and smiled. She walked over to the far wall and flipped several switches. Lights clicked on and then spotlights focused on several large prints.

"Those prints have been on that wall since the day the studio opened." Riley ambled over and stood next to Andrea.

"Mom, that girl looks like you but a lot skinnier," Olivia said.

"Thanks for that, Livy. Believe it or not, that girl really is me." Andrea strolled up to the photos on the wall.

"They let me have the prints when the contest was over. It always makes me smile to see them when I walk into this room."

"Seeing them on your computer screen was one thing, but seeing them on your wall is an entirely different experience. I spent all those years thinking the worst. I honestly thought you hated me." Andrea's words trailed off.

"Nothing could be further from the truth," Riley said, leaning on a table.

"How old were you?" Sydney asked, studying the picture closely.

"I was eighteen. I was two months pregnant with you in that picture." Andrea reached up and touched the glass.

"Did you hire Riley to take your picture way back then?" Olivia asked.

"Would you two like to see some pictures of your mom in Alaska?" Riley asked.

Andrea was grateful for the distraction. She wasn't ready to answer any more questions about that day beneath the apple tree.

Riley walked over to the far wall and shut down the lights in that room. They made their way back through the lobby and then up a wide hallway lined with several photographs that Andrea recognized from the website. The hallway opened up into a sizeable room with a couple of desks, a large worktable, and a monster of a printer.

"This is where we sort through all of the pictures we take." Riley clicked on several light switches and the room lit up. "My desk is back over there in the corner and Jodie sits in this desk up here."

"Why do you need so many monitors?" Sydney asked.

"We each have three so we can work on photos with two of them and see email or whatever we need on the third," Riley answered.

"Who's Jodie?" Olivia asked.

"Jodie works with me. You can meet her later if her flight gets in on time." Riley walked over to the table.

"Is she coming to watch football, too?" Olivia asked.

"No, she kinda lives here." Riley spread out some prints on the table. "I still need to frame these, but here's your mom in Alaska."

"Is she your girlfriend?" Olivia asked. "I thought my mom was your girlfriend."

"No, she's my friend and she works with me," Riley said.

"So, both of you live at work?" Olivia asked.

"The house is above us. We'll go upstairs next. You'll see."

Andrea stood behind Sydney and Olivia. There were several large prints spread out. Shots of her in the black cocktail dress, one of her in the hot springs looking up at the northern lights, another of her in the bridesmaid dress at the hall, and then the last one sitting in the front of the canoe with the reindeer off in the distance.

"Wow, I wish we could have seen all this stuff. The sky was really all of those colors? Green and purple and pink and blue, how cool is that! Mom, you went swimming outside? Didn't you freeze your butt off?" Sydney stared at the photos.

"It was a hot spring, Syd. It was like taking a hot bath outside underneath the sky." Andrea looked at Riley and smiled.

"These are for you, once I get them finished. I have a few others too." Riley squeezed Andrea's hand.

"They turned out beautifully, Riley." Andrea looked up from the photos and into Riley's eyes.

"Who's ready for some tailgate snacks and a football game?"

Andrea stared at the prints on the table even after the lights clicked off. She looked at the print beneath the northern lights and shivered with the memory of what happened after that photo was taken. Who knew when she'd be able to experience that feeling again? Either she was followed by her two young chaperones or Riley was out of town. She had never been this needy, but being with Riley was really that incredible.

Chapter Twenty-seven

The large loft door slid open shortly after the second quarter of the game had started. Riley looked over in time to see Jodie coming through the door backward pulling her suitcase up the last few steps.

"What a whirlwind! Chumly, Maine was the fuckin' bomb! There was this cute little brunette, Cloe, that totally cozied up to me. She was a fun party favor. Get this, she's from Mad—"

"Edit, Jodes, edit." Riley jumped up from the couch and spoke loudly to cover up whatever inappropriately funny thing Jodes was about to say next.

"Edit? Clients? What? Whoa, we have company. A heads up would have been nice." Jodie stood between the kitchen and living room. "Well, hello, everyone."

"I sent you a text."

Jodie pulled out her phone. "Oops. I guess it would help if I took the phone off of airplane mode. Would you like me to get a hotel tonight? Easy peasy, no biggie."

"No, I'd like you to come here so I can introduce you to everyone." Riley shook her head at the whirlwind that was her closest friend. "Jodie, this is Sydney, and Olivia, and this is Andrea."

"Nice to meet you, Sydney and Olivia. Andrea, eh? I apologize now if I call you Andi because that's all I've ever known you as. I've stared at photographs of you since my first day of college. It's nice to finally meet you all. I've heard great things," Jodie said.

"It's nice to meet you, too, Jodie. I've also heard great things. I'm glad you and Riley have each other," Andrea said.

"Ah, Chumly's good people. I couldn't ask for a better friend or a better boss." Jodie smiled.

"Okay, I have to ask. Why do you call her Chumly? There's got to be a story there." Andrea looked from Jodie to Riley.

"Go ahead and tell her." Riley started laughing and rested her hip on the couch. Her worlds were meshing, and she liked the feel of it. A lot.

"Well, for starters, Chumly sounds way better than shark bait." Jodie walked into the living room and sat in an open chair. "Okay, here's the story. Riley and I arrived on campus on the same day and were assigned to the same dorm room. Her walls were quickly covered with photographs of a single favorite subject. So, one day I asked her about the strawberry blonde in the photos and she tells me that she's the one her heart can't let go of. She tells me that the girl in the photos is the one that you'd swim across the ocean for, knowing damned well that you'd be chum for the sharks, but you'd jump in and swim anyway given the chance to be with her just one more time. She gets all dreamy eyed, and says their love was *profound*. Total Shakespeare. It was such an unexpected answer that it earned her the nickname Chumly and it has stuck all these years."

"What was the girl's name?" Olivia asked. "Was she pretty?"

"Seriously, Livy? It was Mom. Mom was the girl in the photos, like downstairs in the camera room!" Sydney shook her head with the kind of disparaging eye roll only available to her age group.

Riley threw a pillow across the room and made contact with Jodie's face. "That was much more detail than was needed." She hadn't expected Jodie to share the conversation word for word. Her face was hot with the embarrassment she felt for allowing that story to be told.

"Oh, that was the condensed version and you know it!" Jodie threw the pillow back. "She called me a few years after we graduated to come and work here. I show up and I'll be damned if those photos aren't still sprinkled everywhere! Did you see them?"

"Like Syd said, we saw the few in the studio room, particularly the shots that won the award." Andrea sat up taller in her chair.

"Oh, there are several others tucked here and there. If you go into her bedroom and close the door there's a black-and-white of—" Jodie ducked before the pillow hit her a second time.

"That hotel room might not be a bad idea." Riley knew her face was flushed.

"Do you and Riley really both live here? You act like sisters. Sydney throws stuff at me too. Where's your stuff? Riley only showed us one bedroom on the tour. Where do you sleep?" Olivia asked.

Jodie looked bemused at the questions flung like more pillows. "Well, Olivia, Riley is going to build a bedroom for me, but in the meantime, I sleep on the couch. My stuff is in the hall closet. I'm only here a day or two a week, and it's not often that Riley and I are here at the same time," Jodie said.

"It's still weird that you both live at your work. Why do you have purple hair? I think I would like to have purple hair. Is that a dog collar on your wrist?" Olivia asked.

Jodie glanced at Riley, who just looked back, smiling. "I like the purple in my hair, and this is a bracelet, not a dog collar, but it would make a cool dog collar, wouldn't it? It matches my belt, here, see." Jodie lifted her shirt to show her belt.

"Liv, seriously! Stop the questions. You're embarrassing me!" Sydney turned toward her sister.

Riley shrugged. "She asks a lot of questions. She's like a little human lie detector. There's no point resisting. There are no defenses."

Olivia giggled and stuck her tongue out at her sister.

"Hey, you two, do you remember when we talked about the camera yesterday?" Riley asked Sydney and Olivia.

"Yeah, but we were told not to bring them up because we aren't supposed to bug you about it," Olivia said. "Isn't that what you said, Mom?"

Andrea nodded. "Way to throw me under the bus, Livy."

Riley smiled. "Well, I didn't forget. Would you like to see what I put together for you?"

Olivia and Sydney nodded. Riley got up from the couch and walked into the kitchen. Andrea followed her.

"Thank you for the diversion. I was squirming in there," Andrea whispered.

"Jodie was there for a lot. I should have given you a heads up," Riley said.

"Not necessary. It's like I have a source to go to on the lost years." Andrea smiled.

"I'll answer any question you have. All you have to do is ask." Riley leaned over and kissed Andrea's cheek, then Riley picked up the two camera bags.

"Those look like backpacks! That's a lot of stuff for two kids who may lose or destroy most everything in the bag," Andrea said. "Can I at least pay for it?"

"Andi, it's okay. I'm giving it without conditions. Jodie and I upgrade gear every couple of years. If they bust it all, so be it, but they both seemed sincerely interested," Riley answered. "Come on, I can hear Olivia bouncing up and down from here."

Riley followed Andrea into the living room with a bag in each hand. She handed one to each of the girls.

"Each bag has different compartments with stuff for you to use with your camera. There's a battery charger in there and some disks and a disk reader to hook up to a computer. There are a couple of lens options and a small tripod. Do you want to play with them for a bit during halftime? I can show you how some stuff works," Riley asked.

Sydney and Olivia were already unzipping the main flap and inspecting items in each compartment.

"It's a blowout game, like the Bears would win anyway. Why wait until halftime? I'd like to stretch my legs a bit after sitting on an airplane all morning. How about I walk them over to the park and show them a few things?" Jodie winked at Riley.

"That would be so cool. Can we, Mom?" Sydney asked. She stuffed items back into the correct spots and zipped up the pack.

"Yeah, can we, Mom?" Olivia jumped up and down.

"Yes, but please don't make Jodie crazy." Andrea smiled and nodded to Jodie. "Riley and I will be over in a few minutes."

"No rush," Jodie said and headed toward the door, her arm up like some kind of tour guide. "Come on, this way."

Riley heard the lower-level door click shut. She turned to Andrea. "Is it bad that I want to drag you into the bedroom and make love to you?"

"It's only bad if you had to drag me. I'm willing. I may drag you. God, I've missed you." Andrea wrapped her arms around Riley's shoulders.

"It's so good to see you. I've missed you too. I'm not sure what is and isn't appropriate in front of the girls, so forgive me if I'm messing up." Riley had a new respect for parents. She had always assumed it was so easy to set rules and have them followed, but seeing the different personalities helped her realize that everything wasn't so easily planned. Her admiration for Andrea continued to grow.

"You're being very respectful, and I appreciate it. The girls aren't here this minute, so will you just kiss me?"

Riley kissed Andrea with all the pent-up passion she'd been feeling since they'd separated. She lifted Andrea's shirt, needing to feel the warmth of her bare skin. She heard the click of the lower-level door and froze.

"Mom, are you and Riley coming? I told Jodie we had to wait. You said a few minutes." Olivia called from the bottom of the stairs.

Andrea pulled away from the kiss and exhaled. "You'll have to accept a rain check for what I was planning on doing to you next." She leaned her forehead on Riley's shoulder.

Riley held Andrea in her arms. "If we ignore her, will she think we didn't hear?"

"We'll be down in a bit, Livy. Go ahead without us," Andrea yelled. She turned to face Riley again. "I'm sure you already know Livy enough to know that answer, but before we head down, can you show me what's behind your bedroom door? I feel like it's something I should see without the girls around."

Riley led Andrea into the bedroom. She opened the blinds and the room filled with light. Riley stepped past Andrea and swung the bedroom door shut. No one but Andrea would know how much this black-and-white photograph of their apple tree held her heart.

"Holy shit, it takes up most of the wall," Andrea said. "When did you take this?"

"The summer after I graduated college. I went back to get the rest of the stuff out of my old bedroom. I ran over to your folks' place and found out they had moved to Florida. So, before I left town, I stopped by the school and walked back into the woods one last time. That spot always meant a lot to me, a sanctuary of sorts. So, after being ignored for a few years, this is what our tree looked like."

"It looks so sad, neglected...forlorn. Everything is so overgrown that it's barely recognizable. Of all the shots you have of our tree, why on earth would you have this version in here?" Andrea asked.

"You'll laugh and think I'm nuts." Riley swallowed the emotion in her throat. She'd felt just as forlorn as this shot for so many years.

"You said I could ask you anything and you'd answer."

"Already using that one against me, eh?" Riley smiled. "When I took the shot, what I saw matched the way I felt without you. I felt like our special place missed you as much as I did, but the memories of us were still there if you looked hard enough. See, our log bench is visible in the tall grass, behind the saplings. The tree is still our tree, the limbs are thicker and the trunk stouter, but it's still the same tree. Our heart and initials are still carved in the bark, they've just taken on a different shape and have grown over some. Our spot evolved over time, much like we did." Riley swallowed, wondering if she sounded too sappy or soft. But it was true, and she didn't need to hide that part of herself from Andi. "Anyway, when I bought the studio and started traveling quite a bit, I decided to enlarge the print and hung it up in here. It might sound silly, but it gave me a little bit of home and helped me feel grounded. Besides, it wasn't anything I had to explain to anyone. Jodie knows about it because she recognized it from the shots on my wall in college."

Tears were running down Andrea's cheeks. "I'm crying because what you said was beautiful and sweet and touched my heart and made me sad, all at once. I'm still the same red hot emotional basket case that I've always been." Andrea wiped away the tears.

Riley wrapped her arm around Andrea's shoulder. "Your emotions are one of the many, many things that I adore about you."

Andrea smiled and wiped a stray tear away. "Come on, you, let's go run around the park for a bit before Olivia hunts us down. You know the girls will be tormenting me with those cameras trying to capture candid shots just like you do."

"I'm counting on it. I may have to show them how to upload to my cloud account so I can see what they capture." Riley laughed.

"Don't you dare! No doubt there will be a photo of me in my not so sexy underwear, or worse!" Andrea chased her down the stairs.

Riley enjoyed having Andrea and the girls in her world. It was nice that Jodie made it back and was able to meet them. The more time they spent together, the more she was willing to admit that she wanted more. Her mother's words echoed in her ears, "Work isn't all there is to life." Truer words were never spoken. Work was fun and rewarding, but days like these were the stuff life was made of. It reminded her of when her family and a handful of friends would gather around to watch a game or enjoy a Sunday barbeque. That's the stuff that made memories.

They played around outside for a while until everyone got hungry, then they headed in and put on the last quarter of the game while munching pizza.

Before the last of the game, Andrea tapped Riley on the arm and nodded toward the kitchen. They left Olivia and Sydney in the living room chatting with Jodie.

"When can I see you again?" Andrea whispered once they were out of sight in the kitchen.

Riley pulled out her phone and moved to the calendar so Andi could see it. "I'm on the road for the next seven days and then back out Wednesday through Saturday morning, but I could switch that flight for late Friday night. What's that weekend look like for you?"

"Actually, that might work perfectly. Scott has to travel for work and needs me to keep the girls this next weekend, so he'll take that one instead. We could finally get some alone time! Plan on the weekend at my place." Andrea smiled and clapped her hands together silently. "I know it sounds needy, but will you still call me whenever you can? I look forward to hearing your voice before I go to sleep."

Riley was glad she wasn't the only one who needed that time each night.

"I look forward to our talks in the evening too. I'll definitely call, including later tonight at our usual time." Riley leaned over and kissed Andrea's lips tenderly. "I'm already looking forward to our weekend."

The day had been so much fun. The need for another photographer continued to become more evident with each passing day. She'd work on an ad tomorrow and get a position listed. She loved her career, and she was starting to figure out that having a life, maybe even a family, could be just as important.

Chapter Twenty-eight

Andrea set her tablet behind the counter at the nurses' station and stretched her back. It had been a long shift. A couple of nurses and an assistant were out sick, and the floor was near capacity. She was too tired to care that it was her birthday, well, tired and perhaps a bit disappointed. So far, she'd received birthday wishes from her parents, her daughters, and her best friend, everyone except the one she most wanted to hear from, Riley. She hadn't brought it up last weekend because Riley had always made such a big deal about it. Cute little handmade cards, notes, flowers, really any romantic gesture imaginable always made her birthdays super special. It never dawned on her that she wouldn't remember. She shook her head. They weren't kids anymore.

Still, even Sara had reached out, and she was on the tail end of her honeymoon. She wouldn't come back to work until the following Monday, but that didn't stop her from sending a short flurry of happy birthday texts and some fun party emojis. She could use a dose of Sara about now. They hadn't talked since before last weekend and so much had happened. No doubt she'd have some unsolicited advice about everything. Andrea smiled. Sharing a shift with her always made the day go by faster. Just a couple more days solo and she'd have her bestie back.

She looked at her watch. Three thirty. There was still plenty of time to get home, relax for a moment, and then get dinner started before she had to rush out to pick up the girls from volleyball practice and dance. Their schedule was always so hectic this time of year, and she was already looking forward to the summer months when the activities quieted down and things weren't always so rushed. What she wouldn't give for a quiet evening at home. She pulled her jacket off the back of her desk chair and grabbed her purse from her bottom desk drawer. The phone on her desk started ringing. She was tempted to ignore it and walk away, but that wasn't something she'd ever been able to do. She sighed and set her purse on the desk.

"Nursing station, third floor east, this is Andrea."

"So glad I caught you. You have a delivery at the welcome desk in the lobby."

"A delivery? What is it?" Annoyance crept in. Now she'd be late and wouldn't have those few precious minutes of quiet time before having to start dinner, since the reception desk was on the opposite side of the hospital to where she needed to go to get to her car. Maybe she'd pick up subs or something.

"I only know that it's perishable, so you should pick it up before you go today."

"Thank you, I'm on my way down." Andrea hung up the phone and picked up her purse.

Who would send her a perishable delivery? Probably some tropical fruit or something from Sara and Kay. She stepped into the elevator, pressed the button for the lobby, and leaned up against the side rail for support. Her feet throbbed. Maybe she should splurge on herself and get a new pair of shoes. She'd had these for at least a year now. The elevator chimed and the doors opened. Andrea stepped out and headed down the long hallway toward the lobby and the welcome desk.

She was just a few feet away when she caught a whiff of a familiar scent. Her heart rate shot up and she looked around the lobby. The top half of a person was completely hidden behind a monstrous bouquet of flowers. A pair of hands supported either side of the large round vase. The arrangement lowered and a pair of green eyes peered over the top of the flowers.

"I hope you still enjoy birthday surprises." Riley lowered the flowers to reveal that amazing half grin.

Andrea stood there in shock, her hand covering her mouth. Riley twisted and set the flowers on a table between two chairs. She looked sexy as hell, dressed in jeans and a nice collared shirt. Andrea was no longer tired. She darted across the lobby right into Riley's open arms.

"You remembered. I'm so happy that you're here." Emotions made it hard to speak. She hadn't forgotten after all. She was here, in person, which was so much better than a text or even a phone call. "How long can you stay?"

"I have to fly out tomorrow morning. Would it be okay if I take you and the girls out for a birthday dinner?" Riley held her close in her arms.

"That sounds heavenly. Where are you parked? You can follow me."

"Actually, I took a taxi on the off chance that you'd give me a ride if I agreed to hold the flowers." Riley kissed the side of her forehead.

"I don't have to pick the girls up until five. Come on, let's get out of here! Where's your luggage?" Andrea stepped back out of Riley's arms. "What can I carry?"

An expert traveler, Riley spun the suitcase and equipment tote back-to-back so that both handles could be managed with one hand. Her briefcase and the camera bag were secured on each of the larger luggage pieces. She picked up the flowers in one arm and rolled the two large pieces of luggage along with the other.

"I'm good, lead the way, birthday girl."

Andrea led them out the front doors toward the parking lot. Even though she had her hand covering Riley's on the luggage, she kept looking over to make sure it wasn't a dream. This was the life she dreamt of. The life where her sweetheart showed up at work to surprise her with flowers and a dinner date. It just didn't get any better than this.

❖

Andrea sat on the couch next to Riley and handed her a glass of whiskey on the rocks. Riley had planned a perfect evening. The restaurant was casual enough for Syd to go in her volleyball sweats and sweatshirt, Olivia in jeans and the top half of her dance leotard, and yet the food was better than several nicer restaurants that she'd been to. Even the dessert was amazing and served with a lit candle, though she'd been spared the singing.

"I didn't think I'd ever get them to bed. Your being here midweek is such a treat. What a wonderful birthday surprise. Thank you." Andrea kicked her shoes off and leaned back into the couch. "Oh, it feels so good to get those damned shoes off."

"Swing your legs up here. Let me see if I can help." Riley cupped one of Andrea's feet in her hands and began kneading the tension away.

"That feels amazing." She leaned her head back and closed her eyes. Definitely the best birthday ever.

Andrea woke up on the couch beneath a blanket a few hours later, but Riley was nowhere to be found. She got up off the couch and found a note on the kitchen counter.

Sweet dreams, birthday girl. You looked so peaceful, I didn't want to wake you. I also didn't want to leave. It took a lot of willpower not to curl up next to you. We haven't talked about me staying when the girls are home, so I forced myself to go to the hotel. I'm looking forward to our weekend in a few days. Happy birthday.
Riley

Andrea held the note to her chest. She wished she had stayed awake long enough to ask her to stay. What she wouldn't give to be curled up in her arms tonight. To know she was in town and alone in a hotel room was almost too much. They'd decided not to label what they had, but there was no question her heart was fully engaged. And for some reason, she had a feeling Riley was in a similar place. It had been so thoughtful that she'd booked dinner not just for the two of them, but she'd included the girls, too. She was clearly trying to fit into Andrea's world. What did that mean? She placed the note on her bedside table and smiled at it as she drifted back to sleep. Things weren't perfect, not yet. But hope made her dreams happy ones.

Chapter Twenty-nine

R iley sat in the window seat on the airplane. Her laptop was open on the tray table connected to the plane's Wi-Fi. She clicked through the portfolios of applicants for the positions she'd posted. The first two took clean shots, but the photos lacked emotion. The third applicant looked more promising. She seemed to shoot memories instead of typically posed photography.

She'd been to three states in five days, and she was completely fried. She'd rearranged things and caught a flight into Madison late Friday night. Her desire to spend more time with Andrea was making for an exhausting travel schedule. The events over the past week and a half were a series of shoot and fly scenarios with no time to sleep, rest up, or explore. She'd had no trouble turning down the unsubtle invitations for companionship at every shoot, preoccupied with thoughts of Andi. The time she'd get to spend with her was better than none, but this kind of thing couldn't continue. It was exhausting, and their time felt rushed and strained.

An email alert popped up in the lower corner of her screen. Riley clicked on the notification and opened the email.

Riley, I can't pick you up at the airport. Scott flipped out. Sydney took off and she's missing. I need to look for her. I'll email as I know more. Please call as soon as you land.

Riley's heart hammered in her chest. She'd never felt more helpless. The plane app on the screen showed that they had another twenty minutes before they landed. Suddenly, that seemed like an eternity. She kept the email up on her screen while the plane started the descent into the Madison airport. It was like watching paint dry. She couldn't imagine what would cause Sydney to take off. She'd only spent a couple of days with the girls, but they seemed like happy kids, neither of them seemed to have an attitude or any particular baggage. Like she knew what baggage looked like for a fourteen-year-old. She still felt inept around children of any age. Regardless, this didn't make any sense.

The moment the plane touched down, Riley took her phone off airplane mode. It buzzed nonstop in her hand while texts and missed calls popped up on the screen. Texts from an unknown number caught her attention.

Riley its Syd where r u. Need help.

Riley didn't take the time to read any of the other messages, she pressed the phone icon next to the number. It rang twice.

"Riley?"

"Hey, Syd, are you okay? Where are you?" Her stomach was in knots. Was this what it meant to be a parent? All-out panic and distress?

"Are you flying to Chicago tonight? I'm at the airport. I'm trying to get to your house," Sydney said.

"Which airport? Chicago? Where are you?" Riley was grateful for the first-class upgrade. She hooked her briefcase onto the camera case and was standing in the front of the line waiting for the door to open.

"I'm at the Madison airport. I don't know how to get to Chicago. Can you help me get to your house?" Sydney's voice was hoarse like she'd been crying. She sniffled into the phone.

"Syd, I'm in Madison too. We just landed. Are you inside or outside?"

"Inside."

"What stores are around you?"

"There's a gift shop and some stairs."

"Perfect. You stay right there and stay on the phone with me. I'm getting off the plane right now." Riley ran up the gangway into the terminal dragging the camera tote behind her, toward a staircase leading down to the main level. This had to be it. "Syd, look up the stairs, do you see me?" Riley lifted the rolling tote out in front of her and hurried down the steps. She searched for Syd and finally spotted her on the far side of the hall. "I see you. Stay right there." Riley hung up the phone and tried desperately not to fall down the stairs.

"Wow, you're really dressed up." Sydney stood there shuffling her feet.

"I left from work and went directly to the airport. Are you okay?"

Sydney nodded. "I'm okay." Her eyes were red and puffy from crying. Tears welled up and her chin quivered.

"We need to call your mom and let her know you're safe. Come on, let's go sit over here, out of the way. You can tell me what's going on." Riley led Sydney to a seating area.

"I'm not going back to my dad's house. Not tonight. I swear I'll bolt." Sydney's jaw was clenched tight.

"Understood, but you gotta let me call your mom. She's worried sick. She's out there looking for you."

"Okay, but just Mom." Sydney crossed her arms.

"You can sit right here with me and listen to every word. Then we'll talk, okay?" She had a feeling that to gain Syd's trust, she'd have to prove it. Adults weren't always the good guys in a teenager's story.

"Yeah, okay." Sydney relaxed a bit.

Riley hit recent calls and then touched the phone icon next to Andi's name. She answered before the first ring finished.

"I haven't found Syd yet. I'm still looking." She sounded panicked and distracted. "Shit, this is all my fault. How could I be so selfish?"

"Andi, stop, she's here. Syd's with me. She's safe. We're at the Madison airport."

"What? Seriously? She's there with you? Will you put her on the phone?"

Riley looked at Sydney. "Your mom needs to hear your voice. She's freaked."

Sydney nodded and took the phone from Riley. "Hi, Mom. I'm okay." She looked over at Riley. "Mom, I couldn't stay there. Dad was being a total dick, even Cathy said so. You two were screaming and screaming and I couldn't take it." She exhaled loudly. "No, I know I didn't answer. I silenced my phone. I came here because I overheard you talking to Riley and knew she was flying back tonight. I thought she could help me get to Chicago for a few days." Sydney shuffled her feet on the floor while listening. "No, I didn't know she was coming here." She flopped back in the chair. "No, none of my friends helped me. It was too late, and I got yelled at for even calling. I took a bus to the airport." Sydney held the phone out to Riley. "She wants to talk to you."

"Andi?"

"Yeah, I'm here. What an unbelievable mess. Scott's gone off the deep end. Let me give him a call and let him know Syd's safe and then I'll head that way and pick you two up. It'll be a half an hour or so. Thank you, I know you didn't sign up for any of this. I'm so glad you were there for her." Andrea still sounded frantic.

Riley wasn't sure what to say. What did she mean by that? Even if they were just friends, she'd be there for her and the girls without question. She was becoming invested in all of them, and it felt...right.

"We're good until you get here. Please be safe," Riley said.

"I will. Sweetheart, I'm sorry about our weekend. Will you accept a rain check?" Andi sounded completely exhausted.

"Absolutely." She hadn't considered that this would derail their entire weekend. "Drive safe."

Riley ended the call. Did that mean she was supposed to go to a hotel? She didn't want to go to a hotel. She wanted to be with Andi, no matter what she was going through. She wanted to be a part of things, not standing on the outside looking in. She looked over at the teenager in the next seat. Her eyes full of concern. Her focus needed to be on Syd at this moment and nothing else. She drew in a deep breath and let it out slowly. "Okay, so your mom will be here in a half an hour or so. How about a cup of hot chocolate while we wait?"

"I hope she doesn't think I'm going back to my dad's house." Sydney flopped back in the chair and crossed her arms in front of her chest.

Riley ran her fingers through her hair. "Come on, let's go get a drink." What she wouldn't give for something stronger than hot chocolate. She put her hand on Syd's shoulder, not so she wouldn't run, but just for a connection. Grounding, maybe, for them both. After ordering, they slid into seats at the sterile café, and Syd poked at her whipped cream with her fingertip.

"I'm sorry, Riley. It's all my fault. All of this is all my fault."

"How about you tell me what happened?"

"The shit really hit the fan tonight. Can I say that with you?" Sydney looked up hopefully.

There was no answer to that Syd would like. "You can be unedited with me, and whatever you say stays between us. So, what happened?"

"It's our weekend at Dad's house, first one since Mom got home from her trip. We went over today after school. While we were eating dinner Cathy asked us about our week, like she always does, and Olivia just couldn't keep her big mouth shut. She starts spouting off about the arcade and the orange pop everywhere and going to your house and how mom has a new girlfriend and how I have a girlfriend, but not her, she has a boyfriend."

"Holy shit." Riley wondered how it felt to be a parent and hear all that secondhand.

"Holy shit is right." Sydney drew her knees up to her chest. "Dad seriously blew a gasket. He wanted to know about you and about mom and about me. He was asking so many questions, so fast, that I didn't know which ones to answer first. Olivia started crying and then she had a total, full on panic attack and just kept gasping for air and screaming that she wanted to go home. Then, Dad and Cathy started fighting. Cathy's cool. She defended Mom. She told Dad that he had no control over what Mom does with her life or who she dates, that it's none of his business. Dad didn't take that too well and said he had a right to know who his kids were spending time with." She flicked at the whipped cream, her hot chocolate still untouched, and it plopped onto the table. She glanced at Riley, who just gave her a quick smile.

"Then he started in on me, asking how I could know I'm a lesbian, that I'm too young. Cathy yelled at him again and that's when Dad got in his car and took off. He squealed the tires and everything. Cathy told us that we could go pack up our stuff and she'd take us home if that's what we really wanted. Liv was still crying, and I had to help calm her down. When we got home, Dad's car was in our driveway, sideways. We went inside and he was screaming at Mom and Mom was screaming right back at him. I took Olivia's hand and pulled her into my room. I had to get her inhaler, she couldn't even breathe. They yelled at each other for a long time, and Cathy was totally on Mom's side, but she couldn't get a word in." She sighed and looked defeated.

"Olivia finally cried herself to sleep. I kept trying to tell her that it wasn't her fault, even though it was totally her fault. Why couldn't she keep her stupid big mouth shut? When she fell asleep, I climbed out the window and took off. They were all still screaming, and I couldn't handle it. There's a bus stop a few blocks away that I take to the library sometimes. The route schedule showed that it came here, to the airport, so I stayed on until it stopped here. Then, I texted you to see how I could get to your place. Riley, I don't want to go home. Not yet. Can't I come to Chicago with you for just a little bit? Jodie can have the couch. I'll sleep on the floor." Sydney was hugging her knees, her heels propped on the edge of the wooden chair.

Jesus. What could she say? What did she have the right to say? "I get it, Syd, but what you have to see, based on everything you shared, is that *everyone* is in your corner. Your mom, Cathy, me, Olivia, and with some time, I'm sure your dad will come around too. It was probably a lot to hear out of the blue like that. Coming to Chicago won't fix anything. It will probably make it worse. Running away always does." She tapped on Syd's finger until she looked up and met Riley's gaze. "You have to face it here with everyone who loves you, okay?"

Syd was silent as she processed before she gave a big sigh. "I guess so, but I feel bad. I know I said it was Olivia's fault, but I know it's really not Olivia's fault. It's all my fault. If I hadn't said all that stuff at the pizza place, then Mom wouldn't have sprayed orange pop everywhere and Olivia wouldn't have thought it was all so funny that she had to tell Dad and Cathy. Dad wouldn't be so mad at me and mad at you and Mom."

"Syd, please look at me." Riley's heart broke at the guilt in Syd's voice. Sydney slowly looked up and met Riley's gaze. "None of this is anyone's fault, certainly not yours or Olivia's. The truth is always best, even when it's hard to deal with. Was anything you said at the pizza place untrue?"

"I don't know. I thought it was all true. Was I right? Do you want to be my mom's girlfriend?"

Wow, so there it was. The black-and-white vision of a child. No beating around the bush. Riley had no idea how Andrea wanted her to answer this, so she decided to shoot from the hip. The truth was the best place to start. She knew she wanted more than just friendship.

"Yes. I'd love to be your mom's girlfriend. I'd love to have the chance to get to know you and your sister better, maybe someday be a part of your lives." Riley took a deep breath. That was all she could say without straying into territory that wasn't hers to traverse. "Okay, now, your turn. Would you rather have a girlfriend or a boyfriend?"

"Dad says I'm confused. That I don't know what I'm talking about, that I'm too young to know who I like."

"Dads say lots of stuff, especially when they're mad, but I'm wondering how *you* feel, not what your dad says. Would you, Sydney, rather have a girlfriend or a boyfriend?"

"I already have a girlfriend. Her name is Amelia. Olivia must have heard me telling Mom about her after you went home." Sydney looked up.

"You're what, eighth or ninth grade? Is Amelia in your class at school? How did you meet her?" Riley asked.

The sadness in Syd's eyes lifted a little. "I'm in ninth grade. She's in a few of my classes and we're both part of the LGBTQ club at school."

"You have an LGBTQ club at your school? How cool is that! We didn't have anything like that when your mom and I were in school."

"Well, you and Mom went to school *way* back in ancient times," Sydney said with a smile. She grew quiet again before asking, "Were your parents mad when you told them about you? How did you tell them that you liked girls and not boys?"

"I wouldn't say they were happy about it, but they were supportive and listened to what I had to say. And we're really close now. Your mom always said that I got the cool parents. I'd have to agree. I don't think there are too many parents who want their kids to be different. Parents are too worried about their kids being picked on or bullied, that life will be harder because of it. My folks admitted much later that they kind of always knew that I was a lesbian."

"How did they kind of always know you were a lesbian. What do you mean?" Sydney asked.

"Well, I was a lot like you. I was a bit of a tomboy. I'd sneak to school on picture day in my football jersey so my Mom wouldn't dress me up in stupid frilly clothes. I traded a brand new pink bike for a nasty beat-up motocross bike. I couldn't stand that stupid pink bike! I got in a lot of trouble for that one. I was never a girly girl. I also never wanted to date boys. They could be my buddies, my friends, but no dates! Even as I got older, I was never interested in boys the way my parents expected me to be. I only ever wanted to be with your mom. I think that's what tipped my parents off, even more than me being a tomboy, since there are plenty of straight women who are tomboys too. But everyone's story is different. My work has taught me that people love who they love. There really are no rules."

"We talk about that in the LGBTQ club too. I'm with you, I won't wear the pink frilly clothes either. No pink anything in my world! Amelia is a girly girl. I like that about her. She's really pretty." Sydney smiled. Her giggle was back. "You wanted to be with my mom when you were my age? How long have you known my mom? You didn't really answer on football day."

"We've known each other since kindergarten. We went to grade school, middle school, and high school together."

"Did you take her to any dances? Oh, did you take her to prom? I want to ask Amelia to the homecoming dance."

Again, this was territory with uneven ground. She changed the subject. "Do Amelia's parents know that the two of you are a couple?"

"Yeah, they're pretty cool about it. They don't care if we hold hands on the couch or anything. I like going over there after school." Sydney smiled.

"You should totally ask Amelia to homecoming. Well, if your mom says it's okay. I couldn't take your mom to any dances back then." Riley would have loved to have asked Andi to a dance.

"Did you date my mom when you two were in school?"

There was no way to keep putting her off, and one thing she believed was that if someone asked direct questions, they deserved direct answers. "Kind of. Things weren't as open or as accepted back then. We kept us a secret, so no one knew. Kids were mean to other kids who were different." Motion caught her eye and she saw Andrea sitting at the table behind them, listening. Olivia was sitting on her lap. Her little eyes were puffy and red. Seeing the two of them tugged at her heart. She tried very hard not to react so Syd wouldn't shut down.

"So, how did my dad date my mom if you were dating my mom?" Sydney asked.

She flicked her gaze over Syd's shoulder and saw Andi wince slightly. "Syd, when you're ready, I'd like you to ask your mom that one, okay? It's really her story to tell."

"Is that why you're around now but not before now? Is that why you've known my mom like, forever, but we're just meeting you now?" Sydney asked.

"Your mom and I lost each other for a long, long time. There wasn't the technology when we were in school that there is now. I had to go to college. Your mom was getting ready to bring you into the world. We didn't know how to find each other and then, after a while, we kinda stopped looking. I was hired by Sara and Kay to photograph the wedding in Alaska. That's how we found each other again. It was completely by chance. Sometimes people just lose touch and then get a second chance to be in each other's lives again. I really want that second chance." She gave that last sentence a little extra emphasis and knew full well Andrea understood. But would she listen?

"I'm glad you were the photographer. Mom's been super happy since she's been home. I'm glad that you and Mom got a second chance to know each other again. I'm happy you're here. You totally get me and you're pretty cool." Sydney finally took a sip of her hot chocolate and made a face when she found it was cold.

The sentiment made Riley's heart ache. Was this what she'd been missing by not wanting a relationship, not wanting kids? "I think we get each other pretty well. Do you feel any better? I know tonight was a little crazy, but you really are loved by so many people. It might just take your dad a little bit of time to come around."

"Yeah, I feel better. Thanks, Riley, I knew I could talk to you. I knew you'd understand."

"I do understand. I'm always here if you want to talk. Well, except when I'm on an airplane." Riley winked at her.

"I didn't know that phones had to be turned off on the airplane. You might have, like, five million missed calls from me."

"No worries. Hey, look who's here." Riley nodded in Andrea's direction. "I'll let you two talk. I have to go see if my suitcases are still here or if they tossed them into the lost and found. I'll see you around, kiddo." Riley gave Sydney a hug before grabbing the handle of her camera tote. She looked over and waited a second. Andrea pulled her arm free from Olivia's grasp and reached out for Riley's hand. She held on, her eyes closed and her lips pursed, blowing out a held breath. She squeezed Riley's hand a little tighter and then let go.

"When you come back with your luggage, we'll go, okay? I'd like to wait here and talk with Syd." Andrea tilted her head back and looked up into Riley's eyes.

She offered a slight nod and walked up the corridor toward baggage claim. It was after two in the morning, and she was shot. The airport was empty. *What a fucking day.* She found her suitcase and the main equipment tote on carrousel two. They were the only two items that remained. She lifted them off and locked her camera tote onto the larger tote and then hooked her briefcase onto the handle of the suitcase. She'd done this a million times at almost as many airports. It was at that moment that she realized she'd had enough. She was burned out, lonely, and just wanted a normal, quiet life. She wanted a family. She wanted to be a part of one specific family. She sat on the edge of the carrousel and buried her face in her hands.

CHAPTER THIRTY

There were tears in Syd's eyes, and Andrea could tell that she'd been crying. The pain in her daughter's expression broke her heart. Andrea wanted to set Olivia off to the side to hug her, but Olivia clung to her like an octopus and Andrea didn't want to risk another meltdown. Olivia was still way too upset to cope. She hoped Riley understood how insane the evening had been and that right now she needed to be there for the girls.

"Syd, come here and sit by me." Andrea continued to rock Olivia in her arms hoping she'd relax and let go. She finally did, five minutes after Riley disappeared down the hall. Andrea carefully set Olivia in the chair next to her and stood up, pulling Sydney into her arms.

"I'm grounded for the rest of my life, aren't I?" Sydney asked when Andrea finally released her from the long embrace.

"We're not deciding any of that tonight. I'm just so thankful that you're safe. I can't imagine my life without you and your sister. You two are my treasures, you know that don't you?" Andrea cupped her daughter's face in her hands. "*I beg you* to never do that again. You scared the living shit out of me."

"I know, I'm sorry, Mom. I won't do it again. Is Dad still totally psychotic?"

"I have no idea. He's back at his house and we're going home to our house. I'll go talk with him tomorrow and we'll go from there." Andrea pulled Sydney into her arms again.

"Mom, stop, you're squeezing all of the air out of me."

"Funny, because that's how I felt when I went into your room and found Olivia sitting next to an open window in a full-blown panic attack. All of the air squeezed out of my lungs and my heart stopped beating. She thought someone had kidnapped you. By the way, all of your friends and their parents aren't very happy with me tonight. I woke everyone up looking for you."

"I'm sorry, but everything Dad said was so nasty. I couldn't sit there and listen to it anymore. Why would he say such mean stuff about you and me? And why does he hate Riley so much? How could you ever love him? I hate him!"

Andrea couldn't blame Syd for feeling that way, since Scott truly had been way out of line. "Syd, please don't say that. He's still your father. His behavior earlier was absolutely unacceptable, but that's something you need to let me take care of, okay? You can hate the behavior, but not the person. Do you hear me?"

"Yeah, I know, but can I hate him, *the person*, for just a few more hours?"

"Only while we're here at the airport. We'll call it Switzerland. What happens in Switzerland, stays in Switzerland, got it?" Andrea shoulder bumped Sydney and smiled when she got a faint giggle.

"Since Livy is sleeping and it's just us, can I ask you something?"

Andrea glanced at Olivia, who was sound asleep, curled up on the hard wooden chair. "What the hell, we're in Switzerland. Ask away."

"Why did Dad say that bi was bullshit and you stopped being queer when you two got together?"

"Heard that, did you?" She should have had this conversation with them after they'd met Riley. Or before, even. But it hadn't seemed necessary. In truth, she could see she'd put if off because she didn't want to face the uncomfortable stuff. Just like she always did.

"Oh yeah, I heard a lot of stuff. A lot! You said I could ask. Why didn't you ever tell me you were bi?"

"And how exactly would you suggest I bring something like that up with my two young children? At what age is that an appropriate conversation? When you're two, five, or ten? Moms don't get a handbook. We're all just winging it, baby girl."

Syd tilted her head, studying her. "I never thought of it like that. I always thought you knew how to do everything."

"I'm glad you think so, because right now, I feel like I'm screwing everything up." Andrea picked up Sydney's hand and held it. It was time to be honest. "Syd, until I found Riley again, there wasn't a reason to explain that I was bi, but I planned on talking with you about it after the arcade. You just kinda stole my thunder. Why didn't you ever tell me you were a lesbian?" Andrea asked. Syd winced. So much for honesty.

"I was getting ready to. We talked about coming out to our parents at club. So, does Dad hate all gay people?"

"Aw, sweetie, I don't think your dad hates gay people. I think his ego took a big hit."

"What do you mean?" Sydney asked.

"I don't think much of tonight had anything to do with you or you being lesbian. Your dad is mad at me because of Riley. Riley's a sore subject with him."

"How come? Riley's awesome." Sydney's face was twisted with confusion.

Honesty. Now. "Riley and I were together before your dad and I got together. I missed her a lot and sometimes I'd cry about it. Okay, a lot of times I'd cry about it. You know what a crybaby I can be."

"That's why we freak if you watch the Hallmark Channel. You cry the entire time."

"True." Andrea smiled and squeezed her daughter's hand. "So anyway, I think that my feelings for Riley always bothered your dad because even after we were married and even after we had you, I still missed her and sometimes I still cried for her. I think your dad felt like I loved Riley more than I loved him, and he could never compete. And that's why he's so mad right now. It's not because I'm bi and not because you're a lesbian. It's because it's Riley and she's back, and to him, it proves that I was in love with her all along. He thinks I never, ever loved him. It hurt his feelings. Does that make sense?"

Sydney thought about it for a minute. "I think so. So, if you had fallen in love with a different woman, he wouldn't be mad, but because it's Riley, he's mad."

"Exactly."

She nodded, looking thoughtful. "I don't think I've ever heard you and Dad scream at each other like that. Do you think he'll get over it?"

"He's going to have to deal with it one way or another, if I haven't totally scared Riley away." Andrea leaned her head against Sydney's. "All I know is that my most important job in the whole wide world is to be a mom, first and foremost. I feel like I lost sight of that for a second because of how much I want to be with Riley. Everything was such a mess tonight, and I can't help but feel like some of it is my fault."

"Seems to me that all of it is Dad's fault, not yours or Riley's. He's the one being a dick. I can say that, we're still in Switzerland."

"How is it you're only fourteen? You give advice like your aunt Sara."

"Not even close, I'd get grounded if I said the f-bomb anywhere near as much as Aunt Sara."

"Indeed, you would." Andrea smiled. Her daughter was proving to be an incredible woman and she was so proud of her.

"How far away are the suitcases? Is Riley coming back?" Sydney asked.

"I don't know. It doesn't seem like it. She's been gone a long time."

Sydney looked up. "I could wait here with Livy if you want to go find her."

"Not a chance in hell. Wherever I go, we go together. I'm not leaving either one of you alone at an airport at, God, it's two thirty in the morning. Help me get your sister into my arms, she's like a sack of potatoes when she's asleep."

"Why don't we just call her?"

"You're so smart. What would I do without you?" Andrea ruffled Sydney's hair. She shifted Olivia into one arm and pulled her phone out of her pocket, tapping the phone icon next to Riley's name.

"Hello." Riley answered on the second ring, sounding despondent and tired.

"Did you find your suitcases? Are you ready to go?" Andrea asked.

"Before we go, I have to know something. What do you mean by rain check? If you mean that I need to get a hotel room, then I can find my own ride." Riley's voice was almost echoing. Where was she?

"No hotel, please no hotel. That is not what I meant by rain check. Come home with me, I need you," Andrea whispered into the phone. The phone beeped. Andrea looked down. Call ended.

She felt like her legs were going to give out. Everyone had a breaking point and she wondered if this was hers.

"Syd, would you take these for me so I can carry Livy?"

Riley's voice was behind her and then hands were on her shoulders slowly spinning Andrea around. Without a word, she held her arms open and Andrea gently handed over Liv, who snuggled into Riley's neck, still fast asleep. The sight made her heart stutter and she wanted to let go of the tears of relief that welled up, but she held off. They still had to get home and then maybe she could let the emotions of the day go. Once she was at home, in bed, wrapped up in Riley's arms. She had stayed, even after all of the day's events.

CHAPTER THIRTY-ONE

Riley opened her eyes and took in her surroundings. She was still in her dress clothes. They'd fallen onto the bed and must have fallen asleep while holding each other, both of them exhausted. She was in Andi's bedroom, but there was no Andi. There was a note on the bed next to her.

Good morning sweetheart,
I hope you were able to get some rest. I have to take care of a few things this morning, but I shouldn't be too long. Syd's with her friend Amelia, and Livy is home watching TV. If you need to go anywhere, she can call Heather, who lives next door, to stay with her. The coffee pot is all set up for you. Just press start.
I'll see you soon.
Andi

She sat up on the edge of the bed and noticed her luggage in front of the dresser. She didn't remember bringing it in here but was happy she didn't have to go look for it. She made the bed and then enjoyed a hot shower. Once she felt a bit more human, she made her way to the kitchen for a cup of coffee.

"Good morning, Olivia," Riley said as she passed by the living room.

"Good morning, Riley." Olivia popped up and skipped into the kitchen. "Do you know how much longer my mom's going to be?"

"Not a clue. What's up?" Riley poured a cup of coffee. It felt weird to be in Andrea's home without her.

"I'm supposed to go to a party this afternoon. I signed up to bring cupcakes. Will Mom be back in time to make cupcakes?"

"What time is the party?" Riley asked.

"I don't know. It's on the fridge." Olivia grabbed Riley's hand and pulled her across the kitchen.

Andrea wasn't kidding when she said she had a calendar on the fridge that was jam-packed. Every square was filled with at least two or three events. It looked like the party started at four and it was already half past noon.

"Can we buy cupcakes?" Riley asked.

"No, we have special sprinkles for Annie. Strawberry is her favorite flavor." Olivia put her hands on her hips.

Riley could see Andrea's personality in the miniature version standing in front of her. "Well then, it looks like we're making cupcakes. Which cupboard has the stuff for baking?"

Olivia walked out of the kitchen. She returned with a step stool and plopped it on the floor to the right of the sink. She climbed up two steps and opened a corner cabinet. She handed Riley two boxes of cake mix, three cans of frosting, and several bottles of sprinkles. Thank goodness they wouldn't be making them from scratch. Boxed cupcakes she could handle.

"Bowls? Whisk?" Riley asked.

Olivia smiled. "On it."

She opened yet another cupboard and handed Riley bowls and measuring cups. She pulled open a drawer and offered a spatula, whisk, and measuring spoons.

"Let's do this!" Olivia looked up, smiling.

Riley picked up the box and looked at the instructions. The store always baked the best cakes for the two birthdays they celebrated each year at the studio. Cupcake liners? What the hell? Oh boy, she was in over her head.

"Do you know what cupcake liners are?"

"Um, yeah, it's the paper that you peel off when you eat a cupcake!" Olivia's little face twisted.

"Got it. Do you have any? What about special cupcake pans? Do they make special cupcake pans?" Riley asked. She did her best to ignore the wide-eyed expression aimed her way.

"Are you serious or are you joking?"

"I'm totally joking!" Riley wasn't joking, but she didn't want to look like a complete fool. "But you have to find it all because I don't know where anything is."

Olivia moved the step stool and opened another cabinet next to the stove. She pulled out a small plastic tub that read "cupcake liners" and held them up, pointing at the words like a game show host before tossing them to Riley. She stepped back down and dug in a lower cabinet. Most of the cabinet's contents were spread out across the kitchen floor when she held out a stack of what Riley guessed to be cupcake pans. Olivia spent the next couple of minutes fitting everything back into the cabinet.

"Okay, there are two different kinds of mixes, strawberry and vanilla. Are we going to mix them together?" Riley asked.

"No way, you'll ruin everything! We make each one in its own bowl. We don't mix them until we put them in the pans, then you do a little bit of one and a little bit of the other. Oh, you'll see. I'll show you."

Riley dumped the contents of the strawberry mix into the first bowl. Olivia grabbed the eggs from the refrigerator and vegetable oil from above the stove.

"We need to get the oven warmed up," Olivia said. "You have to press this button that says bake and then the up arrow until the screen says three hundred and fifty degrees."

Fortunately, all Riley had to do was follow instructions. It was clear Andrea did this with them often. Once the oven was set, Olivia handed Riley a small bowl.

"What's this for?"

"Umm, you crack the eggs in it," Olivia said.

"Why dirty another bowl? I want the eggs in the cake, right?" Riley asked.

"Yes, but you don't want eggshells in the cake. The little bowl is where you crack the eggs so if you get shells in it, you can get them out before they fall in the cake and are lost forever. Mom taught me that. She says, 'Nobody likes crunchy cake!'" Olivia moved the step stool over by Riley and climbed up one step.

"Your mom is one smart lady!" Riley smiled.

She cracked the eggs into the small bowl. Sure enough, a small piece of shell fell in from the second egg. Olivia grabbed a spoon and fished it out.

"See?" She held the spoon up for Riley.

"I'll never doubt you again."

Olivia poured in the measured amount of vegetable oil while Riley whisked up the strawberry batter. They repeated the process for the vanilla batter. Once both batters were ready, Olivia grabbed two pouring measuring cups.

"Okay, you put some strawberry batter in this one and some vanilla in this one." Olivia pointed to each measuring cup. She pulled the cupcake pans apart and placed one liner in each cupcake spot.

"Now, we pour some strawberry in each liner, but not too much. Both kinds together can't be more than halfway full or it will be a big mess. I did that once."

Riley carefully poured some strawberry in one liner and then added in some vanilla to make sure the total per cup was acceptable to her tiny instructor. Olivia grabbed a spoon and turned it upside down. She stuck the handle of the spoon in the cupcake, holding the liner with one finger. She swirled the spoon around about a three-quarters of the way around the cupcake until a line of strawberry showed through the vanilla.

"That's pretty neat. Did your mom show you that, too?" Riley asked.

Olivia nodded her head up and down with a big smile on her face. "I like to help my mom cook."

Riley and Olivia set up two pans' worth of cupcakes and then slid them into the oven. Olivia set the timer for the number of minutes Riley read off from the box.

"Now, where would we find toothpicks?" Riley asked.

Olivia looked confused. "Why do you need a toothpick?"

"It's the only way I know to tell if the cupcakes are done. You poke it with a toothpick and if it comes out clean, then they've cooked long enough. If not, they'll need another minute or two. It's what my mom used to do."

"My mom just touches the top with the tip of her finger. She says they have a bounce when they're done."

"I'm afraid I'll need a toothpick. I have no idea how much bounce a cupcake is supposed to have."

Olivia shrugged and pulled the step stool across the kitchen. She dug in a cabinet next to the stove and found a box of toothpicks.

"Will these work?" She asked.

"Perfect!"

For the intervening minutes, Olivia sat on the floor in front of the oven, watching the cupcakes rise. Riley leaned against the counter, wondering what the hell she was doing. She was growing more attached to the girls every day.

"I hate fighting." Olivia kept staring at the oven, but she didn't seem to be looking at the cupcakes.

"Me too. But sometimes fighting is just part of being human. Emotions get really big and come out like giant waves." Riley took a deep breath. "But the ocean always goes back to normal, after. It doesn't mean people don't love each other."

Olivia nodded, not saying anything else.

When all of the cupcakes were cooling on the counter, Riley washed round one of dishes. Olivia dried each dish and helped put everything away.

"Now, I think it's time for frosting. Why do we have three frostings and only two flavors in our cupcakes?"

"Some cupcakes get white frosting and some get strawberry frosting and then some get chocolate frosting. Everyone has a favorite," Olivia explained. She moved her step stool next to Riley and returned to the first step.

Riley opened each of the three frosting containers. Olivia handed Riley a small spatula and then took one for herself.

"What color do you want?" Riley asked.

"Strawberry. It's Mom's favorite!"

Riley handed the strawberry frosting to Olivia. She swirled about three tablespoons' worth on her small spatula and coated the top of the cupcake like a pro. Riley grabbed the vanilla and tried to do the same, but what she held in her hand didn't look anywhere near as awesome.

"You'll get the hang of it. You have to use your wrist, like this," Olivia said and then frosted another cupcake.

Riley watched Olivia's technique and then practiced a few more times before her cupcakes didn't look like a two-year-old frosted them. A gasp startled the two of them. Riley looked up to see Andrea standing in the hallway. She was smiling; that had to be a good sign.

"Look at you two! You made the cupcakes! I'm so sorry I'm late, Livy." Andrea removed her coat and hung it by the door.

"It's okay, Riley helped me," Olivia said and then frosted another cupcake like there was nothing unusual about the situation.

"I see that. May I try one?" Andrea walked up to the counter.

"Which frosting would you like? Strawberry, vanilla, or chocolate?" Riley asked.

"You are a treasure! Everything is so clean too! Strawberry, please." Andrea reached across the counter and squeezed Riley's hand, and her expression was open and sweet.

"With or without sprinkles?" Olivia asked. "Can we have one, too?"

"Yes, you may have one and I'll take mine with sprinkles please," Andrea said and accepted the bottle of sprinkles from Olivia. She shook a few red and white sprinkles on top before handing the bottle back to Olivia.

Andrea peeled the paper back and took a bite. Her eyes lit up when she noticed the swirled flavors inside the cupcake.

"You two did an amazing job. These are delicious! Perfect swirl too!"

"Olivia deserves all the credit. She taught me all sorts of new skills." Riley smiled.

"Mom, did you know you can stick a toothpick in the cupcake and if it's clean when it comes out, then the cupcakes are all done cooking?" Olivia asked.

"I did not know that! Wow!" Andrea said. "Liv, we need to get going if you want to be on time. Go get cleaned up. Riley and I will finish frosting the last few and get them boxed up."

"Okay, Mom." Olivia jumped off her stool. She put the stool back where it came from and returned to grab a cupcake before darting down the hall. "Thanks, Riley! I had fun."

"You're welcome, kiddo. I had fun too." Riley set down the spatula and turned to Andrea. "I was wondering if we could talk today."

"Do you think we could talk after we drop Olivia off at the party? Syd's at Amelia's for a few hours. We'd have the house to ourselves." Andrea rested her head on Riley's shoulder.

"I'd like that."

Riley held Andrea in her arms. Never before had she been so certain that she was right where she belonged.

CHAPTER THIRTY-TWO

Andrea returned from walking Olivia up to the party at Annie's house and slid into the driver's seat. She pulled the seat belt across her body and exhaled as she leaned her head back in the seat. She was physically and emotionally exhausted. The last twenty-four hours had depleted any energy reserve she had available. Riley had to be just as exhausted, perhaps more so given her schedule the past week. But things had to be said, and there was no reason to hesitate. Not anymore.

"I'm sorry you were pulled into all of that last night. I know it's not what you signed up for." Andrea turned her head on the head rest and looked across the car. Riley's jaw tensed up. Was she upset about something?

"You keep saying that. What exactly did I sign up for?" Riley's tone was sharp.

"Let's not do this in Annie's driveway." Andrea started the car and put it into reverse. She was spent and didn't know if she had the energy for another big conversation. She straightened the car up on the road and put it into drive.

"Andi, can I ask you a few questions before we talk about us?" Riley asked. Her tone was back to normal.

Andrea's chest tightened, the old instinct to avoid conflict rising. She squelched it. No avoidance, time to face this head on. She nodded. "Ask anything."

"How's Syd? Is she in trouble for what happened last night?" Riley asked.

"No, she's not in any trouble. I went to Scott's this morning and talked things through without Syd there. We agreed that the entire night was a cluster fuck of his own making. Syd's spirit seems better today. I can't thank you enough for being there for her last night. She's promised to stay and talk should anything like that ever happen again. No more bolting." She glanced at Riley with a small, sad smile. "She needs to handle things differently than I did. Running away from the hard stuff won't make things better, and I think she gets that now. That's why she's allowed to be at Amelia's this afternoon. I get why she left, and Scott knows he can't behave that way." Andrea turned out on the main street. It was nice having Riley in the car with her. "Scott's blowup had more to do with you than Syd, which I'm sure you know to some degree. He said he's had a hunch about Syd and Amelia. Poor Syd just bore the brunt of his reaction to you being back in my life. He's always been super jealous of you. I don't know if you knew that."

Riley shook her head. "No, I wasn't aware until I talked to Syd last night, but I figured his ego was involved."

Andrea turned left onto the street that headed into her neighborhood. "This morning, Scott and I agreed to some ground rules about respecting my privacy, my life, and my relationship with you. I don't expect anything like that to ever happen again." Andrea pulled into her driveway and put the car in park. She shut off the engine and turned in her seat. "Can we go inside and talk? Please?"

For some reason, everything felt desperate at the moment. The sharpness in Riley's tone while they were parked in Annie's driveway had her flight response on high alert and she had to force herself to face, head-on, whatever was to come.

Riley nodded, opened her car door, and followed Andrea inside. She sat on a stool at the breakfast bar and stared at Andrea.

"Talk to me. There's a lot going on behind those green eyes." Andrea sat in the stool next to her. She reached for Riley's hands.

There was a heavy moment of silence as Riley clearly searched for what she wanted to say. "I feel like I'm always on the outside looking in, the photographer who doesn't get to be in the frame. When I do step inside, it feels so right, and so perfect, but it isn't what we agreed to and I don't know where I stand anymore." Riley's eyes were wet with unshed tears. Her jaw muscles tightened.

"God, I was so worried you'd be scared off by what happened. This isn't what I expected you to say." Andrea felt like she could breathe again. "I was trying to honor what we agreed to. I was trying to make sure we could spend time together without strings or labels or expectations, but I'm not sure that kind of thing can work, not in a situation with kids involved."

"It's not working for me either, but it's not your fault, it's mine. Andi, I want the strings. I want the labels. Could we renegotiate the terms?" A tear escaped and trailed down Riley's cheek.

Andrea's spirit perked up. Her breath caught in her chest. "I'm listening. I'm open to strings. What label did you have in mind?"

"I know we said a relationship wouldn't work because of how different our lives are, especially mine, and now I wonder if we can rethink that. I think girlfriend has a nice ring to it, for starters anyway. I especially like it when Syd and Livy call me your girlfriend, it warms my heart. Andi, I'm still head over heels in love with you. I want a chance at a life with you, just like I wanted a chance at a life with you all those years ago. I want to be there for all of it. The last-minute cupcake frenzy with Olivia, the midnight freak-outs, the talks with Syd, snuggling up with you on the couch looking at photographs or watching terrible movies. I want it all and I hope you want it too. Even if it takes us time to get there, I'm all in."

Andrea realized she was smiling ear to ear and nodding like a crazy woman. Hopefully, she hadn't passed out and this wasn't a dream. She bit down on the inside of her cheek and winced. Nope, not asleep.

"How could I have doubted that we would find a way? No doubts, never again. I love you so much! I've always loved you. I can't imagine letting you go, not having you in my life. I want it all too! I've known it since Alaska. I realized at the wedding that I no longer wanted to be alone, but it was more than that, I no longer wanted to be alone because I wanted to be with *you*. I've dreamt of you all these years. I love you!" She wanted to yell it from the rooftops.

Riley had tears streaming down her face. "These are tears of happiness, just to be clear."

Andrea leaned forward and kissed Riley tenderly. She pulled her in close and held her in her arms. After a bit, Riley's hands were caressing her back and her lips were on her neck. Shivers erupted all over her body, and her need was undeniable. "Sweetheart, we have the house to ourselves for a couple of hours yet. Can I take my girlfriend to bed?"

"You read my mind." Riley lifted Andrea's shirt up over her head.

"You still owe me a real date," Andrea said, standing up from the stool. She let her bra fall to the floor and then turned away from Riley and walked toward the bedroom.

"Indeed, I do," Riley said a moment later and then raced past her, already naked.

Andrea enjoyed the way Riley finished undressing her and guided her down onto the bed. Her touch was sensual and electric creating a powerful need deep within. Her eyes, her expression, was filled with so much love and adoration. She had never felt more cherished by another person in all her life and only hoped that Riley felt all of those emotions from her too.

Riley kissed her with a passion that curled her toes. They explored each other's bodies with experienced hands, knowing when to caress, pinch, tease, or swirl with a delicate touch. Andrea took control and flipped Riley over on her back. She straddled her hips and pushed up against her.

"It's amazing, how I feel when I'm with you," Andrea whispered. "Make love to me, sweetheart, like we did in Alaska."

"The purple prince is in my bathroom bag on your dresser. I didn't forget it," Riley whispered. She cupped Andrea's ass in her hands and lifted her hips into her.

As amazing as that pressure up against her felt, Andrea broke away. She walked over to the dresser and dug into Riley's bag. The purple prince was wrapped up in a side pouch. Riley was up on her elbows watching Andrea. All the times they played with this toy while in Alaska, Andrea had never put it on. She stepped into the harness and tightened the straps. She crawled her way up from the foot of the bed like a lioness on the prowl. She couldn't remember a time when she felt sexier or more seductive. The expression on Riley's face only encouraged her.

The room was dimly lit from the daylight streaming in through the closed blinds. Riley looked absolutely beautiful, lying there, her legs open in invitation. Andrea knelt between Riley's legs and lifted herself up until the tip was close enough to tease. Riley moaned and leaned her head back into the pillow. She circled her clit with the tip and then pushed it gently inside. Riley lifted her hips into the pressure, and it felt unbelievable. Now she understood why Riley loved wearing it. She felt everything. Every ripple, every bit of pressure, and it was all she could do to slow down and savor the moment. She pressed her hips into Riley and was rewarded with a deep moan. Riley wrapped her arms around Andrea's back and flipped her over. She was amazed that they had stayed connected.

Riley drew her knees up and straddled Andrea's hips. She pushed down into Andrea at the same time that she lifted up. Riley was sexy as hell as she leaned forward with a hunger in her eyes that demanded release. She held Andrea's hands over her breasts and thrust into her over and over again until they exploded into each other with wave after wave of orgasm. Riley moved her hips in tiny circles enjoying the many aftershocks until she fell forward into Andrea's arms.

"Babe, that was amazing," Riley said breathlessly. She cupped Andrea's face in her hands. "I love you. I've always loved you."

"Oh, sweetheart, I love you too." Andrea pulled her face closer and kissed her.

She was so grateful for their ability to be honest and open with each other. It allowed her the ability to break through the bad habit of avoidance and to say what she wanted, what she needed. She was so beyond thrilled that it was what Riley wanted too. They were going to work on a future, together, and that alone filled her heart with happiness.

CHAPTER THIRTY-THREE

Riley parked her truck in Andrea's driveway and shut off the ignition. Two weeks had passed since they had professed their love for one another, and despite busy schedules that left the phone as the main communication source, each day had only gotten better. Time together was still an issue, but there was a solution in sight. Riley checked her hair in the review mirror and then made her way to the door for a long overdue date night. Scott had mended fences and had the girls for the weekend and somehow, there wasn't a session booked. Thank the lucky stars for that one.

The door swung open a few seconds after Riley pressed the bell. Andrea looked absolutely stunning, always the perfect balance of sexy and elegant. She stepped back and waved Riley in.

"These are for you. It's not a proper date without a bouquet of flowers." Riley leaned down and kissed Andrea tenderly. "You look beautiful."

"Hmmm. Thank you, so do you, quite sexy. You know I can't resist you when you wear your suit." Andrea accepted the flowers.

"I'm counting on it." Riley smiled.

"Let me put these in water and then I'm ready to go."

Riley helped Andrea into her coat and then into the front seat of her truck. She ran around to the driver's side, trying to settle her nerves. She hoped the evening went as well as she'd planned.

"Where are we going?" Andrea asked.

"You're irresistible. Is back to the bedroom a bad answer?" Riley smiled across the seat.

"It wins you brownie points for later, but I'm starving, so I need food." Andrea flipped up the center console and scootched to the middle seat. She fastened the lap belt.

Riley loved that she took control and sat in the middle, especially when a not so stray hand rested on her inner thigh. Thank God for automatic transmissions. She looked over and smiled, draping her arm around Andi's shoulders before backing out of the driveway.

Given that Andrea knew about Maria and the Italian restaurant, Riley decided on her other favorite and went with Greek Mediterranean instead. A first date had to be unique. A quiet little restaurant that seated about thirty was a few blocks away from her house and it had great reviews. Riley had a table for two reserved.

She ordered two whisky on the rocks and dolmas for an appetizer. Andrea's eyes lit up, and that's all she was hoping for.

"I had no idea this place was here, let alone so close," Andrea said between bites of stuffed grape leaves. "You couldn't have picked a better place for our date night!"

Riley smiled, thrilled that this was a hit. "I'm so glad you're enjoying yourself. A toast, to one of many amazing dates."

Andrea smiled one of her deep dimple smiles. "I'll toast to that, one of many amazing dates. I'll hold you to it, too."

"I'm counting on it, love." Riley drew in a deep breath, a lifetime of dreams coming true.

Dinner was exquisite and the baklava for dessert was just as amazing. Andrea sipped on a second whiskey, while Riley had switched to water, so she was safe to drive.

"Do I get to take you home now and relieve you of that suit?" Andi looked playfully over her glass once the waiter had picked up their check.

"One more stop and then I will relieve you of that sexy dress." Riley raised her eyebrows a few times playfully.

"What more is there? Dinner and dessert are accomplished, now I get my second dessert." Andrea smiled.

"You'll see."

Riley signed for the check and walked with Andrea to the parking lot. She helped Andrea up into the passenger side of the truck and then made her way over to the driver's side. She hoped this next stop was everything she'd wished for.

About ten miles up the beltline, she exited and turned right instead of left toward Andrea's house. She didn't miss the quizzical look but decided to ignore it for now. Another flick of the blinker and she turned right into a parking lot before parking and shutting off the truck. She hopped out of the driver's side and ran around to help Andrea out of the truck.

"Why are we at the old art museum? What are you up to?" Andrea held onto Riley's hand. Another car pulled in and an older woman climbed out of the driver's seat, waving to Riley.

"Why do you have to be so versed on the area around your home? Of course you'd know this is the old art museum." Riley waved back and guided Andrea to the doors. "Hi, Peggy, thank you for meeting us out here tonight."

"No problem, happy to do it. I'll unlock it and duck out if you don't mind, I have some grocery shopping to do. I'll swing by after and lock up." Peggy nudged Riley with her elbow and winked.

"No problem at all. We'll make sure the lights are out. I'll touch base tomorrow, okay?" Riley guided Andrea inside and flipped a bank of light switches. Peggy nodded and made her way back to her car.

"Did she just wink at my girl?" Andrea smiled.

"Yup, you found me out!" Riley leaned down and kissed Andrea. "So, that brings us to the old art museum. It was listed on the market a few weeks ago. I've been scouring the internet for something close, but not too close. This one is close enough to your place that we could walk back and forth, but hopefully not so close that you feel smothered. The lower level is perfect for a photography studio and office space. The bonus is that there are four small apartments above, which would be perfect for me and my nomadic photographers. All I know is that it would be a lot easier to see where life can take us if we're in the same city and can spend some time together that doesn't involve a six-hour commute or two o'clock in the morning airport pickups."

Andrea looked like she was going to burst with happiness. She looked around the large open floor plan. "This is going to make a beautiful studio. The tall ceilings are perfect. But, sweetheart, if you move up here full-time, you're never sleeping here!"

"I love the sound of that." Riley wrapped her arms around Andrea. They continued the tour around the lower level of the building. "I know that moving up here doesn't change my travel schedule. But I've hired a couple of new photographers to distribute the workload, and that way, maybe all of us can have a chance at a somewhat normal life. Jodie's on board with all of this. We'll train the newbies and shoot side by side for a while until we can get a feel for their perspective. My goal is to eventually travel less and run much of the business behind the scenes. There's plenty to do without getting on a plane two or three times a week."

"It's like a dream come true."

Riley took a deep breath and leaned in closer to Andrea. "My sweet Andi, I have no ties to Illinois, it's just where I landed after an internship, and there's nothing keeping me there. Nothing keeping any of us there. I also understand that *everything* is keeping you here. I'm excited to see how it could all come together. It all started to fall into place after Syd's night at the airport, when I randomly started looking for something in this area. I wanted to see what you thought of the idea before I put in an offer."

"You'd really move up here to be with me, with us?" Andrea's eyes sparkled. The smile on her face said everything Riley needed to know.

"Yes, without a doubt." Riley nodded.

"Are we really going to get a chance at being a couple?" Andrea leaned over and cupped Riley's face in her hands. "Yes, please, put in an offer. I want more of everything with you."

Riley pulled her in close. "I've listened, too, babe. I get that you want time for everyone to adjust to a new normal. I get the need to make sure we're going to work out before the girls get too attached. I realize it's about more than just you and me. I respect that. I need a studio, either way. We can take it slowly until everything is settled."

"The girls are already attached. They've each asked if you could move in with us, so we don't have to do that drive to Illinois ever again. They hated that car ride but loved seeing you." Andrea laughed. "This was some date night. I don't know how you plan to top this."

"I think someone was interested in a second dessert." Riley leaned down and kissed Andrea with all the passion that their two weeks apart had created. Their future was calling, and she intended to answer in the best possible way.

CHAPTER THIRTY-FOUR

A fter four long months and countless delays, the renovations on the new studio and apartments were finally complete. The new display walls were painted in a variety of bright and bold colors, selected specifically to enhance the elements of the prints hung as the foreground. Riley took one final lap around and checked on the lighting for each and every print on the walls. Everything was perfect. She heard the bell jingle above the lobby door and caught a whiff of Andrea's perfume. Riley inhaled deeply and turned around.

"Wow."

It was the only word that Riley could come up with. Andrea looked absolutely stunning. She'd seen the red dress on the hanger in the closet, though it looked much more incredible on Andrea's curvy frame. She wore her hair down and the choker from Sara's wedding. Riley's mouth was dry, and she found it difficult to swallow. The click of Andrea's heels on the stained concrete floor was mesmerizing as she walked across the room with that sexy swagger.

"Everything looks amazing!"

"Thanks, I'm happy with the result."

"Where's Jodie and Cloe and the new additions?"

"They're upstairs, they'll be down in a bit," Riley said. "My parents will be here in about an hour or so. My mom can't wait to see you again. She really missed you."

"Could I have a tour before the guests start to arrive?"

Riley lifted her suit jacket off the back of a chair and slid her arms into the sleeves. She picked up the two rocks glasses that she'd prepared and handed one to Andrea.

"To us." Riley held up her glass.

"Hmmm, to us." Andrea tapped her glass against Riley's.

The whiskey was warm on her throat and seemed to steady her nerves. She set down the glass on the table and reached for Andrea's hand. It was time for the tour. She'd been a bundle of nerves all day in anticipation of this moment. They had about a half an hour before the guests began to arrive.

She walked with Andrea from section to section. There were a few prints from the studio in Illinois, but the majority of the prints were newer shots from more recent events. Each of the four photographers had a pod of their favorites and the lobby was filled with a variety of portraits and one-off shots. Miss Charlotte, their wonderful contact from the sex shop they'd popped into on their road trip, was larger than life on the wall before Riley's pod. It was a great shot with Times Square in the background. Her space was twice the size of the other photographers, mostly because she couldn't narrow down the prints that she wanted to display. She figured it was owner's prerogative.

Riley stopped outside of the pod and reached her free hand into her suit jacket pocket. It was still there. She drew in a deep breath and clicked on the lights before walking with Andrea through the doorway. She smiled when she heard Andrea's breath catch. She turned in time to see the surprise in her eyes and her hand instinctively come up to cover her mouth.

Two of the walls in the pod were covered with a variety of shots from their time together along with the inside wall around the entrance into the pod. There were a couple of the shots from their high school days, a shot of their tree, and then so many more shots of their trip to Alaska. Riley could spend all day in this pod staring at these walls. She loved each and every print.

"Riley, this is incredible." She wrapped an arm around Riley's waist.

"The shot of you in bed will move into our room after tonight." Riley smiled.

"It's a little weird that my image is plastered all over the walls in this area. At least you have a few of us together." Andrea turned to take it all in.

"Most of these will move up to the apartment or to your place after tonight." Riley had staged this pod for one very specific purpose.

"You have so many other incredible shots that you've taken. Why is this wall on the left still blank? I find it hard to believe you couldn't pick something to hang there."

"Oh, I know exactly what's going to hang in that spot. I have a photoshop mockup if you'd like to see it?" Riley raised her eyebrows. She knew she was blushing.

"Based on the look on your face, I'm a little scared to see it."

"Stay right here."

Riley jogged into the back office and grabbed the poster-sized printout of her creation.

"Close your eyes." Riley walked back into the pod and hung the print up on the wall. It was corny but she couldn't resist. She stood next to Andrea and pulled the small box from her suit jacket pocket. She opened the lid and drew in a deep breath. "Okay, open your eyes."

Andrea opened her eyes. She looked at the print on the wall. Riley looked, too. She'd cropped in pictures of the four of them. Riley and Andrea decked out for a wedding in the back, Sydney and Oliva in the front in their best dress clothes. The lighting was a little off, but the gist of the shot still shined through.

"How on earth? What is this?" Andrea stepped closer to the print. "I just bought the girls these outfits for the school dance."

"Like I said, a mockup. I'm hoping to replace it with our real wedding photo." Riley swallowed. Her mouth was suddenly so dry.

Andrea slowly turned back to Riley and then finally looked down to the box in her hand. She squealed and covered her mouth with her hand. Riley couldn't stop smiling.

"My sweet Andi, I love you with all of my being. I've loved you my whole life, and I'll love you till the end of time. So, with Sydney and Olivia's permission, I wonder, would you marry me?"

"You asked the girls for their permission?" Andrea kept looking from the ring up to Riley's eyes and then back to the ring.

"I did," Riley said. She lifted the ring out of the box. "What do you say? Would you marry me?"

Andrea rushed into Riley's arms. "Yes, a thousand times yes! I love you too! *Yes!*"

She cupped Riley's face in her hands and kissed her. When she pulled back, Riley accepted her left hand and slid the ring in place. It fit perfectly and seemed to sparkle even brighter on Andrea's hand.

"Yes?" Riley smiled.

"Yes!" Andrea held her hand out and stared at the ring. She stepped into Riley's arms and kissed her again.

"Can we have a big wedding with the dress and everything?" Andrea asked. Her eyes were sparkling brighter than the diamond on her hand.

"Absolutely! The whole thing. I might know some photographers." Riley smiled.

"Would it be crazy if we honeymooned in Alaska? Maybe a September wedding and an Alaskan honeymoon in the hot springs?"

"Babe, I'd love nothing more. Our little oasis is perfect for our honeymoon!"

The bell above the door jingled. Voices echoed back to them. Everyone must have arrived at once.

"Andi, Riley, where are you? Get your clothes back on and get your asses out here! This place looks awesome." Sara's voice called out.

"Oh my God, I can't wait to show Sara!" Andrea said. She held out her hand again and then leaned in for another kiss. "I love you, Riley."

"I love you, too."

Riley turned back to the photographs in her pod, allowing herself to be in the moment. An image of Andrea turning away from the bar at the welcome party in Alaska caught her eye. It was still unbelievable that a fluke encounter could give her a second chance at a life with her soul mate. She'd spent so long convinced she couldn't have it all, but she was about to have exactly that. Love, a family, and work she loved, but on a more practical level. There were still bucket list places to tick off, but now she'd have her best friend and soul mate beside her to capture every special moment. Their lives would truly be picture perfect.

About the Author

A vivid imagination spurred Nance Sparks's desire to write lesbian romance. Nance lives in south central Wisconsin with her spouse. Her passion for photography, homesteading, hiking, gardening, and most anything outdoors comes through in her stories. When the sun is out and the sky is blue, especially during the golden hour, Nance can be found on the Wisconsin River with a camera in hand capturing shots of large birds in flight.

Books Available from Bold Strokes Books

A Convenient Arrangement by Aurora Rey and Jaime Clevenger. Cuffing season has come for lesbians, and for Jess Archer and Cody Dawson, their convenient arrangement becomes anything but. (978-1-63555-818-0)

An Alaskan Wedding by Nance Sparks. The last thing either Andrea or Riley expects is to bump into the one who broke her heart fifteen years ago, but when they meet at the welcome party, their feelings come rushing back. (978-1-63679-053-4)

Beulah Lodge by Cathy Dunnell. It's 1874, and newly engaged Ruth Mallowes is set on marriage and life as a missionary…until she falls in love with the housemaid at Beulah Lodge. (978-1-63679-007-7)

Gia's Gems by Toni Logan. When Lindsey Speyer discovers that popular travel columnist Gia Williams is a complete fake and threatens to expose her, blackmail has never been so sexy. (978-1-63555-917-0)

Holiday Wishes & Mistletoe Kisses by M. Ullrich. Four holidays, four couples, four chances to make their wishes come true. (978-1-63555-760-2)

Love By Proxy by Dena Blake. Tess has a secret crush on her best friend, Sophie, so the last thing she wants is to help Sophie fall in love with someone else, but how can she stand in the way of her happiness? (978-1-63555-973-6)

Loyalty, Love, & Vermouth by Eric Peterson. A comic valentine to a gay man's family of choice, including the ones with cold noses and four paws. (978-1-63555-997-2)

Marry Me by Melissa Brayden. Allison Hale attempts to plan the wedding of the century to a man who could save her family's business, if only she wasn't falling for her wedding planner, Megan Kinkaid. (978-1-63555-932-3)

Pathway to Love by Radclyffe. Courtney Valentine is looking for a woman exactly like Ben—smart, sexy, and not in the market for anything serious. All she has to do is convince Ben that sex-without-strings is the perfect pathway to pleasure. (978-1-63679-110-4)

Sweet Surprise by Jenny Frame. Flora and Mac never thought they'd ever see each other again, but when Mac opens up her barber shop right next to Flora's sweet shop, their connection comes roaring back. (978-1-63679-001-5)

The Edge of Yesterday by CJ Birch. Easton Gray is sent from the future to save humanity from technological disaster. When she's forced to target the woman she's falling in love with, can Easton do what's needed to save humanity? (978-1-63679-025-1)

The Scout and the Scoundrel by Barbara Ann Wright. With unexpected danger surrounding them, Zara and Roni are stuck between duty and survival, with little room for exploring their feelings, especially love. (978-1-63555-978-1)

Bury Me in Shadows by Greg Herren. College student Jake Chapman is forced to spend the summer at his dying grandmother's home and soon finds danger from long-buried family secrets. (978-1-63555-993-4)

Can't Leave Love by Kimberly Cooper Griffin. Sophia and Pru have no intention of falling in love, but sometimes love happens when and where you least expect it. (978-1-636790041-1)

Free Fall at Angel Creek by Julie Tizard. Detective Dee Rawlings and aircraft accident investigator Dr. River Dawson use conflicting methods to find answers when a plane goes missing, while overcoming surprising threats, and discovering an unlikely chance at love. (978-1-63555-884-5)

Love's Compromise by Cass Sellars. For Piper Holthaus and Brook Myers, will professional dreams and past baggage stop two hearts from realizing they are meant for each other? (978-1-63555-942-2)

Not All a Dream by Sophia Kell Hagin. Hester has lost the woman she loved and the world has descended into relentless dark and cold. But giving up will have to wait when she stumbles upon people who help her survive. (978-1-63679-067-1)

Protecting the Lady by Amanda Radley. If Eve Webb had known she'd be protecting royalty, she'd never have taken the job as bodyguard, but as the threat to Lady Katherine's life draws closer, she'll do whatever it takes to save her, and may just lose her heart in the process. (978-1-63679-003-9)

The Secrets of Willowra by Kadyan. A family saga of three women, their homestead called Willowra in the Australian outback, and the secrets that link them all. (978-1-63679-064-0)

Trial by Fire by Carsen Taite. When prosecutor Lennox Roy and public defender Wren Bishop become fierce adversaries in a headline-grabbing arson case, their attraction ignites a passion that leads them both to question their assumptions about the law, the truth, and each other. (978-1-63555-860-9)

Turbulent Waves by Ali Vali. Kai Merlin and Vivien Palmer plan their future together as hostile forces make their own plans to destroy what they have, as well as all those they love. (978-1-63679-011-4)

Unbreakable by Cari Hunter. When Dr. Grace Kendal is forced at gunpoint to help an injured woman, she is dragged into a nightmare where nothing is quite as it seems, and their lives aren't the only ones on the line. (978-1-63555-961-3)

Veterinary Surgeon by Nancy Wheelton. When dangerous drugs are stolen from the veterinary clinic, Mitch investigates and Kay becomes a suspect. As pride and professions clash, love seems impossible. (978-1-63679-043-5)

A Different Man by Andrew L. Huerta. This diverse collection of stories chronicling the challenges of gay life at various ages shines a light on the progress made and the progress still to come. (978-1-63555-977-4)

All That Remains by Sheri Lewis Wohl. Johnnie and Shantel might have to risk their lives—and their love—to stop a werewolf intent on killing. (978-1-63555-949-1)

Beginner's Bet by Fiona Riley. Phenom luxury Realtor Ellison Gamble has everything, except a family to share it with, so when a mix-up brings youthful Katie Crawford into her life, she bets the house on love. (978-1-63555-733-6)

Dangerous Without You by Lexus Grey. Throughout their senior year in high school, Aspen, Remington, Denna, and Raleigh face challenges in life and romance that they never expect. (978-1-63555-947-7)

Desiring More by Raven Sky. In this collection of steamy stories, a rich variety of lovers find themselves desiring more, more from a lover, more from themselves, and more from life. (978-1-63679-037-4)

Jordan's Kiss by Nanisi Barrett D'Arnuck. After losing everything in a fire, Jordan Phelps joins a small lounge band and meets pianist Morgan Sparks, who lights another blaze, this time in Jordan's heart. (978-1-63555-980-4)

Late City Summer by Jeanette Bears. Forced together for her wedding, Emily Stanton and Kate Alessi navigate their lingering passion for one another against the backdrop of New York City and World War II, and a summer romance they left behind. (978-1-63555-968-2)

Love and Lotus Blossoms by Anne Shade. On her path to self-acceptance and true passion, Janesse will risk everything—and possibly everyone—she loves. (978-1-63555-985-9)

Love in the Limelight by Ashley Moore. Marion Hargreaves, the finest actress of her generation, and Jessica Carmichael, the world's biggest pop star, rediscover each other twenty years after an ill-fated affair. (978-1-63679-051-0)

Suspecting Her by Mary P. Burns. Complications ensue when Erin O'Connor falls for top real estate saleswoman Catherine Williams while investigating racism in the real estate industry; the fallout could end their chance at happiness. (978-1-63555-960-6)

Two Winters by Lauren Emily Whalen. A modern YA retelling of Shakespeare's *The Winter's Tale* about birth, death, Catholic school, improv comedy, and the healing nature of time. (978-1-63679-019-0)

Busy Ain't the Half of It by Frederick Smith and Chaz Lamar Cruz. Elijah and Justin seek happily-ever-afters in LA, but are they too busy to notice happiness when it's there? (978-1-63555-944-6)

Calumet by Ali Vali. Jaxon Lavigne and Iris Long had a forbidden small-town romance that didn't last, and the consequences of that love will be uncovered fifteen years later at their high school reunion. (978-1-63555-900-2)

Her Countess to Cherish by Jane Walsh. London Society's material girl realizes there is more to life than diamonds when she falls in love with a non-binary bluestocking. (978-1-63555-902-6)

Hot Days, Heated Nights by Renee Roman. When Cole and Lee meet, instant attraction quickly flares into uncontrollable passion, but their connection might be short lived as Lee's identity is tied to her life in the city. (978-1-63555-888-3)

Never Be the Same by MA Binfield. Casey meets Olivia and sparks fly in this opposites attract romance that proves love can be found in the unlikeliest places. (978-1-63555-938-5)

Quiet Village by Eden Darry. Something not quite human is stalking Collie and her niece, and she'll be forced to work with undercover reporter Emily Lassiter if they want to get out of Hyam alive. (978-1-63555-898-2)

Shaken or Stirred by Georgia Beers. Bar owner Julia Martini and home health aide Savannah McNally attempt to weather the storms brought on by a mysterious blogger trashing the bar, family feuds they knew nothing about, and way too much advice from way too many relatives. (978-1-63555-928-6)

The Fiend in the Fog by Jess Faraday. Can four people on different trajectories work together to save the vulnerable residents of East London from the terrifying fiend in the fog before it's too late? (978-1-63555-514-1)

The Marriage Masquerade by Toni Logan. A no strings attached marriage scheme to inherit a Maui B&B uncovers unexpected attractions and a dark family secret. (978-1-63555-914-9)

Flight SQA016 by Amanda Radley. Fastidious airline passenger Olivia Lewis is used to things being a certain way. When her routine is changed by a new, attractive member of the staff, sparks fly. (978-1-63679-045-9)

Home Is Where the Heart Is by Jenny Frame. Can Archie make the countryside her home and give Ash the fairytale romance she desires? Or will the countryside and small village life all be too much for her? (978-1-63555-922-4)

Moving Forward by PJ Trebelhorn. The last person Shelby Ryan expects to be attracted to is Iris Calhoun, the sister of the man who killed her wife four years and three thousand miles ago. (978-1-63555-953-8)

Poison Pen by Jean Copeland. Debut author Kendra Blake is finally living her best life until a nasty book review and exposed secrets threaten her promising new romance with aspiring journalist Alison Chatterley. (978-1-63555-849-4)

Seasons for Change by KC Richardson. Love, laughter, and trust develop for Shawn and Morgan throughout the changing seasons of Lake Tahoe. (978-1-63555-882-1)

Summer Lovin' by Julie Cannon. Three different women, three exotic locations, one unforgettable summer. What do you think will happen? (978-1-63555-920-0)

Unbridled by D. Jackson Leigh. A visit to a local stable turns into more than riding lessons between a novel writer and an equestrian with a taste for power play. (978-1-63555-847-0)

VIP by Jackie D. In a town where relationships are forged and shattered by perception, sometimes even love can't change who you really are. (978-1-63555-908-8)

Yearning by Gun Brooke. The sleepy town of Dennamore has an irresistible pull on those who've moved away. The mystery Darian Benson and Samantha Pike uncover will change them forever, but the love they find along the way just might be the key to saving themselves. (978-1-63555-757-2)